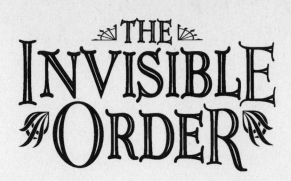

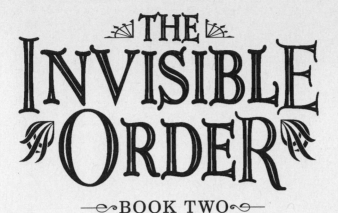

THE INVISIBLE ORDER

BOOK TWO

THE FIRE KING

PAUL CRILLEY

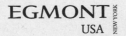

EGMONT

USA NEW YORK

EGMONT

We bring stories to life

First published by Egmont USA, 2011
443 Park Avenue South, Suite 806
New York, NY 10016

Copyright © Paul Crilley, 2011
All rights reserved

1 3 5 7 9 8 6 4 2

www.egmontusa.com
www.paulcrilley.com

Library of Congress Cataloging-in-Publication Data is available
LCCN number: 2011024161
ISBN 978-1-60684-032-0
eBook ISBN 978-1-60684-279-9

Printed in the United States of America

CPSIA tracking label information:
Printed in August 2011 at Berryville Graphics, Berryville, Virginia

For Caroline,

*Without your constant support
none of this would be possible.*

*And for our children, who have
a whole life of dreaming ahead of them.*

With love.

⊹⊱ ⊰⊹

CONTENTS

⊱ CHAPTER ONE ⊰

*London, 1666. In which Emily and Co. find themselves
in a spot of bother. A Murder of Ravens.*

Emily woke up in darkness.

She yawned, her mind going through the usual check-list of hopes and fears that accompanied every awakening. Would there be snow today? Would she get to the market in time? Would she sell enough watercress to feed William and herself?

She rolled lazily onto her back. Motes of dust glowed in the sunlight that skewered through gaps in the wooden walls. Emily frowned, sleepily confused. Wooden walls? Their room in Cheapside didn't *have* wooden walls. And what on earth was that *smell*?

Then it all came back to her in a rush of disjointed images. The battle in Hyde Park. Grabbing the key from the Faerie

Gate just in time to stop the Faerie Queen's soldiers from invading London. And in the process leaping through the gate and finding herself trapped here. In 1666. She quickly felt around beneath the old sacks that covered the dirt floor. The key was still there, safely hidden away.

It was only then that Emily realized how quiet it was. She sat up and looked around their hiding place—an old tanning shed on the north bank of the Thames. (Jack had suggested it. He said the smell of old animal hides would make sure no one bothered them.)

She was alone. The others had gone.

A wave of panic threatened to overwhelm her, but Emily struggled against it. Keep calm, she told herself. Obviously, they hadn't just deserted her. She had dozed off while they had all been talking about finding something to eat. The others must have simply slipped out to get some food. .

But why had William gone? She had told him not to leave the shed. He was too young—only nine years old. The city would be far too dangerous for him.

He hadn't been happy with that. But then, he hadn't been happy with anything she had told him to do for a very long time. There had been a brief period of reconciliation after he, Corrigan, and Jack appeared through the gateway after defeating Queen Kelindria, but that hadn't lasted long, and he had quickly slipped back into his old ways of arguing with her whenever she tried to tell him what to do.

The door to the small shed opened slightly, then got stuck on the sacking that littered the ground. A mop of untidy hair appeared in the gap as Jack tried to see what was jamming the door. He shoved with his shoulder, pushing the gap wider, then slipped inside and pushed the door closed. He turned with a grin.

"I come bearing gifts," he proclaimed. His grin faltered as he took in the interior of the shed.

"Where's Will?"

"What do you mean? Isn't he with you?"

"No." Jack held up a bundle of grubby paper. "I went out to get food. Meat pastries." He looked dubiously at the paper. "At least, I *think* it's meat."

"Then where is he?"

Jack tore his gaze away from the pastries. "Probably wherever Corrigan is," he said darkly. "They seem to have taken quite a shine to each other. We need to watch that piskie, Snow. He's trouble."

Emily tended to agree. Corrigan *was* trouble, but not in the way Jack meant. He had a knack for getting into mischief, but that was about it. Yes, he had betrayed her to the Faerie Queen, but he also came back for her. He had rescued William and herself from the Queen's cells. That was what counted.

3

But that didn't matter to Jack. He and Corrigan had clashed from the moment they met, and that didn't look set to change anytime soon.

As to whose idea it was to sneak out of the shed while Emily slept—both Corrigan *and* William were capable of making such a rash decision.

"We should find them," she said. "Before they get into trouble."

"Agreed. But one of us should stay here. If they come back and find the shed empty, they'll just head right back into London again."

Jack was right. And as much as Emily wanted to feel as if she was doing something other than sitting around, Jack had already been into the city. She'd probably only get herself lost.

"Then you should go," she said. "But if you don't find them in an hour, come back so we can figure out what to do next."

Jack nodded and yanked the door all the way open. Hazy afternoon light spilled inside, illuminating moth-eaten pelts and three large barrels that had been shoved up against the sidewall. Outside, a dusty avenue lined with more half-ruined sheds led down to the brown waters of the Thames, the sun glinting on small waves as they lapped against the muddy riverbank. Jack handed her the small package of pastries (Emily briefly thought about asking him where he got the money to buy them, but she wasn't sure she would like the answer, so decided against it), then he hurried along the weed-choked road.

Emily watched until he disappeared behind one of the tumbledown shacks, then sat down on a smooth boulder outside the shed.

She fished around in her jacket and once again pulled out the pocket watch the Dagda had given her. The metal was covered in patterns so delicate they were hard to see unless you tilted the watch to catch the light. Emily gently rubbed her fingers across the engravings, then pressed the gold button at the top. The lid clicked open, revealing a circle of plain, dark glass. What did it mean? Had the Dagda tricked her after all? Back in Hyde Park the watch had shown Emily her ma and da, sitting in a room in an old castle, dragons circling overhead. But ever since she'd come through the Faerie Gate, all it showed was a blank face. How could she tell if the images had even been real? She'd been tricked and lied to over and over since this whole thing began. It was hard to know what the truth was anymore.

A loud caw echoed forlornly through the ramshackle buildings. Emily looked up, startled by the sound. A large raven was perched on the rotting roof of one of the sheds. But it wasn't like any raven Emily had ever seen. Instead of the normal black color, this one was totally white, with eyes that were a bright, startling blue. The bird tilted its head to

5

the side, staring down at the package of pies in Emily's lap. It cawed again. This time, the caw sounded demanding, as if the bird was giving her an order.

Emily hesitated, then put the watch away and unwrapped the flimsy paper. She broke off a chunk of crumbly pastry and threw it onto the path. The raven let out a triumphant caw and flapped down from the roof, its pale beak stabbing violently at the food, throwing it up into the air and catching it before it touched the ground. Emily watched the bird with a mixture of curiosity and nervousness. It was the biggest raven she had ever seen. Its beak alone was about the length of her middle finger.

The bird finished the morsel of pastry. Then it tilted its head again so it could stare at her with one pale blue eye.

"No more for you," she said firmly. "Shoo." Emily tried to wave the raven away, but the bird simply followed the movements of her hands, watching expectantly for more food. When nothing was forthcoming, it hopped closer, snapping its beak rapidly together, making a *click-click click-click* noise that Emily found vaguely threatening. "Shoo," repeated Emily. "Away with you."

The bird ignored her and hopped even closer, still clicking its beak. Emily searched around for something to throw at it, but as she was doing so, she saw Jack reappear at the end of the lane, followed closely by William and Corrigan.

Emily surged to her feet. The raven let out a startled cry and danced backward. It launched itself into the air and fluttered to the roof, all the while cawing its raucous displeasure. Emily ignored it and hurried toward the others. As she approached, she could hear Corrigan complaining loudly from his position on Will's shoulders.

"I don't see what all the fuss is about," he snapped. "We went to look for food. What of it? What if you hadn't found anything for us? Then we'd all be starving."

"I *did* find something," replied Jack, grim-faced. "But *you* didn't."

Corrigan waved this observation away. "It was only a matter of time," he said. "We only came back because William didn't want Emily to worry."

"Bit late for that," said Jack.

Emily met up with them halfway along the avenue. One look at Will's sullen face told her she shouldn't say anything. She knew that. But she couldn't help it. The words were out of her mouth before she had a chance to stop them.

"What were you thinking?" she snapped. "Oh, how silly of me. You *weren't* thinking, were you? That is patently obvious."

"It's not my fault if you fell asleep," responded William hotly. "Corrigan wanted to wake you up, but I said we should let you rest. I was doing you a favor!"

"Then don't! Don't do me any favors, William. Wandering

off like that was a foolish thing to do. What if something had happened? We'd have had no idea where you were."

"Nothing happ—," started Corrigan, but Emily just turned her glare on the piskie, and he quickly clamped his mouth shut.

"Anyway," said Jack uncomfortably. "We're all here now, eh? No harm done. Let's just eat our pastries, then we'll decide what to do next—"

"I can tell you what you'll be doing next," said a voice. "And it won't be eating. Less you can eat with a knife in your guts."

Emily whirled around. A girl who looked about the same age as Jack was leaning against one of the unused sheds. She wore a dirty shirt that might once have been white but had been washed so many times it had faded to a dull yellow. The shirt was tucked into leather breeches, which were in turn tucked into a pair of well-worn boots. Her outfit was topped off by a wide-brimmed hat with a white feather sticking jauntily from the top.

The girl was holding what looked to be a very sharp knife. She tossed it into the air, letting it turn end over end a few times before catching it again. She repeated this over and over, never once taking her eyes from the group.

After a brief moment to recover from his surprise, Jack sauntered forward, the cocky grin Emily always found so annoying flashing across his features. "Good day to you, miss.

Spring-Heeled Jack's the name," he said. "And who do I have the honor of addressing?"

The girl snorted, and for a moment she and Emily locked gazes. Emily only just stopped herself from rolling her eyes in commiseration.

"You have the honor of addressing Katerina Francesca. And most men bow when addressing me." She looked at him critically. "Although I see you are no more than a boy, so your lack of knowledge of polite etiquette is perhaps understandable."

Jack's smile slipped from his face. "Boy?" he spluttered. "You don't look any older than me!"

"Maturity doesn't come with age," said Katerina. "Something most wise people already know. But again, allowances must be made for your obvious lack of upbringing." For a moment the girl lost her haughty tones and frowned at Jack. "And what kind of a name is Spring-Heeled Jack? It's silly."

"It's not silly. It's what everyone calls me."

"Why? Don't they like you?"

Jack opened his mouth to respond, but Katerina raised a hand to stop him. "It doesn't matter. You will all come with me now."

Jack glanced over his shoulder at Emily. His look was half confused, half irritated, like he didn't know quite how to respond. Emily thought that maybe she should take a turn.

"Why should we go anywhere with you?" she asked.

Katerina smiled. "Because if you don't, you'll be killed where you stand."

"Oh, is that so?" snapped Jack. "And are you going to be the one doing this killing?"

He stepped forward, but before he had taken two steps, an army of children appeared from nowhere, stepping out of the shadows, emerging from between buildings, popping up on the broken roofs.

"Among others," said Katerina.

Actually, it wasn't quite *an army,* thought Emily, as she looked around for some means of escape. But it might as well have been. There were about thirty children, ranging from Will's age to a year or two older than Jack. Their clothing was ragged. Torn and dirty. They all had the familiar hollow-cheeked look that she was so used to seeing in London. A gang of street children.

Street children they may be, but they had blocked off all means of escape, surrounding them in a slowly constricting circle.

Jack was still standing a pace or two ahead of the others. Will tried to position himself in front of Emily, but she grabbed his arm and pushed him behind her, nearly knocking Corrigan off his shoulder in the process.

She studied the children as they approached. They were all armed, gripping knives and short swords. This surprised Emily. The swords looked like they were worth something. Why didn't they sell them for money?

"What do you want with us?" asked Emily. "We haven't harmed you."

"You're a traitor," said Katerina. "And we hunt down traitors. It's our job."

"What are you talking about?" snapped Jack. "A traitor to who?"

Katerina blinked in surprise. "To the human race, of course."

"The human . . ." Jack looked around to see if anyone else knew what Katerina was talking about. Emily simply shrugged, her eyes scanning the ranks of children for a gap through which they could run. She caught sight of movement on one of the roofs. It was the white raven, perched on a broken chimney and watching them with its unsettling blue eyes.

There was a flutter of wings, and from out of the clear sky came a second white raven. It landed on the chimney next to the first. They leaned toward each other and bumped heads as if in greeting, then turned their attention back to what was happening below them.

Strange, thought Emily absently. She'd never seen a white

raven before today, and here she was seeing two at the same time. *They must be from the same family, surely?*

"You seem pretty caught up on etiquette," said Jack to Katerina. "So why don't you explain to us exactly why you think we're traitors."

Katerina leveled her knife directly at William. "Because of him."

William's eyes widened in surprise. "Me? What have I done?"

"Stop playing the fools," snapped Katerina. "You know perfectly well who I'm talking about."

And then it struck Emily. She scanned the faces that surrounded them. The angry, fearful, hateful faces. They weren't looking at William. They were all looking at one thing, and one thing only.

Corrigan.

They were talking about Corrigan.

"You can see Corrigan?" exclaimed Emily. How was that possible? Humans couldn't see the fey unless they were given the second sight. A few, like Emily, had natural talents, but not so many as now surrounded them. It didn't make any sense.

"Why do you want to hurt him?" asked William, stepping out from behind Emily. "He's done nothing to harm you."

"Give me a chance," muttered Corrigan. "I've only just met them."

"He doesn't need to *do* anything," said Katerina. "His existence is crime enough. Our fight is against *all* the fey. And against those who associate with them," she added pointedly. "That is our charter."

Emily was about to ask about this charter when an odd sound distracted her. It was like a sheet, billowing and rippling in the wind. She looked up to where the noise was coming from and took a fearful step back.

The sound wasn't a sheet rippling in the wind. It was the sound of wings. White ravens, hundreds of them, were descending from the sky to settle on the roofs of the dilapidated structures all around them. As soon as they landed, they furled their wings and gazed at the confrontation taking place below them, their blue eyes alert.

Katerina followed Emily's gaze. As soon as the girl spotted the ravens (and as soon as the ravens had *seen* her spot them), they started snapping their beaks as the first one had done when trying to get Emily's pastry. *Click-click. Click-click. Click-click.*

Emily shivered. It was an unsettling experience, to say the least. The white ravens staring down at them while the clicking and snapping eddied through the ranks of the birds like a wave in the ocean.

"Oh, that can't bode well," said Corrigan, staring up at the birds.

13

Katerina whirled back to face her gang. "The enemy is upon us!" she shouted. "Ready yourselves."

The order was hardly necessary. As soon as the birds had been spotted, Katerina's gang broke away from the circle they held around Emily and the others to find positions that weren't so exposed. And while they readied themselves, the *click-click* sound rained down on them from above, getting louder and louder as more and more white ravens descended from the sky.

"I don't know what's going on here," Jack said, "but now would be the perfect time to leave, don't you think?"

Emily nodded. Jack pointed to a gap between two of the old sheds and was just about to cross the dusty lane when the clacking noise suddenly stopped. The abrupt silence seemed to echo around them, the absence of sound louder than anything that had come before.

Emily looked up at the ravens.

They had all turned to stare toward the end of the avenue, where the lane turned aside and followed the muddy banks of the Thames.

Slowly, ever so slowly, Emily followed their gaze.

A dark figure was rising from the water, a figure draped in a black, sodden cloak. The figure rose to its full height and pulled the hood back to reveal the wrinkled face of an old crone, her eyes the cold, uncaring black of the deep ocean.

The murky river water dribbled from her mouth and nose as a second figure rose up behind her, its slimy, lank hair framing a skeletal, pale green face.

Emily felt her breath catch in her throat.

Black Annis and Jenny Greenteeth.

⊰━CHAPTER TWO━⊱

In which Emily discovers that the enemy of her enemy is not necessarily her friend. Enemies old and enemies new.

Black Annis and Jenny Greenteeth waded slowly out of the Thames, the brackish water dripping from their rotting clothing. Jenny smiled, baring her sharp black teeth as she stared hungrily at Katerina's gang.

Strangely, the sight of them gave Emily a brief surge of hope. How had they managed to follow her here from 1861? Was there another way besides the Faerie Gate in Hyde Park? And more important, did that mean she could use the same method to get them all back home?

But her hope was short-lived. Black Annis carefully patted down the slimy, decaying hood of her cloak, her oily black eyes passing over Emily without a hint of recognition. That was when Emily realized that this Black Annis and Jenny

Greenteeth belonged here, in 1666. They hadn't even met her yet.

"Hello, my poppets," called Annis.

Emily turned to see Katerina's response. There was no surprise in the girl's face. Fear, yes. But no surprise. Which meant Katerina had seen Black Annis and Jenny Greenteeth before. None of this was new to her.

Yet another puzzle to add to an already long list.

The street children formed into a line across the lane, their knives held ready before them. This meant Emily and the others were caught in a slowly constricting vice, with Black Annis and Jenny Greenteeth approaching along the path from the right, and Katerina's gang unmoving to their left. Emily glanced at Jack and William. On an unspoken signal they all took a few steps back, leaving the lane altogether and sheltering between two of the deserted shacks.

"What's going on here?" Emily whispered to Corrigan. "How can they all see you?"

"What are you asking me for?" replied the piskie. "I have no idea."

Jack frowned at him. "How can you not know? This is your history, isn't it?"

"Not mine. I only came to London in the eighteen hundreds."

"Where were you then—now, I mean?" asked Emily.

Corrigan shrugged. "All over. Eire. The mainland. Doing

17

the bidding of the Cornwall Spinster Queen. There were other battles to fight."

"Stay back, Annis!" called Katerina. "You know we can hurt you."

Black Annis smiled. "I don't think so, poppet," she said. "Times are changing. We're taking London back."

"Not if we have anything to say about it," snapped Katerina—rather bravely, Emily thought.

"Oh, but you don't have anything to say about it. You and your little gangs are finished. I'm going feed you all to young Jenny here. She needs a good meal, don't you, Jenny?"

"I do, Black Annis. Their fear makes me all shivery. I like to eat their screams."

Black Annis fondly stroked Jenny's seaweedlike hair. "Of course you do, poppet. That's all they're good for."

Emily looked over her shoulder, searching for a way out. But their hiding place backed straight onto a wall of earth. If they wanted to get away, they would have to leave their cover and head back onto the lane. Emily turned back . . .

. . . and saw something that made her blood run cold.

"Behind you!" she screamed without thinking.

Katerina and the others whirled around.

Stalking out from a small lane that ran between the sheds on the other side of the road were three . . . Emily wanted to call them dogs, but they were too big to be dogs. They were the size of small ponies, black wolflike creatures with eyes the color of congealed blood. They slunk out from the alley, huge muscles bulging and rippling beneath dark, matted fur. Heavy black chains were wrapped around their necks, the chains disappearing back into the dark lane from which they had appeared.

"What are they?" whispered William fearfully.

"The Hounds of the Great Hunt," said Corrigan, in a worried voice.

As he talked, one of the hounds tried to leap ahead, but there was a sharp tug on the chain and it jerked back, snarling into the air.

"Who's holding—," began Emily. But she didn't get a chance to finish, because following the hounds were three massive horses. One was white, one was black, and the other was a deep crimson. Sitting on the backs of these horses were three knights, each wearing armor matching the color of his steed. The Crimson Knight held the chains that were attached to the hounds. The Black Knight held a long metal lance, while the White Knight held a massive spiked ball hanging from the end of a chain. He swung the chain in lazy circles, the spiked ball whistling through the air.

"Corrigan?" said Emily in a trembling voice, unable to tear her gaze away from the massive horses and the knights. "Who are they?"

Corrigan nervously licked his thin lips. "The Three

Riders," said the piskie. "Huntsmen. And if they're here, then *she* isn't far away."

"She? Who are you talking about?" asked Jack.

"The Morrigan," said Corrigan quietly, his voice filled with foreboding. "The Phantom Queen."

As he spoke her name, a cold wind gusted through the deserted sheds, whipping dry earth and dust into the air. The wind formed tiny tornados that danced and skittered across the ground. One of the whirlwinds passed in front of them, and from inside it, Emily thought she could hear a high-pitched howling and shrieking. The white ravens cawed their displeasure, ruffling their feathers and gripping the roofs tight with their claws to prevent being blown into the sky. One of the shacks started to creak, then collapsed in on itself with the rumble and crack of splintering wood. The Three Riders moved to the side of the lane. They waited, silent, as the wind grew stronger. Another shack collapsed. The hounds strained against their chains, howling and snarling, but the Crimson Knight effortlessly held them in check.

Then the wind suddenly stopped, debris pattering to the ground in the sudden silence.

A tall figure emerged from the lane. She wore a dark red cloak, the hood drawn up over her face. She walked forward until she had passed the Riders, then paused and looked slowly around, taking in the scene before her.

"Children," she said in a quiet and menacing voice, "should be boiled alive at birth and fed to the crows. You are like little fleas, always biting, always there, an itch that never goes away."

She reached up and lowered her hood. Emily stifled a gasp as her face was revealed. It was as though someone had taken every storybook witch, every terrifying painting created to scare a child, and combined them to form the woman who stood before them. Her nose was long and curved, covered in red veins, the nostrils flared in a way that reminded Emily of Ravenhill. At the same time, her chin was long and misshapen, curving upward so that the tips of her nose and chin almost touched. Her skin was wrinkled and creamy white, giving her the coloring of a week-old corpse. Her eyes were black and set against her anemic skin, they burned with feverish light.

"We should leave," said Corrigan firmly. "Now. This is going to be a slaughter."

"They've still got their weapons," said Emily. "They're made of iron, aren't they?"

"Doesn't matter. The hounds can only be killed by witchbane. Their knives won't make a lick of difference."

Katerina and her gang were still standing defiantly, their weapons held defensively before them. They obviously had no idea that their knives and swords wouldn't work against the hounds. Without another thought, Emily stepped out of concealment and cupped her hands around her mouth. "Run!" she shouted. She was vaguely aware of Black Annis turning sharply in her direction. "Your knives won't—" she started to shout, but at a sharp signal from Black Annis, every single white raven cried out at once, cawing and flapping their wings, creating such a racket that Emily's words were swallowed by the din.

Black Annis was now staring directly at Emily. The old hag smirked at her and waggled her finger in a no-no gesture.

Emily ground her teeth in frustration. There was nothing else for it. She wasn't about to let Black Annis and her stupid birds get the better of her.

She ran straight for Katerina.

"Snow!" shouted Jack, but Emily ignored him and kept going. She sprinted forward and grabbed hold of Katerina's arm. The girl whirled around, knife raised to strike. Emily held her hands up to show they were empty.

"You have to run!" she gasped. "Iron doesn't work against the hounds. Only witchbane can kill them."

Katerina narrowed her eyes, then turned back to face the creatures. Their heads jerked and twitched, lips pulling back in snarls and growls. They were terrifying to look at, but it was the eyes that got to Emily. They were frenzied, insane, hungry for death.

Katerina hesitated, then stared hard at Emily. "Why are you helping us?" she asked.

"Because I think we're on the same side," said Emily.

Katerina pursed her lips, then nodded abruptly. "Fine. You'd better stick with me then. Things are about to get confused." Then she cupped her hands around her mouth. "*Scatter!*" she shouted.

Her command was obeyed instantly. The street children abandoned their line and ran in every direction. As soon as they moved, Jenny Greenteeth was after them, reaching out to grab any who came within reach of her clawed hands. At the same time, the Crimson Knight released the chains, letting the metal trail noisily through his gauntlet. The hounds tilted back their heads and howled into the sky, then leapt forward to attack. They moved with a speed that stunned Emily, lunging forward into the chaos. She sprinted back to the others. "We have to follow Katerina," she said. "She'll take us to safety."

"What are you talking about?" snapped William, casting fearful glances at the avenue, where cries and shouts filled the air. "She was going to kill Corrigan! We should just get away from here. Away from all of them."

"No," said Emily firmly. "We need someone who can tell us what's going on. We follow her." Emily felt a brief pang of regret at the look of anger on William's face. But there was no time to talk him round to her thinking. How could she explain it anyway? She didn't even know why she was following Katerina. William would just have to deal with his hurt feelings on his own.

She turned to ask Jack how he felt, even though she thought she knew the answer to that. Jack was always proud of his quick mouth, and Katerina had easily matched him in that department. Which meant he probably hated Katerina already.

But Jack wasn't even looking at her. He was gripping the ruined wood of the shed, his knuckles white as he stared out into the street.

Emily followed his gaze.

Despite Katerina's command, some of her gang—Katerina included—were actually facing up to Jenny Greenteeth and Black Annis, trying to rescue one of their own whom Annis held by the neck. The street children had surrounded the two hags as they tried to drag their victim into the Thames.

But doing this left their backs exposed to the attacking hounds. Some of the other street children were attempting to hold off the massive dogs, and while the iron did not have any magical effects, the weapons still managed to draw blood. But it was a lost cause. As Emily watched, one of the hounds leapt forward and bit the arm of a small boy who had strayed too close. He struggled, screaming for help. The others tried to grab hold of him, but the hound was too strong, too quick. It turned and disappeared between the sheds, dragging the boy across the ground like a rag doll.

His screams soon stopped.

Katerina had seen this. She shouted something to those closest to her. On her words, they all moved away from Black Annis, fleeing the scene of battle. Katerina caught Emily's eye and gestured for her to follow.

Emily faced the others. "We have no choice. We follow her at least until we're safe. Then we can go our own way if we have to." She looked to Jack, waiting for him to contradict her. But she was rather surprised when he simply nodded and clapped a hand on William's shoulder.

"Come on, squire. Let's move."

They darted from their hiding place and headed for Katerina. The hounds had all vanished, chasing Katerina's gang between the sheds. The knights and the Morrigan had disappeared as well, moving through the dark lanes as if hunting animals.

That left only Black Annis and Jenny Greenteeth, but they were both occupied. As Emily threw a quick glance in their direction, she saw them disappearing beneath the water with the girl Katerina's gang had failed to rescue.

Emily, Jack, Will, and Corrigan hurried across the road. Emily could see Katerina up ahead, a few of her gang following close behind as they sprinted through the narrow spaces between the ramshackle structures. There was no sign of the hounds or the knights, though she could hear a furious snarling somewhere off to her right.

It was at that moment that Emily remembered the key to the Faerie Gate. She had left it back in the tannery, hidden beneath the moldy sacking. She staggered to a halt, watching as the others disappeared around a corner. She had to go back for it. She couldn't just leave it there.

She wondered whether she should try to catch up with Jack and tell him what she was doing, but quickly decided against it. There was no time. Emily moved off the path, squeezing between a narrow passage formed by the walls of two sheds standing back to back. She edged along in the general direction of the tannery shed. Every now and then she could see the avenue through missing slats of wood. The first time she saw nothing. But the second time she had to freeze as the White Knight passed by not ten paces from her.

She waited till she was sure he had gone, then peered into the open. A grass-covered path lay beyond, and on the other side of the path was a rocky bank that dropped away to the river. If she could get down the bank, she should be able to move around to the rear of the shed they'd been resting in earlier and work her way inside without being seen.

Emily peered along the path to the left. She could see the

back legs of the black horse, but the Rider's attention was focused elsewhere. Emily took a nervous breath, then ran across the path and over the rise.

As soon as her feet hit the grass, she slipped. She went down onto her back and slid down the hill, barely managing to stop herself from rolling into the brown water.

She waited, lying flat on her stomach, but it didn't seem as if she had been heard. Emily pushed herself into a crouch. She could see their shed from her position. It was only about thirty paces away. She hurried along the shoreline at a low run.

Emily arrived at the rear of their shed and dropped to her knees. She pulled at one of the rotting planks, but it creaked and groaned alarmingly, so she gave that up and started digging the soft earth around the base of the structure instead. After a few minutes she had dug a hole big enough to admit her. She got down on her back and pulled herself through, wincing as the wood scraped against her back.

Emily threw aside the moldy sacking, breathing a sigh of relief when she saw the tangled branches of the circular key sitting exactly where she had left it. She had half feared Black Annis or one of the others would be able to sense its presence, much the same as the Dagda had done back in Hyde Park.

Emily scooped up the key and hurried back to the hole.

27

She wriggled through on her stomach. The dry earth got up her nose and into her mouth as she did so. She wrinkled her nose and spat the dirt out as she tried to free her ankle, which had become wedged beneath the wooden planks.

"Look at that, Jenny. Disgusting is what it is. Expectoratin' all over the ground. No manners at all."

Emily yanked her foot free and rolled onto her back. Black Annis and Jenny Greenteeth were standing over her, their hideous faces framed against the blue sky.

Black Annis reached down to grab hold of her. Emily lifted her hands up to ward the hag off, forgetting that she still held the key.

Annis's black eyes widened in amazement. They darted to the key, then to Emily, then back to the key again, as if she couldn't believe what she was seeing.

"The key, Jenny," she said in a shocked voice. "She has the key."

"Can't do, Miss Annis. Titania holds it tight, she does."

"I know that, cretin! But what do you think that is? Chopped children's liver? I can feel the power. It's the real thing."

Emily took advantage of their confusion to whirl around and dive back into the hole, thinking perhaps she could escape through the front door. She got halfway through before she felt clawlike hands grab hold of her ankles. Emily

28

kicked and struggled with all her strength, but it was no use. She was pulled slowly backward. She grabbed at the wooden slats, her fingers scrambling for purchase. She managed to get a grip, her backward movement stopping. Then her eyes fell upon something on the dirt floor. A nail. An iron nail. She could use it as a weapon. But if she let go of the slats, she would be yanked back through the hole. And the nail looked like it was just out of reach.

Emily took a deep breath. Well, she couldn't just lie here forever, could she? There was nothing else for it.

She let go of the wooden slat with one hand and stretched out for the nail. Her fingertips brushed against the cold metal, but then she slid backward.

"No!" she screamed, and kicked behind her with a sudden burst of anger. She must have connected with something, because she heard a grunt of pain, and the pressure on her legs lessened. Emily quickly pushed forward, grabbing the end of the nail just before the hands took hold of her legs once again and jerked her from the hole with a violent yank that sent pain shooting up her legs.

She rolled over and tried to scramble away, but Black Annis grabbed her by the neck and lifted her into the air. She brought Emily close, studying her face curiously. Emily could smell stagnant water and rotten fish on the crone's breath.

"Now where did someone like you get that key?" Black Annis's hand tightened around Emily's neck. She couldn't answer even if she had wanted to.

"Not talking? Ah well. I'm sure Kelindria will get the truth from you. Isn't that right, Jenny?"

"Oh yes, Mistress Annis. Kelindria will poke things into her till she talks."

Kelindria? Emily couldn't let the key fall into her hands. Not after all she had been through to keep it from the Faerie Queen in the first place. If she got her hands on it now, everything they had done would be for nothing. Kelindria would be able to open the gate and summon her armies, and this time Emily might not be able to stop her.

Emily stabbed the iron nail hard into Black Annis's hand. The crone shrieked in pain and released Emily. She dropped to the ground and scrambled backward, gasping for breath. Black Annis's hand was spewing oily smoke and black blood. Jenny Greenteeth lunged toward her, but Emily slashed out with the nail, and she jerked backward out of reach.

Emily didn't wait to see what they did next. She turned and ran back along the shore. Black Annis raised her voice and shrieked for help. Emily forced herself to run faster, dashing across the small path and back between the sheds. She could hear the sound of running feet somewhere behind her. She pushed on through the tight space and into the lane where she had been separated from the others. She ran on. A stitch stabbed into her side, but she ignored it, concentrating on getting every bit of speed she could from her legs. She could still hear Black Annis's wailing in the distance, but thankfully the sound didn't seem to be coming any closer.

She rounded a corner and collided with someone coming the other way. She fell onto her backside and looked up, ready to use her nail once again.

But it was only Jack. Emily almost sobbed with relief.

"Where have you been?" he snapped, yanking her to her feet.

"Don't speak to me like that," said Emily. "I had to go back for this." She brandished the key in front of his face. "Seeing as no one else was going to remember it."

Jack looked confused. "But you were the one in charge of it," he said. "Remember? You said you didn't trust any of us to look after it."

"So what are you complaining about? I went back and got it, didn't I?"

"I'm not complaining—" Jack stopped, mid-argument. He shook his head. "It doesn't matter. We have to hurry. Corrigan says those hounds will be hunting us. Katerina wants to take us to some place called the Warren."

Emily quickly walked on ahead. She glanced back over her shoulder. "Come on then. What are you waiting for?"

⊷ CHAPTER THREE ⊷

In which Emily and Co. travel through a city that is almost,
but not quite, familiar. Ancient tunnels. A surprise awaits.

This wasn't Emily's London. She *knew* this, obviously,
but the truth of the statement became more and more apparent as they fled through the cobbled alleys and dirty streets
of the city. Everything was much smaller than she was used
to, more stifling. The roads were narrower, filled to bursting
with Londoners and horses and boys driving sheep and cows
from one side of the town to the other.

Instead of brick, most of the buildings were made from
timber and shoved right up against one another. As a result of
this, the only way to make houses larger was to build upwards,
each precariously built floor larger than the one beneath and
jutting farther and farther out over the street until only a
small section of sky was visible from the shadowy road.

But despite these differences, there was still a lot that was similar. For instance, there were the carriages of all sizes and types that jostled for position on the heaving streets, some rickety, some elaborately carved and painted. (Although, the clothing of the people inside these carriages was odd to her. Men wore frock jackets and curly, shoulder-length wigs, and women held scented kerchiefs to their noses to block out the stench.)

When Emily first saw this, she felt a sharp stab of envy, because the stench was another thing that was familiar to her. Everyone she passed stank of stale sweat or bad breath. There was nowhere she could turn to escape it. The smell of vomit wafted from dark alleys, the stink of burned food from an open door, the revolting smell of rotting meat from an abattoir.

And added to this was the stink that came from having all kinds of animals walking through the streets. The inevitable buildup left by the animals either buzzed with flies or crawled with writhing maggots. Back home, there were people whose job it was to clean up this type of mess. Obviously, this simple idea hadn't occurred to anyone here, though Emily fervently wished it had.

She stepped over a pile of something she would rather not identify, following Katerina as she slipped into a dark alley. The buildings that formed the two sides of the narrow lane were linked by a plank of wood resting on windowsills high above them. As Emily watched, someone climbed out of one of these windows and clomped over the plank to the house opposite. The wood creaked alarmingly, a fine dust sifting down through the air. Emily blinked the dust away and lowered her eyes. Katerina stood at the entrance to the alley, checking back over their route. The other members of her gang had disappeared as soon as they had left the river. It was just the four of them and Katerina now.

"Where are we going?" Emily asked.

Katerina glanced quickly over her shoulder. "To see Rob Goodfellow," she said. Her eyes lingered on Corrigan. "I can't figure you lot out. Maybe he can."

She turned her attention back to the street. Emily followed her gaze. It looked the same as all the other streets they had moved through. Except here the people going about their business looked slightly less well off, their clothes dull, and most of them had short hair. (Emily assumed this was to keep the nits away.) One or two beggars tried their luck, but anyone could see this wasn't the best area of the city for them. There were no plump merchants. No rich people to take pity on them. Those who went about their business here were only a few steps up from begging themselves. They didn't have anything to give.

Corrigan hopped across from William's shoulder. "Notice anything?" he said in a low voice.

Emily took another look. No sign of Black Annis or Jenny Greenteeth. No sign of those hideous hounds. Or the knights. It all looked perfectly normal. She shook her head.

"Look," said Corrigan. "What's missing here?"

Emily took another look, trying to see what it was Corrigan was talking about. A moment later it struck her. She couldn't see any of the fey. Not a one. Back in her time, there would be brownies hitching rides on the passersby; the fey would be wandering between the humans, going about their own business. But here there was none of that.

"Where are the fey?" she asked softly.

"Maybe we should ask your new friend," replied Corrigan.

"Come on," said Katerina, apparently satisfied that they had managed to shake off pursuit. "We've still got a ways to go."

<hr/>

Katerina led them on for another hour or so, keeping to the stinking back alleys as much as possible. That was another thing that was similar to Emily's London. There were a lot of warrens and courts, twisting lanes and mews that snaked around and behind the main streets, leading to hidden courtyards and forgotten houses. It seemed that London had always been like that, the passing years only adding to the confusion and mystery.

They finally stopped before a stout brick wall with thick, flowering bushes growing at its base.

"Where are we?" asked Jack.

"Bonehill cemetery," said Katerina. She got down to her knees and stuck her head inside the bushes, wriggling forward until only her legs remained in view. A moment later, they, too, were gone.

Emily crouched down and peered through the leaves. Katerina's face stared back at her from the other side of a large hole in the wall.

"What are you waiting for?" she whispered fiercely. "Get in here. Unless you want Black Annis to catch you."

Emily straightened up and turned to Will. "In you go," she said. William frowned, folding his arms across his chest.

"Why do I have to go first? Do you think I'm going to run off and get into trouble if I'm out of your sight for a couple of seconds?"

"Come on, Will," said Jack. "Smallest first. In case I get stuck."

Will hesitated, then nodded at Jack. He got down onto his stomach, pointedly ignoring Emily, and squirmed through the hole.

Emily frowned but didn't say anything. What was the point? Any time she tried, Will took what she said the wrong way. It was like he *wanted* to fight with her.

Emily went next. Branches snagged her clothing and hair, scraping against her skin, but she managed to pull herself through to the other side without too much difficulty.

She stood up and surveyed their surroundings. Everywhere she looked she saw weathered headstones and small, stone crypts, some of them topped by statues of angels. Off to their right, nestling amidst the dry, brittle grass, stood a small church. Some distance away were long rows of freshly turned earth.

"What are those for?" she asked, nodding at the long piles of earth.

Katerina looked at Emily strangely. "The plague," she said.

Emily nodded thoughtfully, even though she didn't really understand Katerina's response. Katerina must have sensed Emily was none the wiser.

"Last year? That spot of bother we had where thousands of people died? There wasn't any more room for single graves, so they had to use those. How could you not know that?"

Emily was spared having to answer Katerina's question when Jack pulled himself through the hole and stood up. Katerina threw a suspicious look at Emily, then set off across the grass, heading deeper into the graveyard. After a few minutes, she stopped before a tall tree and proceeded to break off some of the smaller branches.

"What are you doing?" asked Emily.

"Arming ourselves. You said we needed witchbane." Katerina handed Emily a branch about as long as her forearm. "Or, to give it its more common name, rowan wood. We can sharpen these up and use them as weapons if the hounds come back."

Katerina handed one each to Will and Jack, then led them along a stone path choked with weeds. It was obvious to Emily that the path wasn't used very often, but they followed it anyway until it passed a small crypt with a hideous gargoyle perched above the closed doors. It was leaning over the roof, glaring at them, as if daring them to enter.

Here Katerina stopped. She checked their surroundings carefully, then pulled open the doors and disappeared into the dark interior.

William was the first to follow. He hurried through the opening after Katerina, moving before Emily could say anything. Emily watched him go. What was he doing? Trying to beat her? Did he think this was some kind of race? Or that he had to score points? Jack just shrugged awkwardly and followed after. That left Corrigan and Emily standing outside.

"You're very quiet," she said.

Corrigan looked around the graveyard. "It's very peaceful here," he said after a while.

Emily glanced around. A sparrow flitted past, disappearing into the foliage of a nearby tree. It *was* peaceful.

"And soon the Fire King is going to sweep through and burn it all."

Emily blinked, looking around with fresh eyes. "Is there any way we can stop it?"

Corrigan shrugged. "Can you change the past? I don't know anything about that. All I know is that the second war of the races is about to start, and a lot of fey are going to die. A lot of humans as well." He stared earnestly into Emily's eyes. "I don't want to be here, Emily Snow. Things are going to get very dangerous very soon."

Corrigan turned and entered the crypt. Emily swallowed nervously. She didn't like it when Corrigan talked like that. He was usually so sure of himself, so cocky. If he was scared, then things were about to get very bad indeed.

As she stood there, the bells of the church rang out in the distance, signaling the new hour. In the pleasant surroundings of a warm summer's day, the bells should have been cheerful. But to Emily they sounded desolate, the echoing peals marking the beginning of the end.

She shivered and stepped through the door, blinking as her eyes adjusted to the dim interior. Jack was waiting next to a statue of a fierce wolf. As Emily approached she could see a hole in the wall behind it. From the scrape marks on the floor, it was evident that the heavy base of the statue had once blocked the opening.

"Where's Will?" she asked.

"He's already gone through," said Jack. "So has the piskie."

Emily eyed the hole doubtfully. "Where does it go?"

"No idea," said Jack. He grinned. "Shall we find out? There might be treasure."

In spite of everything going on, Emily couldn't help but smile. "You've got treasure on the brain," she said. "If there was any treasure, why do Katerina and her gang look like they live on the streets?"

Jack thought about this. "Disguise?" he suggested. "If you think about it, it's really cunning. *I* certainly wouldn't advertise the fact that I had piles of treasure stashed away."

"Jack, if you had any treasure, you'd be living it up at Claridge's until you'd spent every last penny."

"Fair point," he said. "But that still doesn't mean they don't have any." He gestured at the opening. "Shall we?"

Emily ducked, finding herself at the top of a rough-hewn tunnel that sloped away from her at a steep angle. A single, flickering torch lit the darkness, the flame giving off a putrid, greasy smoke that drifted up the tunnel, cloying the air with its rotten smell.

Emily and Jack followed the slope down. At the bottom was an old stone wall that had collapsed sometime in the past. The stones still littered the ground, shifting precariously underfoot as Emily climbed through another rough opening.

Katerina, Will, and Corrigan were waiting for them on the other side. Katerina held another of the foul-smelling torches, and by its light Emily could see that Corrigan had taken up residence on William's shoulder and that the two of them were whispering about something. She wasn't sure she liked that. Corrigan was a bad influence on *anyone*, never mind someone as young as Will. Emily moved closer to her brother while Katerina started leading the way along the low tunnel.

"Why don't you let me take Corrigan?" Emily suggested.

"Oh, *now* you want to give me a ride," snapped the piskie. "Every time I've asked it's been 'I'm not your slave, Corrigan,' or 'you've got feet—use them, Corrigan.' Why do you want to help me now?"

"Because she doesn't want me having any fun," said Will.

"Fun? William, you think this is fun? You saw those knights! Those hounds! They tried to kill us."

"I'm not scared of them," snapped William.

"You should be, squire," said Jack, edging past them to keep Katerina in sight. "I know I was."

"You were not!" scoffed William.

Jack turned a solemn face to Will. "I was," he said. "It's a fool who doesn't know when to be scared, squire. Fear's what keeps you alive. Trust me."

William clearly didn't know what to say to that. He looked slightly betrayed, as if Jack had turned on him.

"Well I know *I* wasn't scared," boasted Corrigan. "Takes a lot more than a few ugly hags and their little dogs to scare *me*. Why, if it wasn't for the fact that I had to look after you lot, I would have been right on top of those knights, sticking my blade in their necks." Corrigan demonstrated his killing thrust into the air. "Hyah! Like that."

"Really?" said Will.

"Of course. Have I ever lied to you?"

"I don't think so."

"Just wait, squire," called Jack over his shoulder. "You've only known him for a few days. It'll come."

"Ignore him," said Corrigan airily. "He's just jealous of my lightning reflexes. Did you hear about the time I saved him and your sister from Black Annis and Jenny Greenteeth?"

"No," said William.

"Allow me to set the scene. Your sister abandoned me to the cruel London streets. . . ."

Emily gritted her teeth and moved on ahead until she could no longer hear Corrigan.

"You'd better watch your brother," said Jack, falling into place beside her. "That piskie will have Will eating out of his hand before the day's out."

"I know," said Emily. "But what can I do? If I tell Will off, he'll just do the opposite of what I want. All I can do is leave him be and hope he shows some common sense."

They both turned and looked behind them. Corrigan was balancing on Will's shoulder, thrusting his sword at imaginary foes. Will's eyes were wide with wonder as he listened to the piskie's stories.

"Mmm," said Jack doubtfully. "Good luck with that."

⟊ ⟋

After walking for some time, they found themselves in a tunnel with a high, arched roof, the bricks that lined the walls all neatly placed despite their apparent age. When Emily asked Katerina about it, the girl looked around as if seeing her surroundings for the first time.

"I think it's Roman," she said. "Not sure what they used the tunnels for, but they've been a godsend to us."

"Do you and your . . . friends all live down here?"

Katerina nodded. "Nowhere else to go, is there? Can't live on the streets. Not safe. Especially not nowadays."

"How many of you are there?" asked Jack.

"Hundreds."

"And you all follow this . . . what was his name? Goodman?"

"Goodfellow. Rob Goodfellow. Yes, we follow him. He looks after us. Trains us. Keeps us alive." She threw a warning look at Jack. "And I'll not hear a word said against him."

Jack raised both his hands in a gesture of surrender.

Katerina glared at him for a moment, then turned her attention back to navigating the dark passage.

+⇒ ⇐+

After about an hour of walking, the tunnel opened up into a large, echoing room, with crumbling pillars receding into the darkness. Something crunched underfoot when Emily entered the chamber. She tried to see what it was, but Katerina had walked on ahead, taking the torch with her. She looked back, though, as if able to read Emily's thoughts.

"It's human bones," said Katerina. "Rob says the Romans tried to hide here during one of the fey/human wars, but they died of starvation."

"Charming," muttered Jack.

The chamber opened onto a wide set of smooth stairs that led down into a second room, this one much smaller than the first. A flickering orange light came from beyond an arched doorway. Emily could see shadows moving against the portion of wall visible through the arch. Many shadows, crossing over one another, stretching and distorting as their owners moved around the room beyond.

What was odd about it was that Emily couldn't hear any sound. Going by the amount of shadows, there were quite a few people in the room. But there was no noise whatsoever. Not even whispering.

She and Jack exchanged an uneasy look. She checked to make sure Will and Corrigan were close by. The two of them were right behind her, their faces reflecting the same uneasiness she felt.

But Katerina didn't seem at all bothered. She marched toward the doorway, her torch held high. When she noticed their hesitation, she paused and turned toward them.

"Come on then. You can get some food inside you while Rob decides what to do."

Without waiting for a response, she stepped through the doorway, taking the torch with her. The others hurried forward, unwilling to be left standing in the darkness.

As they approached, Emily saw that the shadows on the wall suddenly started moving faster, as if their owners were rushing forward to greet Katerina.

Emily stepped through the archway and found herself in a large room with niches set into the walls all around them. The niches contained beds and wooden chests, clothing laid across threadbare covers. This was obviously where Katerina and her gang lived.

But she saw this only in the first glance, because her attention was quickly taken by something else.

Besides Katerina, there was only one other person in the room. A boy who looked to be about eleven years old. As Emily watched, the shadows she had seen moving on the walls rushed across the brickwork from all directions, joining together into a single shadow that belonged to the boy. He grinned at them and bowed, his lone shadow mimicking his movement, although to Emily, it seemed there was a slight delay before it moved. "Greetings," he said. "And welcome to the lair of Robin Goodfellow."

Emily heard a noise of surprise and irritation coming from Corrigan. She turned around to find him staring at the boy with a mixture of confusion and annoyance.

"Puck," said Corrigan. "Just what are you up to now?"

"You know him?" Emily asked in surprise.

"Know *of* him," replied Corrigan. "He's fey, Emily. Just like me."

⇥ Chapter Four ⇤

*In which Puck explains what is going on
and reveals troubling news about the Invisible Order.*

Emily, Jack, William, and Corrigan were seated around a table eating bowls of soup that Katerina had brought to them before disappearing into another room to talk to Puck. It was turnip soup. Emily *hated* turnip soup, but she was so hungry she forced herself to swallow every last mouthful. One of the things she had learned over the last few years was that when you were given food, you ate it, because there was no telling when the next meal would turn up.

They were all finishing up when Katarina and Puck reentered the room. As he walked toward them, Emily couldn't take her eyes off his shadow. Or rather, *shadows*. She counted at least ten, all of them attached to Puck. They danced around the chamber and darted across walls, constantly moving and shifting under their own guidance. But whenever Puck stopped moving, the shadows paused to see what he was doing. If it seemed remotely interesting, the shadows darted back to their proper place, joining together to form a single shadow as would be cast by any normal human being.

It was as if they were separate, self-aware beings who were listening to and watching everything that was going on.

Puck sat down and drummed his fingers on the wood.

"Katerina tells me you may have saved my soldiers," he said, a frown marring his young face. He surveyed them with large, green eyes. "That's the only reason you aren't dead already. To be honest, I'm still not sure if I shouldn't just kill you all now. You, boy," said Puck, turning to William, "what do you think I should do?"

Will blinked in surprise. "Uh . . . definitely not kill us."

"Mmm," said Puck thoughtfully. "Maybe I should just kill the piskie, then?" he said hopefully. "Save you lot for later."

Emily leaned forward. "You won't kill any of us. We helped you."

"So you say. Could be a trick, though." Puck cocked his head, looking for all the world as if he were listening to someone speak. For some reason, Emily found her eyes drawn once again to Puck's shadows. After a moment, Puck nodded, muttered something beneath his breath, cracked a grin, then turned serious again, all in the space of two seconds. "The piskie could be a spy. You could all be spies. Sent here to destroy my army. Take me down from the inside."

"Spies for who?" snapped Jack. "If you're going to sit there accusing us of spying, at least tell us what's going on."

Puck opened his mouth, then paused and turned his head to listen once again. "Think you . . . ?" he muttered. "Could still be a trick." He listened again, then slapped his hands angrily on the table. "Well, fine then!" he shouted. "Have it your way!" The boy folded his arms and stared sullenly at the table.

"Well?" prompted Emily.

"Well what?" he snapped.

"What's going on? We helped Katerina. It's only fair you give us an explanation."

"Oh, it's only fair, is it?" asked Puck sarcastically. "Well, if you put it that way, then I suppose I *have* to tell you, don't I? Don't want to be seen as *unfair*, do we? No. Not at all."

Katerina sat down next to Puck and laid a hand on his arm. "They did help us," she said softly. "I'd be lying in that lane with the midnight rider's lance through my back if it wasn't for her." She nodded at Emily.

"Then you talk to them," said Puck. "Because I'm not sure I like them. Especially him." Puck nodded at Jack. "Looks a bit shifty, that one."

Katerina sighed. She patted Puck's arm, then turned to face the others. "Ask, then. I'll try to answer your questions."

"What's going on?" asked Emily immediately. "Why are you fighting the fey? Why are Black Annis and the others after you?"

"The first question to answer," interrupted Corrigan, "is who rules the fey. There were a lot of changes going on now. Changes for the worst."

"*Were* a lot of changes?" said Puck. "You speak like it's all over. Believe me, things are just getting started."

"To answer your question," said Katerina, "Titania is the Faerie Queen. She and Oberon rule over the fey."

Emily turned to Corrigan in confusion. "Titania? But isn't the Queen's name—?"

Corrigan held up a hand to cut her off. He leaned toward Puck. "Who are you fighting?" he asked. "Not Titania, surely. You're Oberon's Puck. And Oberon was always loyal to Titania."

"I'm my own Puck," said Puck, offended. "But no, we're not fighting them. There are others . . ." He sighed. "Things are difficult at the moment. Rebellion in the ranks. Some of the fey think that Titania and Oberon have grown too soft, that they have too much fondness for the humans. They want the King and Queen deposed."

"Who leads these rebels?"

"A fey called Kelindria," said Katerina. "At least that's what everyone is saying. That she fancies herself as the next Queen. And she has support."

"Black Annis," said Emily.

"And the Morrigan." Katerina shivered. "She's a bad piece of work, that one."

"She defeated Baba Yaga, you know," said Puck. "Over in Europe. Baba Yaga ruled over the Winter fey. They called her the Bone Mother. But then the Morrigan stepped right in and killed her. Those knights used to be Baba Yaga's protectors, but now they're loyal to the Morrigan."

"And that means they're loyal to Kelindria?" asked Emily.

Puck nodded. "The split goes right down the center of our people. Titania can't do anything outright, because a lot of fey are wondering whether Kelindria doesn't have a point. If Titania arrests Kelindria, some will think she felt threatened. It will give Kelindria's cause strength, turn her into a martyr."

"And while Titania dithers, Kelindria grows stronger," said Katerina. "She's gathering her forces together. There will be a war soon, and I don't think Titania can stop it."

"And that's what you're doing?" Corrigan said to Puck, jerking his head in Katerina's direction. "Building your own army? You gave them all the Sight, I suppose?"

"Aye," Puck said, a note of defensiveness creeping into his voice. "What of it?"

"They're just children."

"Hah! Shows what you know," said Puck. "They're hard as nails. Tough. Besides, who else is there? I don't trust adults. Treacherous, they are. I'm fighting the war Titania can't. Understand? If it can't be traced back to her, then no one can accuse her of being scared of Kelindria."

"Are you under her orders?" asked Corrigan.

"No. I'm doing this of my own will. No one else has the courage to act. They're too scared to make a move in case it's the spark that ignites the inferno."

"And you don't have that fear?"

Puck shrugged. "What happens, happens. All you can do is make the most of the situation and try and turn it to your advantage."

"What about the Invisible Order?" asked Emily. "Why aren't they fighting?"

Puck's shadow suddenly split into ten separate shadows again, fanning out along the wall behind him and leaning toward Emily. "What do you know of the Order?" Puck asked, surprised.

"Just . . . things."

"What kind of things?" asked Puck, a note of danger entering his voice.

"Keep your distance, Puck," said Corrigan. "You took your humans into your confidence. I've done the same. I told her about the Order. And her question stands. What of them?"

"Where have you been for the last ten years?"

"Not here."

Puck snorted. "That's obvious. The Order is gone."

"What do you mean, 'gone'?" asked Jack.

"Gone. Finished. Ceased to exist. Dead."

"Dead?"

"Dead. Every single one of them. Hunted down and killed."

"Who by?" asked Will.

"Who do you think? Kelindria and her followers. Least, that's what I think. She wanted the Order out of the way for when she makes her move. Anyway, that's why I took matters into my own hands." He grinned. "You could say we're the new Invisible Order."

"But what about Christopher Wren?" asked Emily. "He can't be dead."

"Who?" asked Puck.

"Christopher Wren. He was an important member of the Invisible Order."

"'Fraid you've been misinformed. Never heard of him."

"Are you sure?" asked Corrigan. "He's a scientist of some sort. Member of the Royal Society."

"The Royal Society? I've heard of that lot," said Puck.

"They meet over at Gresham College. Bigwigs. Think they're going to change the world with mathematics." He fixed his eyes on Emily. "But they've got nothing to do with the Invisible Order. Never have."

"If they did they'd all be dead by now," said Katerina.

Emily glanced helplessly at the others. None of this made any sense. Christopher Wren was supposed to be a member of the Invisible Order. He was the one who had made sure Emily got the clues she needed to find the key back in her own time. He had to be involved.

"We need to speak to him," she said. "You said it yourself. Members of the Order have been targeted. Maybe he's just keeping his head down."

"And you think he's just going to open up to you?" scoffed Puck. "What are you going to do? Bat your little eyelashes at him?"

"I've never batted my eyelashes at anyone," said Emily firmly. "And all I can do is try. It's better than sitting here doing nothing." She turned her attention to Katerina. "Will you take us?"

Katerina hesitated, looking to Puck for some kind of signal. He waved his hand at her.

"Take her," he said. "But the rest of them stays here."

"Why?" asked Emily.

"Because I'm still not sure I trust you. With these three

still here I can at least make sure you don't get into mischief."

"What kind of mischief?" asked Jack.

"Like bringing Black Annis and the Morrigan to my hideout," said Puck.

"We've already explained that we're on your side!"

Puck leaned back and folded his arms. "Those are the conditions."

"So you're saying we're prisoners?" asked William.

"Not prisoners. Not as such. More like a guarantee."

"And what if we were to simply get up and walk out of here?" asked Emily.

"You can certainly try. But these tunnels go on for miles. Easy to get lost if you don't know the way."

Emily looked at the others. Jack stared at Puck in frustration. Corrigan simply shrugged.

"Your decision," said the piskie.

"Fine," said Emily. She looked at Katerina. "Can you take me now?"

⊰⊱ CHAPTER FIVE ⊰⊱
Lady Kelindria of Faerie.

The cottage stood at the end of a dark alley, low and squat, like an animal lurking in the dirt and debris. The roof was made from thatch that had turned black and patchy with age. A thin trickle of sweet-smelling smoke writhed reluctantly from the crooked chimney, like a snake stirring slowly in the heat.

Lady Kelindria of Faerie wrinkled her nose in disgust as she took in her surroundings. She didn't like dirt. She liked things to be beautiful. Perfect. Like herself.

She glanced over her shoulder to make sure her pets were keeping her gown off the ground. The children cowered in fear when her gaze passed over them, but they were doing their job adequately, so there was no reason to punish them. Not yet, anyway.

Kelindria had never been to the Morrigan's dwelling before. There was never any need. Besides which, it was dangerous. If any of those loyal to Titania saw them talking, there would definitely be trouble. As it stood, Titania may have suspicions that Kelindria was behind the strengthening rebellion, but she had no proof, and Titania was nothing if not fair. Another point against her. If it had been Kelindria in Titania's position, she would have sent assassins to deal with her as soon as she suspected who was behind the trouble. Titania's sense of fair play would prove her undoing.

But Kelindria had to be here. The Morrigan had sent one of her ravens with a message. She was to come straight away. It was important. Ordinarily, Kelindria would have bridled at such a summons, but there had been something urgent about the note that made her decide to attend.

Four small green lights flared to life as Kelindria approached the cottage. The lights shone from the empty eye sockets of two skulls mounted above the gate. The gate itself and, in fact, the whole fence were made from bones. Human bones, if Kelindria was any judge. She sniffed in disapproval. She wanted to say that it was all theatrics, that the Morrigan was simply being dramatic, but Kelindria had learned to tread carefully when it came to the witch. She was old, older than Kelindria, and had powers that ran down to the bones of the earth. Kelindria had found it wise not to underestimate the crone. Besides which, Kelindria still had need of her.

But once the crown was in her hands, Kelindria would see to it that the Morrigan disappeared.

Kelindria put her hand to the gate. As soon as she did so, a quiet voice whispered out of the air.

"Who seeks entry? Be you here of your own free will, or be you sent?"

"You know exactly why I'm here," snapped Kelindria. "Now invite me in before I lose my patience."

There was a pause, then the gate swung silently inward. Kelindria walked through, ignoring the skulls that turned to follow her movements. She walked up the short path, snakes and spiders scurrying away from her feet into the long grass that fronted the dwelling. There was a fluttering sound from above. Kelindria looked up and saw that the Morrigan's white ravens had appeared, perching on the roof of the cottage as well as the roofs of the buildings that formed the walls of the alleyway.

Kelindria ignored them and stood expectantly before the crooked door. If the Morrigan expected her to knock, then she was going to be disappointed.

The door swung inward. Kelindria allowed herself a small smile of triumph, but a moment later the smile faltered. The Morrigan was not one to pander to others. Why was she being so accommodating? Kelindria suddenly wondered if it had been wise to come here without any bodyguards. What if the Morrigan had turned against her? What if she had decided to give her support to Titania? Or worse, what if she fancied the crown for herself?

There was nothing else for it, though. She was here now. She couldn't simply turn away. It would be seen as weakness.

So instead, Kelindria straightened her shoulders and swept imperiously into the cottage, the children who held her dress scrambling to keep up.

The door led into a dim sitting room. The only light came from a low fire that had burned down to the embers. The Morrigan was sitting in a chair by the hearth, staring at the flickering red coals. Black Annis and Jenny Greenteeth stood behind her.

"Well?" demanded Kelindria. "What say you? Why did you summon me?"

The Morrigan slowly shifted her gaze from the fire, the red glow sliding across her features as she did so. The light pulsed and flickered against one side of her face, glinted in her black eyes.

"I think you know," said the Morrigan quietly.

Kelindria frowned. "I don't like games, old one. Whatever grievance you have, out with it."

"Fine." The Morrigan pushed herself to her feet. "I want

59

to know why you have gone behind my back." She took a step forward. "I want to know why you have broken our pact." Another step, but Kelindria refused to back away. "I want to know"—and here the Morrigan's voice rose to a shout— "why there is a girl running around London town with the key to Faerie hidden about her person!"

Kelindria's eyes flicked between the Morrigan and Black Annis. What was this? Some kind of trick? "What are you talking about?" she asked in amazement. "Is this a jest?"

"No jest, I assure you," snapped the Morrigan. "So I ask again, is this your doing? And why weren't we told?"

"You talk in riddles," said Kelindria. "The key to Faerie, you say?" She shook her head. "Impossible. You must be mistaken."

The Morrigan had calmed down somewhat in the face of Kelindria's obvious confusion. "Then see for yourself," hissed the hag. "Annis?"

Black Annis stepped around the chair and approached Kelindria. Jenny Greenteeth followed close behind her, clutching a jar made from smoked glass. The Morrigan turned away and dropped a log of wood on the fire. The embers flared to life, sparks exploding upward and floating into the chimney.

Greenteeth handed the jar to Annis. The crone lowered her damp hood and smiled at Kelindria, revealing the rotten stumps of her teeth, like craggy rocks, in the black, glistening cave of her mouth. Annis pulled the lid from the jar and reached inside with her bony fingers, withdrawing what looked like a fat tick about the size of an acorn.

Kelindria couldn't hide her surprise when she saw this. "Is that a nostalgae?"

"It is," said the Morrigan, without looking up.

Annis quickly popped the nostalgae into her mouth and closed her eyes. Kelindria knew this was not from any kind of distaste, but rather because she was concentrating. Kelindria watched, fascinated. She could see little bumps form on Annis's hollowed cheeks as the nostalgae searched for a way out. But this soon stopped.

There was a minute of silence. Then Kelindria saw Annis's mouth open. Slowly, ever so slowly. The nostalgae's legs poked out of her mouth, scrabbling over the crone's weathered lips. Her mouth grew wider and wider, and as it did so, Kelindria could see this was because the nostalgae was growing in size, pushing Annis's mouth open as it enlarged.

Just before Kelindria thought Annis's mouth must split apart, the crone breathed in through her nostrils, then exhaled sharply. The nostalgae flew from her mouth with a pop and landed on its back. Still the parasite grew, until a few moments later it was the size of Kelindria's head, its gray skin stretched tight and translucent.

Images flickered inside this bulbous sphere. They were grainy and faint, but Kelindria could see them clear enough. For that was the magic of the nostalgae. Instead of blood, it fed on thoughts and memories, sucking them from someone's mind and storing them inside its body. Kelindria bent over and watched the flickering images. She saw the Thames. A small, dark-haired girl running along the shore and behind a shack. She saw the viewer (Black Annis) confronting the girl.

She saw the key.

For there was no doubt about it. The girl held the key to Faerie, the key Titania was supposed to be in possession of.

But how? Was it some kind of trick? No, you couldn't fool a nostalgae. It didn't feed on imagination. Only real memories.

Then what had happened? Had the girl stolen the key? Preposterous. The Dagda was a member of Titania's court. He would have alerted her if anything had happened to jeopardize their plans. And if not him, then she would have heard it from somewhere else. This wasn't the kind of thing that could be kept secret.

She turned to Black Annis. "You're sure it was real? It wasn't a replica?"

"It was real. I felt its power, I did."

"Then what does this mean?"

"You really had nothing to do with this?" asked the Morrigan suspiciously.

"No! You think if I had the key we'd be sitting here right now? I would have opened the doors to Faerie. London would be ours."

They sat in silence for a while.

"This troubles me," said the Morrigan. "It is yet another element we seemingly have no control over." She stared moodily into the fire. "What of this so-called *Raven King*? Are we at least any closer to finding him?"

"We are not," said Kelindria shortly.

"Then maybe it is time to abandon your search. We don't even know if he is real."

"But what if he is? What happens when we take London? The story says the magic in him will sense the danger. He will awaken into his powers and come for us. That is what he does. No. We must find out the truth first. And if he is real, we must deal with him *before* we make our move."

"I tell you one thing," said the Morrigan. "Despite his name, he has nothing to do with ravens. They are my creatures. I would know if they were linked to such a being."

"Then why is he called the Raven King?" asked Kelindria.

"I know not."

Kelindria stared at the nostalgae. The image was replaying once again. She stared thoughtfully into the frightened eyes of the girl.

"Do you know, this may be a good thing," she said slowly.

The Morrigan shifted her gaze from the fire. "How so?"

"Think on it. What has been holding up our plans? The fact that Titania has the key to Faerie hidden away. The fact that she could summon her armies from Faerie if she needed to. But if there is a second key . . . How much simpler to find this child and take the key from her? We could open our own gate to Faerie. We could bring our own army through and storm the tree. Titania would be caught unawares."

All eyes turned to the nostalgae. The image showed the girl running away along the banks of the river Thames.

"We must find that girl," said Kelindria.

The Morrigan nodded. "I will send the Crimson Knight back to the river. His hounds will soon find her scent."

⇥CHAPTER SIX⇤

*In which Emily visits Gresham College
and speaks to Christopher Wren.*

Gresham College had certainly sounded impressive to
Emily. Especially when Katerina told her it was where
Christopher Wren taught his lessons. So she expected something large. Something impressive. A large building fronted
with statues, perhaps. But when Katerina finally stopped on
Bishopsgate Street and pointed the college out to her, Emily
couldn't help but feel slightly let down.

The afternoon sun shone hot against her cheek as she
stared at the short gravel path leading up to an untidy jumble
of stone houses. It didn't look like any college *she'd* ever
seen. "I think there might be more of it on other side," said
Katerina doubtfully.

Emily glanced along the dusty street as she readied to

cross. Two maids struggled to carry a basket overflowing with white linen. A woman with a tray of matches and pegs around her neck rested against a tree. Emily was slightly heartened to see the tray also held a small group of fey creatures, their legs swinging idly over the edge as they sat and enjoyed the sunshine. It seemed some parts of London weren't affected by Puck's attempts to root out those loyal to Kelindria. "I'll wait for you here," said Katerina. She smiled self-consciously. "Places like this make me nervous. All that learning."

Emily nodded, hurrying across the street and slipping through the open gates. The gravel path forked into two, one section leading to the main house, the other along the side of the wall. She followed the second path, passing more buildings and catching glimpses of one or two men in wigs and neat clothes.

Emily decided the best thing to do would be to approach one of them. She picked a short, fat man with a flushed face. He was furiously scratching beneath his wig.

"Excuse me, sir," she said.

"You don't happen to have a quill about your person, do you?" he asked, barely giving her a glance.

"I'm afraid not."

"Pity." The man scratched some more, then heaved a heavy sigh and yanked the wig off his head, revealing gray hair cut almost to the scalp. He peered into the underside of the wig. "Blasted lice," he muttered. He rubbed his hand over his head and sighed happily. "Much better. Now," he said, turning his attention to Emily. "What can I do for you?"

"I'm looking for Christopher Wren," she said. "Do you know him?"

"Wren? Course I know of him. Lovely fellow. Sometimes think he's a bit dilly in the head, if you know what I mean. You can't get that clever without it pushing a few things loose up there." He tapped his head, then trailed off and frowned at the wig hanging limply in his hand like an exhausted animal.

"Um . . . do you know where I can find him?"

"Hmm? Oh, I do beg your pardon. I'll take you to him, shall I? Nothing better to do. No one turned up for my lecture. The name's Barnaby, by the way. Barnaby Stephens."

He turned and led the way past the jumble of buildings and through a short tunnel that opened onto a covered walkway. The walkway formed a path that led around a huge grass-covered courtyard that was in turn surrounded by three rows of drab-looking buildings. "The professors' lodgings," said Stephens, nodding at the buildings. He pointed to the other side of the square. "Wren's apartments are over there."

They walked around the courtyard until Barnaby stopped in front of one of the many doors and rapped sharply on the wood. It was yanked open by a tall, pinch-faced man with cold gray eyes. He had a thick pile of parchment tucked under his arm.

"Afternoon, Cavanagh," said Barnaby. "Is Wren in? Young girl to see him."

The man called Cavanagh turned his cold eyes to Emily. "What on earth for?" he asked, his lips curling in distaste.

Barnaby shrugged good-naturedly. "Didn't think it was my business to ask," he said.

Before Cavanagh could respond, a man with white hair and bright blue eyes appeared at the door. He gave Barnaby and Emily a cursory glance, then nodded at Cavanagh.

"See you next week," he said, leaving the apartments.

"Who is it, Cavanagh?" called a voice from inside the dim room.

Cavanagh half turned. "A . . . *child*, Christopher. A small girl."

Emily fought back the urge to tell Cavanagh she wasn't actually all *that* small.

"A girl?" asked the first voice, surprised. "Whatever does she want?"

"I have no idea, Christopher. Perhaps you should come and see?"

There was a pause. "Er . . . yes. Good idea."

Emily heard the clumping of shoes on wood, and a second man appeared at the door. His face was kinder than the skinny man's. Not good-looking (his nose was rather large), just . . . friendlier. His eyes were distracted at first, but they sharpened to attention when he focused on Emily.

"Yes? Hello?" he said politely.

Now that she was here, Emily didn't really know how to start. Should she just ask him about the Invisible Order outright? Or maybe ask to speak to him in private?

"I'm afraid I must rush you, my girl. I'm due to give a lecture soon, and I'm fairly confident someone may turn up." He smiled.

Another man exited the room, nodding a farewell at Christopher Wren and Cavanagh as he went. Emily waited to see if Cavanagh or Barnaby would leave as well, but it seemed they wanted to hear what Emily had to say. Oh well. Best just to get it out.

"Um . . . I wanted to talk to you about the Invisible Order," she said. As Emily spoke, she kept a careful watch on Wren's features, but they showed not the slightest hint of recognition.

"The Invisible Order?" asked Wren, puzzled. "What is that? It has the sound of subterfuge about it, eh?" He smiled at the other two men before returning his attention to Emily. "A secret communiqué perhaps? Something to do with spies?"

"No, it's . . . a group of men. Scientists, mostly, like yourself. They meet . . . and . . ." Emily glanced at Cavanagh from

69

the corner of her eye. He was glaring at her. She knew what he was thinking. That she was wasting Wren's time. "They protect people," she said. There was no turning back now. She just had to say it. "They protect people from faeries."

Silence followed her words. Then there was an explosive laugh from Cavanagh and a kinder chuckle from Barnaby. Wren glanced at the others, puzzled, as if he thought this was some kind of trick they had concocted. He smiled tolerantly at Emily.

"Faeries?" he asked. "A group of scientists that protects people from faeries?" He shook his head. "My dear child. I wish I had the time to stand here and listen to stories, but flights of fancy are not for me." He tapped his head. "I have no space for them. My mind's filled up with numbers and theorems."

And that was that. Emily stared up at Wren as her world collapsed around her. She had thought that Wren would know what she was talking about. After all, he was her connection to the Faerie key's hiding place. She had thought she would tell him, and he would nod wisely and take her under his protection. That he would know what to do. Would know how to get them back home. But unless he was an actor of amazing skill, it seemed he really didn't know what she was talking about.

Which meant they were utterly alone. They had no one to turn to, no one to help them.

"But . . . but you're the key," she said numbly. "You're the reason the fey didn't win. It was all down to you."

Something of her feelings must have shown on her face, because Wren guiltily fished around in a purse and took out a dull coin.

"Here you go now. Take this and get something to eat, yes?"

Emily stared blankly at the coin for a second. Then she slowly reached out and took it from his hand. "Thank you, sir," she said automatically.

Wren was staring at her quizzically, as if she was a problem he was trying to solve. "Are you taught, child? Do you know your letters?"

"Yes, sir. Numbers, too."

"Good manners on the child," said Barnaby. "Even though she's got a bit of an imagination. That's what comes of letting women read. Overheats the brain."

"Don't talk nonsense, man!" snapped Cavanagh. "The reason Gresham left us this college was to eradicate thinking like that."

"I was only jesting," said Barnaby, clearly hurt. He smiled at Emily. "Honestly. I don't really think that way."

"Where are you from, child?" asked Wren. "Do you have a place to stay?"

Emily sighed. When adults started asking questions like that, it meant they were thinking about doing this "for your

71

own good," as they liked to put it. What it really meant was that they were trying to ease their own nameless guilt. "Yes, sir. I've got a place to stay."

"Good. Yes, good," muttered Wren. "Well, I really must be going." He pulled the door closed behind him so that they were all standing on the doorstep in front of his rooms. "Well . . . good-bye then."

"Good-bye," mumbled Emily.

Wren turned and headed along the walkway, Cavanagh at his side. He had gone only a few steps before Emily thought of something else to ask. She almost didn't, but she'd already made a fool of herself. It couldn't get any worse.

"Mr. Wren?" she called.

Wren and Cavanagh stopped and turned around.

"What about Merlin? Do you know nothing of him?"

"Merlin?"

"Yes, sir."

"The magician? King Arthur's adviser?"

A brief flutter of hope flared to hesitant life. "Yes."

"Stories, child. As I said, I have no time for them."

He turned away and resumed walking. Cavanagh stared at Emily for a second or two more, then he shook his head in irritation and hurried to join Wren. Emily could hear them talking as they left.

". . . to speak with you," Cavanagh was saying.

"I'm busy at the moment, Cavanagh. It will have to be later."

"Tonight, then? I'll come to your quarters."

"Fine. Tonight it is. After supper—"

A jovial hand clapped Emily on the shoulder. "There now," said Barnaby. "Not sure what that was all about, but at least you can say you got to meet Christopher Wren, eh? Great mind, that man. Great mind. Come along. I'll escort you back to the gate, shall I?"

"He was the key," Emily repeated quietly.

"I'm sorry?"

Emily looked up at Barnaby. He was smiling rather nervously at her. "Nothing," she said.

"Good, good. Come along, then."

"Nothing."

This time they simply cut across the large sward of grass as they headed for the front of the college grounds.

"What was all that about then?" asked Barnaby.

"Nothing. Just me being silly."

"Oh." They walked in silence for a while. Then Barnaby cleared his throat. "Do you really have a place to stay? Because I know someone. A lady. She would be more than happy to take you in for a while. Give you some food."

"No, thank you. It's very kind of you, but I have a friend I'm staying with. She's waiting for me outside."

"Oh, I see. Well, just thought I'd offer."

They left the grass square behind them and stepped onto the gravel, the small stones crunching noisily underfoot. As they approached the gate, Katerina saw her and hurried across the road.

"Is that your friend?" asked Barnaby.

"Yes." She smiled wanly at Barnaby and held out her hand. "Thank you. For everything. You've been very kind."

Barnaby solemnly shook her hand. "It was my pleasure, miss. Good-bye."

An hour or so later, Emily and Katerina were back with the others, seated around the table while she explained what had happened.

"I thought you said Wren was the key?" Jack asked.

"He is!"

"Then why doesn't he know anything?" asked William. "What if you were wrong, Em?"

"I wasn't wrong. It was Wren who wrote the clues so we could find the stone. Even the Faerie Queen said he was involved. She said it was Wren who closed the gates to Faerie, remember?"

"Then he was lying," Corrigan said.

Emily shook her head. "No. He really didn't know what I was talking about."

"So what do we do now? We need a new plan."

"I did think of something," said Emily hesitantly.

"Well? Out with it," snapped Corrigan. "I'm not a mind reader."

Emily took a deep breath. "You reveal yourself to Wren."

"No," said Corrigan immediately. "Forget it. I'm tired of you using me like that. Look what happened last time you made me do it." He nodded his head at Jack. "We ended up stuck with him."

"In case you're short on memory as well as short on brains, I rescued you from Black Annis and Jenny Greenteeth, remember?"

Corrigan ignored this. "And he's a scientist. You know how annoying scientists are? With their logic, and . . . and their sums." He shook his head. "No. And when I say no, I mean no. Never. Won't happen. Not now. Not tomorrow. Not the next day. And that's my final word."

Emily stared at him for a moment. "Are you finished?"

"Yes."

"Good. We'll leave in a few hours. Wren is giving some kind of lecture this afternoon, so we'll only be able to see him after that." She looked at William. "In the meantime, you should get some sleep. We all should."

"I'm not tired," he said immediately.

Emily suppressed the urge to snap at him. Instead she

said, "Fine. Do what you want. But I'm getting some rest."

"Aren't you forgetting something?" asked Puck.

"What?"

"I haven't said you can leave," said the fey boy smugly.

This was just about enough for Emily. "Oh, is that right? Well you just listen here, Puck, or Rob, or whatever you want to call yourself. It seems we're on the same side, whether you believe it or not. You don't want the fey taking over London, and neither do we. So my advice to you is to be quiet and give us what help you can. Honestly, I'm tired of all this subterfuge. Everyone needs to grow up. And right now!"

Emily stamped her foot on the ground as she said these last words. She was aware this slightly ruined the effect of trying to act like a grown-up, but there was nothing she could do to stop it. She was just so frustrated with everyone.

But Puck didn't appear to notice. He stared at her in some surprise, then finally nodded. "Fair point," he said. "And actually, I agree with you. Bringing someone else into the mix might shake things up a bit."

"Just one thing," said Jack, leaning toward Puck. "Why are you doing all this? What's in it for you?"

Puck looked offended. "What—you think you lot are the only ones who want to do any good?"

"Well . . . ," said Jack, looking at the others. "Not really, but—"

"But nothing," said Puck. "You've probably heard the stories, yes? 'Oh, don't trust that Puck. He'll stab you in the back, he will. Only thinks of himself, he does. Bit of an imp. Full of mischief. Always thinking of the moment, never looking ahead.' Yes?" He glared at the others.

"Actually," said Emily, "I've never heard any of that."

Jack shook his head. "Me, neither."

"Nor me," said William.

"Oh." Puck deflated slightly. Emily thought he seemed slightly disappointed.

"They may never have heard any of that," said Corrigan. "But *I* have. And it's all true. Didn't you once put a hedgehog on Queen Elizabeth's throne?"

Puck leapt suddenly to his feet with a crow of laughter, startling everyone at the table. His shadows separated, linking arms and dancing an excited jig across the walls. "Aye. That was funny, that was. I was hiding in the ceiling beams. You should have seen her face. The funniest thing I'd ever seen."

"Yes. Some of her courtiers couldn't help but crack a smile," said Corrigan.

"No wonder. It was a truly remarkable jest."

"They were all executed."

This just seemed to please Puck even more. He clapped his hands together, his shadows doing somersaults of delight on the walls. Then he saw the looks on their faces and dropped immediately back into his seat.

"Yes. Terrible affair, that. Tragic. Tragic." He shook his head sadly. "'Twas a silly prank." He hung his head in shame. His shadows slunk slowly back along the walls to take up their accustomed place.

But then Puck looked up again, his eyes dancing with delight. "But you should have heard her scream," he said gleefully.

⊱ CHAPTER SEVEN ⊰
A traitor revealed.

Barnaby Stephens hurried through the late-afternoon streets of London. The sun was sinking just below the skyline, sending hazy shafts of golden light past the roofs of buildings to spear the ground.

Beyond a brief, cursory glance, Barnaby ignored such things. Beauty had no place in a city such as London.

He held a kerchief to his mouth as he walked. To get to his destination, he was forced to travel through some of the less desirable areas and, although the plague had finally left the city last year, he wasn't taking any chances. Who knew how long it would linger in the damp and dirty corners, waiting for the opportunity to take down the unwary.

Even though, if things went according to plan, there would be other means of combating the disease, of cleaning up the city. Less . . . *scientific* ways.

It was dusk when Barnaby finally arrived at the house. It was nondescript, very much like any other house in London. Yes, the garden was slightly overgrown, but again, most gardens were. Those who had returned to London after the plague hadn't quite gotten round to tidying up what Nature had wreaked in their absence.

It was the first time he'd been here. He had been ordered never to come. That if he was seen it could ruin everything. But this was important. She would want to hear the information he had uncovered.

Barnaby pushed open the wooden gate and stepped onto the paving stones that formed a winding path up to the front door (half hidden behind a clump of bushes).

He hesitated for the first time. The deepening dusk drew shadows out of the undergrowth, patches of darkness where anything could be hidden. A strong wind was gathering, warm and dry. It flicked against his face, doing nothing to soak up the sweat on his brow. If anything, it made it worse.

He moved tentatively forward. Just walk, he told himself. Walk up to the front door and knock. He wasn't doing anything wrong. In fact, he should be praised for his actions.

So thinking, Barnaby squared his rounded shoulders and set off at a brisk pace.

Until he heard the noise.

It sounded like a hundred people whispering at the same time, a dry, sibilant hiss that made his neck prickle with fear. Barnaby whirled around in a circle, searching for the source.

Then he saw it. A patch of oily, heaving darkness that detached from the shadows and floated through the air toward him. He hesitated a second too long. When he finally decided to retreat to the street outside, the cloud was upon him, enveloping him in thick, cloying strands that probed and prodded his face. He opened his mouth to scream, but the strands (strands that now felt like fingers), crawled down his throat, choking off any sound. He couldn't breathe. His eyes opened wide with horror. He saw faces in the darkness, defined by darker shadow and brief flashes of light, as if he were watching lightning flickering in thunderclouds. The faces whispered nonsense in his ears, threats and promises of what was going to happen to him for trespassing.

Depart, Sluagh, said a disembodied voice. *He has my . . . reluctant blessing to attend.*

The whispers in Barnaby's ears changed to hisses of frustration. The strands pulled slowly from his throat, from inside his ears, his nose, leaving Barnaby on his knees, gasping and retching.

Through a haze of pain he heard a curiously comforting sound: the clicking of a door latch. He looked up through streaming eyes and saw the front door of the house swing open.

Barnaby scrambled to his feet and ran as fast as he could through the undergrowth, ignoring the twists and turns of the path in his haste. He tripped over some creeping ivy, but quickly righted himself and lunged through the door, slamming it shut behind him.

He leaned up against the heavy wood, gasping with relief.

"You are ordered to follow," said a voice.

Barnaby looked down. An ugly, goblinlike creature stood in one of the doorways that opened from the front corridor. It blinked its sickly yellow eyes, then stepped into the room beyond.

Barnaby quickly followed, finding himself entering a large, empty sitting room. There was another doorway on the opposite wall, and Barnaby reached the room just in time to see the creature disappear through the door.

Barnaby stepped through the door and found himself in another corridor, this one lit by flickering torches. He frowned, doing some quick calculations in his head. There was no way this corridor could be part of the house. It would extend out into the garden if it were.

The goblin was already at the far end of the passage. It had stopped before a huge wooden door that slowly swung open to reveal yet another room.

"Attend me," called a rich, commanding voice. Barnaby knew that voice. Knew it didn't like to be kept waiting.

Barnaby hurried along the corridor and into the room beyond. The door slammed shut behind him. He jumped but kept his eyes fixed firmly on the floor, staring at the black-and-white tiles as he waited for his cue. There was a strange noise in the room, a soft ruffling sound he couldn't place.

"You may look up," said the voice.

Barnaby raised his eyes to behold Kelindria of Faerie.

For a brief moment, he thought she was sitting on a throne made from white ravens. But then he caught glimpses of the black wood of her seat as the many birds shifted their weight, casting their unnerving blue gaze over Barnaby.

His eye shifted to Kelindria. She did not look pleased.

"Approach."

Barnaby shuffled forward until he stood at the foot of her throne.

"Why have you come here? Did I not tell you to stay away?"

"F-forgive me," stammered Barnaby. "But I bring news. I . . . I thought you should know straightaway."

"Tell me then."

"A girl came to the college today, seeking Christopher Wren. She spoke to him of the Invisible Order—"

Kelindria stiffened in her throne. The ravens cawed, then snapped their beaks in displeasure.

Click-click. Click-click.

Barnaby froze, then swallowed nervously, wondering if he should go on.

"This girl," snapped Kelindria, "what did she look like?"

"She looked about twelve or thirteen. Dark hair. Large eyes—"

Kelindria pushed herself up from her throne, a look of fury darkening her beautiful features. Barnaby stumbled backward, squeezing his eyes closed against the anticipated blow. But when nothing happened, he opened his eyes to find Kelindria standing before him. After a moment an image formed in the air between them, an image of a girl lying on the ground next to a river.

"Is this her?"

"It . . . it is. How—?"

"Never mind. Who is this Christopher Wren?"

Barnaby couldn't take his eyes off the image hovering before him. "He's an astronomer. Among other things. A scientist."

"And is he a member of the Order?"

Barnaby wrenched his gaze away from the image. "No! I would have told you if he was."

"Perhaps you did not know."

"Impossible. I had access to all the names. Besides, he had no idea what the girl was talking about."

"Unless he was simply acting."

Barnaby shook his head. "My lady, if I may be so bold, I really do not think Wren knows anything."

"What of the girl? What exactly did she say?"

"She asked if he knew of the Invisible Order. She looked most upset when he said no." Barnaby searched his memory. "Oh, and she also asked him about Merlin."

Kelindria narrowed her eyes. "Merlin? What of him?"

"That was all. She asked if he knew of Merlin the Enchanter."

"And what did he say?"

"He said that they were childish stories, and that he had no time for such things."

Kelindria sat back thoughtfully in her throne. The ravens cawed as she did so, but she raised a hand to quiet them.

"Where is the girl now?"

"I . . . I do not know. I came here straightaway."

"You let her go?" asked Kelindria incredulously.

"I had to!" whined Barnaby. "There was someone waiting for her outside. I . . . I tried to get her to accompany me, but I didn't want to draw attention—"

Kelindria sliced her hand through the air, cutting him off. "I like this not," she said. "I feel as if someone is making moves behind my back."

Kelindria stared at the black-and-white tiles. Barnaby waited, unsure whether he had been dismissed or not.

Finally, Kelindria straightened. "We can afford no mistakes," she said. "Go back to the college. I will send one of the Morrigan's ravens to her and ask for one of her knights. Show the knight this Christopher Wren and bring him to me. I wish to speak to him."

"But, my lady, I assure you, he's not a member. He will know nothing."

"When I want your opinion, you sniveling worm, I will be sure to ask for it. And since that will never happen, I advise you to keep your mouth shut. Nothing can be left to chance, do you understand? You have been through the Invisible Order's records. I have captured and tortured every member we could find, and yet I am *still* no closer to finding the Raven King. The Order knows who he is, they must do! So if there is even the remotest chance that this Wren is one of them, I want him brought here!"

"Yes, my lady," said Barnaby meekly.

"Now go, before you try my patience any further."

Barnaby bowed. "Yes, my lady."

He turned and walked back toward the door. The ravens snapped their beaks as he went, a chorus of disapproval.

Click-click.

Click-click.

⇥ CHAPTER EIGHT ⇤

In which the foundations of Christopher Wren's world are torn asunder. A rooftop battle. Death stalks the Invisible Order.

Christopher Wren sat at his desk, the guttering light of beeswax candles illuminating his plans for the dome that was to replace the dilapidated spire of St. Paul's Cathedral. He blinked, realizing he had been drifting once again. He couldn't help it. His thoughts kept returning to the young girl who had visited him that afternoon. Why had she asked such strange questions? They were patently ridiculous, and yet she had seemed so . . . solemn. So serious. Perhaps she was touched in the head?

Wren shook his head in an attempt to clear it of distracting thoughts. He needed to focus his energies now. His plans had been approved by the King only a day ago. That meant he had to deal with the logistics of the project. Hiring stonemasons and laborers, sourcing building material. He sighed. It wasn't his favorite part of a job. Not by a long way.

A sharp knock came from the front door. Wren rose from his desk, chiding himself for the relief he felt at having a legitimate distraction. He took one of the candles and made his way along the short passage outside his office, his shoes clumping loudly on the wooden floorboards.

A second knock echoed through his rooms, this one louder, more urgent. Wren turned the key and pulled open the door to find Cavanagh standing on his doorstep, rooting around in a battered leather satchel.

"Cavanagh?" said Wren in surprise. But then he remembered. The man had wanted to see him about something, hadn't he? Wren had totally forgotten about it. Truth to tell, he wasn't really in the mood for company. He'd intended to have an early night.

"Wren," said Cavanagh. "We must talk. It's terribly important that we talk. Now." Cavanagh glanced nervously over his shoulder.

Wren felt himself becoming rather worried. Cavanagh was usually the most stoic of fellows. Wren had never seen him moved to fear. Irritation, yes. Annoyance—definitely. But fear? Worry? Never.

Wren quickly stood aside. "Of course. Please, come in."

Cavanagh hastily entered Wren's rooms and headed

straight for his study. Christopher followed after, watching while Cavanagh dropped into a chair. But he was obviously too agitated to sit still, for he quickly leapt to his feet and paced back and forth. He glanced up at Christopher's collection of books, his lips curling in disgust.

"So many books, and yet you know nothing," said Cavanagh angrily.

"Steady now," said Wren. "I'm not sure what's got into you, dear fellow, but I do not appreciate being insulted in my own rooms."

"Hmm?" Cavanagh looked over at Wren as if seeing him for the first time. "Oh, it wasn't an insult, I assure you. More a regret. A deep, abiding regret." He sighed. "I wish there was another time to tell you this, Wren. I need more time to prepare." He laughed bitterly. "But isn't that always the case? We always need more time, yes? We never have enough, and we never use what we do have in a wise fashion."

"Cavanagh, what on earth has gotten into you? I've never seen you so agitated. Perhaps some tea to calm your nerves?"

Cavanagh shook his head. "No time."

"Are you in some form of trouble?" asked Wren.

"Oh, yes." Cavanagh laughed. "Have been for some time now. It was just a matter of seeing how long I could stay ahead of it." He paused in his pacing. "Do you remember that girl today?"

"Of course I do. How could I forget?"

Cavanagh hesitated, then ploughed on. "What if I were to tell you that everything she said was true?"

This time it was Wren's turn to pause, waiting for Cavanagh to crack a smile. He didn't. "I'd say you probably needed a rest," he said carefully.

"I know how insane it sounds, Wren, but I'm afraid it's true. Faeries exist, and they're not adorable little creatures with wings. They're dangerous, conniving, selfish creatures who want to wipe out humankind. That, or make us their slaves."

"Cavanagh, really—"

"No, let me finish. The Invisible Order is a secret society. We have fought the fey down through the centuries, making sure their plans came to naught, attacking them, fighting them, foiling their schemes. But lately . . . something happened. I don't know what. The fey found out who we were and started eradicating us one by one. Killing us all until only one remained."

Cavanagh drew himself up to his full height. "I'm the last member of the Order," he said proudly. "Gresham, he was one of us. That's the real reason he left all these buildings as a college. To serve as a meeting place for the Invisible Order. To serve as a repository for our knowledge, our records."

Wren found it extremely hard to believe he was having

this conversation. He shook his head dumbly. "But what of the girl? What is her involvement?"

"I have no idea. But if she *is* involved, then her life is in danger. The fey have spies everywhere. It's how they managed to get to us."

"Then how do you know I'm not a spy?" asked Wren.

"I just know. We were going to approach you to join the Order before all this started. Lucky for you we didn't. You might be dead by now."

"But . . . but why are you telling me this now? Not that I believe a word you are saying."

"Because I think something is going to happen. The girl had information she shouldn't have had. When she mentioned Merlin, I nearly had a heart attack—"

"Oh, come now," scoffed Wren. "Merlin the magician is a story, a myth."

"He's as real as you or I," said Cavanagh. "He was one of the founding members of the Order. Thousands of years ago he helped King Lud defeat the Old Ones and lock them away. This was before London even existed. But then he fell in love with a fey who tricked him and took him prisoner. No one has seen him for over a thousand years. But Wren, no one should know about his connection with the Order. *No one.* And yet this girl just strolls in here, obviously thinking you should know what she is talking about. Why?"

"Don't ask me!" snapped Wren. "I think you're all insane."

"Not insane. More's the pity."

"And what do you intend me to do about all this?"

"I think you should leave London. At least for a while."

Wren burst out laughing. "I'm not leaving London. Are you mad? The King has only just approved my plans to improve St. Paul's. I can't leave now."

"Wren, you must—"

Cavanagh was interrupted by another knock at the door. He grabbed Wren by the arm, digging his fingers into Wren's skin.

"Are you expecting anyone?" he whispered.

"Only you, but I do occasionally entertain visitors, you know."

The knock came again.

"Cavanagh, I must insist—"

Cavanagh raised a warning finger to Wren and moved stealthily along the hallway and stopped before the door. But he made no move to open it to whoever was outside.

Wren had had enough. He marched along the passage just as a voice called from outside.

"Wren? It's Barnaby. Are you still up?"

"There," said Wren, reaching around Cavanagh to unlock the door. "It's only Barnaby."

"Wait!" Cavanagh tried to stop Wren from opening the door, but he already had it halfway open. Barnaby was standing on the step.

"Wren? I'm very sorr—"

Before Barnaby could finish his sentence, Cavanagh glanced outside, gave a strangled curse, and slammed the door shut, turning the key quickly in the lock. Just before he did this, Wren was surprised to see a look of murderous hatred flash across Barnaby's face.

"Cavanagh, what—?"

Cavanagh shoved Wren back along the passage toward his study. As he did so he frantically searched through his leather satchel.

"I *told* you they had spies, Wren! All this time, he's been right here, hiding within our ranks. How could I have missed it?"

"Barnaby?" asked Wren, still struggling to catch up. "A spy? For the Spanish?"

"Not the Spanish, you fool!" shouted Cavanagh. "Haven't you listened to a word I've said? The fey! He's with *them*." Cavanagh finally found what he was looking for, a small jar filled with green paste. He yanked the lid off with shaking fingers just as there was a furious banging against the door.

"What—?"

And then a number of things happened at once. The

knocking stopped for a brief second, only to be replaced by a thunderous blow that smashed the door from its hinges, sending broken planks of wood spinning through the corridor outside Wren's study. Wren and Cavanagh ducked for cover. A portion of the door flew lethally through the air, disintegrating into fragments against Wren's desk.

The next thing Wren knew, Cavanagh was dabbing something wet and cold onto his eyelids.

"What are you doing, man?" Wren tried to wipe the sludge away, but Cavanagh kept Wren's arms in a tight grip while he whispered urgently into Wren's ear.

"We must find the child. It seems you are involved in all this, whether you know it or not. The girl said you were the key, the reason why the fey didn't win. Remember? She knows something. We need to find out what she meant. Do you understand?"

But Wren was no longer listening. From his position, he could see down the corridor to where his front door had once stood. His eyes widened in shock.

A huge figure—a man easily seven feet tall and dressed in black plate armor—stood on the step outside. As Wren watched, dumbfounded, the figure ducked beneath the doorframe and entered Wren's lodgings. He was so big he had to turn sideways so his shoulders would fit through the opening. His old-fashioned helmet almost touched the ceiling.

The figure looked ridiculous standing there, flanked by the commonplace wood panels of Wren's rooms and dull paintings of the Thames. He didn't belong.

Barnaby entered behind the knight. He was smiling. "So you're the last of them, eh, Cavanagh? Funny. You were one of the few I never suspected. You were good at hiding. You should have kept it up." Barnaby stepped aside and turned to the knight. "Kill him, but remember to take Wren alive," he said.

The knight tilted his head down and stared at Barnaby through the thin eye slit in his helm. "Do not give me orders, worm," he said, his voice deep and echoing.

Barnaby paled and took a step back. The knight kept his gaze fixed on Barnaby for a few moments longer, then turned to face Wren and Cavanagh. He tilted his head back and let out a terrifying, animal-like roar.

The horrific sound echoed through Wren's rooms. Wren and Cavanagh staggered back as the knight lashed out with his arms, smashing them into the walls. The wooden panels splintered, paintings flying into the air, ripped canvas fluttering to the floor. He started moving, his arms still embedded in the walls. He was like a plough digging up soil, thought a distant part of Wren's mind. The walls ripped apart, the knight moving effortlessly through them, leaving huge furrows in his wake. The noise was horrific and constant, like a forest of trees being felled, splinters flying through the air like tiny daggers.

The top half of the wall behind the knight started to sag, then it separated from the ceiling with the screeching of tortured nails and dropped to the floor, revealing the sitting room on the other side. Barnaby yelped and jumped back outside.

Wren slammed the study door shut. Not that it would do any good against that monstrosity, but he couldn't think what else to do. He whirled around to face Cavanagh, who was fishing around in his satchel again. This time Cavanagh yanked out a short sword about the length of Wren's forearm. He clutched it like a poker and grimaced at Wren.

"Never been one for weapons."

The rending and crashing of wood from the passage stopped. They both looked nervously at the study door.

"We need another way out," said Cavanagh. "Any thoughts?"

"The attic?" Wren suggested. "It opens onto the roof."

Cavanagh nodded. "Lead the way."

Wren hurried through another door that led from his study. It opened onto a short passage with a set of stairs leading up to the second floor. Wren clambered up the steps, his heart racing erratically. He had no clear idea what was going on. Just that what had only this morning been a clear and ordered—albeit a slightly humdrum—existence had been turned on its head. Was he really running from a seven-foot-tall knight? Did faeries actually exist?

It didn't seem possible, and for a brief second he wondered if he had fallen asleep at his desk. But then he heard his study door being ripped from its hinges and the knight venting his blood-chilling roar once again, and he realized this was all real. Horrifyingly, dangerously real.

The attic stairs were at the end of the second-floor landing. Wren quickly led the way up into the low, dusty attic. Moonlight shone through the small window, illuminating old crates and pieces of junk, the detritus of previous tenants. When Wren saw how small the window was, he had a sudden fear that they would be trapped up here. It didn't look big enough for them to fit through.

He fumbled with the latch and tried to push the window open. It didn't budge. He tried again, bracing his feet and pushing. Nothing. Wren leaned closer and inspected it by the silver moonlight. Successive coats of paint had sealed it shut. They were trapped. Cornered. The roaring of the knight came closer. He must have found the stairs to the second landing.

Which meant he would soon discover the attic door. They were as good as dead.

Cavanagh pushed him aside and started digging around

the window frame with his sword. "Not exactly the use I had in mind, but needs must when the devil drives, yes?"

"Devil is an apt choice of word," said Wren, keeping a nervous eye on the door. "Are they demons?"

"I told you. They are faeries. All the myths. All the legends. All true. You really need to understand this if you want to stay alive, Wren." Cavanagh gave the window a shove. It still didn't budge. He sighed, then shoved the point of his sword between the window and the frame, pushing down on the hilt. There was a tearing sound as the paint reluctantly separated and the window moved slightly. Cavanagh wrenched his sword free and pushed the window the rest of the way open. "After you?"

Wren dragged an old crate across the floor and used it to climb up onto the windowsill.

"Hate to hurry you," said Cavanagh in a tight voice. "But that clumping sound you hear is the knight on the attic stairs."

Wren wriggled the top half of his body out the window. It was a tight fit. The grass of the commons lay far below him. Strange. He'd never thought the professors' lodgings to be overly high, but from this perspective, it was absolutely terrifying. One wrong step and that would be the end.

Wren twisted around so that his backside was on the sill, then grabbed the eaves above the window, using them to steady himself while he shuffled back and finally got his legs free. He pulled himself up onto the roof, swaying slightly as he tried to keep his balance.

Cavanagh joined him moments later, and they hurried up the incline to the peak of the roof. A loose slate gave way beneath Cavanagh's boot. He slipped onto his knee, the impact causing more of the slates to part ways from the roof beams. He started to slide. Wren staggered down the slope, only barely managing to stop himself falling over, and grabbed Cavanagh's arm, bringing him to a lurching stop.

Cavanagh pushed himself to his feet and nodded gratefully at Wren. "I suggest we run now. With much alacrity."

Wren shook his head. "You always were a one for the understatement, Cavanagh." The long roof stretched ahead of them. At the end of the long row that made up the professors' lodgings he could see the lecture halls and the reading rooms, an untidy jumble of structures that eventually gave way onto the street outside the college.

They started to move but hadn't gone five steps before there was a furious crash from beneath their feet. The whole roof shook. Wren and Cavanagh paused, exchanging a look of alarm. The crash came again, harder and louder.

Wren and Cavanagh turned just as the roof of Wren's lodgings exploded upward in a lethal cloud of shattered tiles and broken wood.

Wren ducked and shielded his face from the spiraling shards. They scattered all around him, fragments stinging exposed skin. He straightened up and found himself staring at the knight as he pulled himself up through the massive hole he had torn in the roof. Tiles cracked underfoot as the knight slowly straightened up to his full height. The moon was full and round behind him, limning his black armor in silver light.

Then, to Wren's utter horror, Cavanagh held the small iron sword before him and readied himself to face the knight.

"Cavanagh! Are you insane? We must flee."

"No time, Wren," said Cavanagh bleakly. "Not anymore." He unshouldered his satchel and tossed it through the air. Wren caught it with fumbling fingers. "You're now the last of the Invisible Order, Wren. It falls to you to stop the fey. If you don't, then humanity is lost."

"I won't abandon you—"

"Wren! Just go! This is my time. Don't let me die in vain."

The knight had started to walk forward by this time. But he was having trouble moving, as every step of his heavy tread sent broken tiles sliding away beneath him. Cavanagh let out a scream of defiance and charged the knight with his sword held out before him, braced in both hands. He aimed the point at the eye slit in the knight's helm, but the knight brought his arm up to deflect the blow. The sword hit with a flash of sparks and a screech of metal, sliding away to the side. Cavanagh braced his legs and swung again. Once more the knight deflected. More sparks leapt into the night sky, glinting against the black armor.

Wren hesitated briefly, then turned and ran as fast as he could along the sharply pitched roof, tears stinging his eyes. Cavanagh had made his choice. There was nothing Wren could do to help, no weapon he could wield to assist him. The only thing he could do was honor Cavanagh's request and take advantage of any delay his attack would cause.

He reached the end of the roof. The astronomy lab was a few feet below him. He readied himself to jump, but a deep roar of pain behind him caused him to whirl around. The knight's arm was raised to the night sky. Cavanagh stood below him, his sword piercing the creature through the gap in the armor just below the armpit.

The tableau was frozen for a brief second. The moon hung low behind them both, illuminating the scene in clear ivory light. Cavanagh's face registered surprise that he had actually wounded the knight with his iron blade.

Then the knight lashed out with his free arm and hit Cavanagh in the chest. Cavanagh let out a grunt of pain and sailed backward through the air, the force of the blow sending him clear over the roof.

Cavanagh dropped out of sight. A moment later, Wren heard a distant thud.

The knight fell to his knees in pain. There was a moment of silence, and then the whole roof collapsed beneath his weight and he disappeared in a cloud of dust and the screaming of splitting wood.

╼CHAPTER NINE╾
In which Emily and Co. battle the Black Knight.

It was dark by the time Emily and the others arrived back at Gresham College. Katerina had joined them, even though Puck hadn't wanted her to go. He had thrown up quite a fuss, his shadows raging around the room as he and Katerina argued. But in the end, he had no choice. Katerina wouldn't back down. She said that she felt it was where she was meant to be. Helping the others instead of sitting in an underground room listening to Puck relive past glories. That had sent Puck into another tirade, and the others had used the opportunity to slip away through the tunnel and out into London.

The gate to the college still stood open, something Jack found a bit *too* exciting. "If it's still open now," he said eagerly, "I bet it's open all night long." He stared keenly across the street. "And not even a gatekeeper to keep watch." He shook his head in mock sorrow. "These professors are very trusting."

"Barnaby mentioned something about most of the professors being away on leave," said Emily. "Something about restoration to the college."

"The perfect time," said Jack, rubbing his hands together.

"Perfect time for what?" asked William.

"Nothing," said Emily quickly, throwing a stern look at Jack.

"Will you stop doing that?" said William forcefully. "How am I supposed to learn anything if you keep trying to hide things from me? Let me make up my own mind!"

"The lad's got a point," said Corrigan, from his position on Emily's shoulder. "And to answer your question," he said to William, "he's talking about theft. Stealing the belongings of the professors."

"Oh. Yes. Obviously, I knew *that*," said William quickly, flushing with embarrassment. Emily knew that look. He felt humiliated because he hadn't known what Jack was talking about. And by not knowing it, he more or less proved that Emily was right. That he really *was* too young to take part in such discussions. He turned away, but not before throwing an angry glare at Emily, as if it was all her fault.

That really was it. Emily decided she would have a talk with William soon. His behavior was getting out of hand. She was the eldest, so it fell to her to look after them both. It was as simple as that. He wouldn't treat their parents like this. Or if he did, he'd probably get a cane across his hide, something Emily couldn't do. (And wouldn't, even if she had the chance. She had been caned while at school, and her backside had hurt for days afterward.)

But that was for later. Right now, they needed to get Corrigan in front of Wren so he could see she hadn't been talking gibberish. That there really were fey creatures who lived alongside the people of London.

Emily led them across the road and past the jumble of houses and rooms that made up the front side of the college, then through the short tunnel to the grass-covered quadrangle that was surrounded by the professors' lodgings.

As they emerged onto the covered walkway, a bellow of pain burst across the college grounds, bringing them all up short.

Emily's eyes darted toward the source of the shout. There were two figures on the roof above Christopher Wren's rooms, outlined against the full moon. Her breath caught in her throat. The taller of the figures was one of the knights they had seen that afternoon, one of the Morrigan's knights.

The other figure was a man. He was standing braced

against the roof as he tried to push a sword or something deeper into the knight. Was it Wren? Had he lied to her? Did he know about the fey after all?

But a moment later all such questions were driven from her mind. There was a blur of movement, then a meaty thud as the knight struck the man in the chest. The force of the blow lifted him high into the air and sent him tumbling from the roof.

There was a brief moment of silence, a brief instant when everything seemed to freeze. Then the moment was gone, and the man landed heavily on the ground and lay still.

Emily tore her eyes away from the horrific sight and looked up. The knight sagged to one knee, and then the roof gave way beneath his weight and he fell into the rooms below amidst the screams of shattering wood and breaking tiles.

Emily started running. She didn't think about how dangerous it was, only that she had to see if she could help. She sprinted across the grass, drawing closer and closer to the dark form lying outside Wren's lodgings. She dreaded what she would find. Was the person dead? Wounded? Maybe he was unharmed. Maybe he'd fallen in such a way that he was somehow cushioned from the worst of it.

But no. As she drew closer to the figure, she could see how unnatural his legs looked, jutting out at such an angle that anyone could see they were broken.

She also realized something else—something that flushed her entire being with relief, which was followed immediately by a hot rush of guilt at feeling such a thing.

It wasn't Christopher Wren. The figure was too tall, too thin for it to be the man she had spoken to. In fact, it looked more like . . .

Cavanagh?

Emily slowed down. She glanced warily around her, not sure what to expect. Why was Cavanagh fighting the knight? What did he have to do with anything?

The others caught up with her, slowing down to stare at the figure lying on the grass. "Snow?" said Jack. "Care to tell us what's going on?"

"I have no idea," she said, carefully approaching the prone figure. There was blood on his face. An old-looking sword lay by his side.

"Is this Wren?" asked Katerina, squatting down to peer at Cavanagh's face. She had her own sword drawn. She clutched it tightly as she cast wary glances around them.

"No. It's Cavanagh. He was with Wren this afternoon."

"Is he dead?" asked William, peering in fascination at the figure.

"I . . . I'm not sure," said Emily. She moved closer. He certainly looked dead. If the crushing blow from the knight hadn't finished him, then surely the fall had? Emily moved around the figure so that her moon-cast shadow wasn't falling across his features. His eyes were closed. There was blood soaking through his clothes.

"Yes. I think he's—"

Cavanagh's hand shot out and grabbed hold of Emily's arm. She screamed in fright and tried to pull away, but the man's bony fingers only bit deeper.

"You . . . ," he gasped. He tried to say something more, but all that came out was a moan of pain. His hand dropped away.

"Come on," said Jack nervously. "If this isn't Wren, we should get out of here."

"We can't just leave him like this," said Emily. "He needs help."

"There's nothing we can do for him," said Katerina. "Jack is right. It's Wren we're looking for. We should go."

"Wait," said Cavanagh weakly. "I . . . I am a member of the Invisible Order."

Emily locked eyes with the others. Jack hesitated, then shrugged. Corrigan looked at Cavanagh with some interest and sauntered casually into the man's field of vision. When Cavanagh saw him, he groaned and fumbled for his sword. But the movement was too much, and he cried out in pain.

"Well, he can certainly see me," said Corrigan in amusement.

"Corrigan!" snapped Emily. "Stop that."

Corrigan stuck his tongue out at her.

"You . . . you command the fey?" asked Cavanagh weakly.

Emily moved closer to Cavanagh. "Not really. I keep trying to make him behave, and he keeps ignoring me."

"This . . . this is your fault. You brought the fey to our door. I have tried to stay hidden from them. Tried to make sure at least one of us remained. But you have undone all of that. You have put Wren's life in danger. They must think he is a member of the Order."

"Isn't he?" asked William from behind Emily.

"No. It was too dangerous. They were hunting us down. Seeking information on . . . on the Raven King. They are getting ready. Getting ready for something big. Something terrible. You must go to my house. There are things . . . things that can help you. I . . . I have notes . . ." Cavanagh coughed, and Emily was alarmed to see blood coming from his mouth. When Cavanagh's coughing fit had subsided, he reached out and touched Emily's wrist with his cold fingers. "It falls to you . . . you must protect Wren. Teach him. The Order must live on."

His fingers dropped to the grass.

"Mr. Cavanagh?" Emily gently prodded him. "Sir?"

Jack gently moved Emily out of the way. He bent over and felt at Cavanagh's neck.

"Is . . . is he dead?" asked a voice from behind them.

Emily and the others whirled around to find Christopher Wren standing a few paces away, staring at the still form. His face was almost as pale as Cavanagh's. He clutched a battered leather satchel to his chest with trembling hands.

"Not yet," said Jack. "But he's not looking very good. Christopher Wren, I presume?"

"What?" Wren blinked and tried to focus on Jack. "Yes. Christopher Wren," he said absently. "Pleased to meet you."

"Are there any doctors nearby?" asked Emily urgently. Wren turned his dazed eyes onto Emily. "Oh, it's you. Hello again. Cavanagh told me I had to find you. Well done, me."

"Snow, we need to get him somewhere safe," Jack said.

"Nice thought," said Katerina, "but we have other problems at the moment."

She was standing off to the side, looking across the grass at Wren's rooms. Emily followed her gaze. Dust was drifting through the empty doorway.

She was just about to ask Katerina what she was talking about when she heard it.

The sound of breaking wood.

Katerina moved forward a few steps so that she was standing in front of the others. Jack scooped up Cavanagh's sword and hurried forward to join her.

"Careful you don't stick yourself with that," said Katerina, glancing at Jack.

"Hah! You just . . . make sure you don't stick *your*self," Jack replied weakly.

Katerina smiled, turning her eyes back to the gaping black door ahead of them. "Nice retort. I hope your feet move faster than your mind. Because if they don't, you should just stay out of my way."

Emily searched around for a weapon of her own. All she had was her stake of witchbane, and she didn't think she'd have much luck penetrating the knight's armor with it.

But that didn't stop William. He gripped his own stake and joined Jack and Katerina. Emily hurried forward and grabbed him by the arm.

"What are you doing?" she asked furiously.

"Let me go!" William tried to shake her off, but Emily wouldn't release her grip.

"You can't fight one of those knights with a piece of wood! You'll get killed."

William finally managed to wrench his arm free. His face was pinched with fury. "So is that what you plan on doing, Em? Standing here and watching someone else die for you? Well, I won't do that. I won't stand here and watch them fight on their own. I can help."

He turned away and moved to stand next to Jack. Emily watched him go, crestfallen. She hadn't meant it that way. Is that what Will thought of her? That she would just stand back while the others put themselves in danger? Surely he knew her better than that.

While she had been arguing, Wren had been carefully dragging Cavanagh across the grass until he was out of the way. Now he was busy fumbling inside his leather satchel. Emily hurried over to him.

"Cavanagh gave me this," he said. "There are all sorts of things—"

Emily grabbed the satchel and dumped the contents on the grass. Corrigan scurried over and began sorting through the odd assortment of items. Wren eyed him warily but didn't say anything.

"Movement!" shouted Jack.

Emily looked up to see the clouds of dust swirl into little circles, as if a breeze had wafted through the courtyard. Then the Black Knight emerged from the shadows of Wren's rooms. He staggered onto the grass, clutching the wound beneath his arm. He stopped short when he saw William, Jack, and Katerina standing in a line, their weapons raised before them.

He watched them for a moment. Then he put his head down and charged straight at them.

Emily frantically searched through the items from the satchel, but there didn't seem to be much that would help. A key, a small crossbow (but nothing to put in it), and a few iron daggers.

That was it.

The knight had almost reached the others.

"Scatter!" shouted Katerina. Jack and William did as instructed, moving aside so that they surrounded the knight. He skidded to a halt, eyeing them warily. Without warning, he lunged forward and swung his arm around, trying to smash it into them. Only Jack was close enough for contact, and he threw himself backward. The knight's armor-covered fist sliced through the air only inches from his face.

Katerina darted around to his back and stabbed at him with her blade. The metal skittered uselessly off his armor. At the same time, William lunged forward with his rowan stake, looking utterly ridiculous to Emily, and stabbed at the back of the knight's knee. To Emily's amazement (and William's), the wood slipped past the join in the armor and sunk into the knight's leg. The knight jerked away, whirling around to face his attacker. When he saw William, he raised his other leg and brought it down hard, intending to crush William beneath his weight.

Jack barreled into Will, sending them both flying out of the way. The knight's foot came down with a heavy thud, leaving his imprint deep in the grass.

He turned to face them as they rolled across the ground, but once again, Katerina struck him with her sword, distracting him so they could get to their feet.

But William had given Emily an idea. She pulled her own rowan stake out of her coat and used one of the iron knives to saw it quickly in half. She scooped up the small crossbow, wondering how you were supposed to get it working.

"Turn the thing, the handle," said Corrigan urgently.

Emily saw the handle he was referring to. She wound it round and round, watching as the bow-shaped wood at the front bent more and more, pulling back toward her hand. She kept going until a small clicking sound told her it was locked in place. Then she slid one of the pieces of rowan into the track and aimed it at the knight. He was only ten or so paces away. She had a clear shot. None of the others were in the way.

Emily pulled the trigger.

The crossbow released with a solid *thunk*. The rowan bolt flew into the air, turning end over end. It hit the knight's arm, then bounced off his armor and embedded itself in the ground, narrowly missing Katerina's ear as it did so.

"Do you mind?" she shouted, then dove to the side and rolled to her feet again as the knight lunged at her.

Emily quickly wound the crossbow again. She slid her last piece of rowan onto the weapon, then aimed it once again. She had to get it right. This was her last shot.

She aimed . . .

A hand closed over hers, stopping her from firing. It was Wren.

"It won't work. The wood isn't straight. It won't fly true."

"I have to try," said Emily. "How else are we supposed to stop that thing?"

Wren took the crossbow from her hands. "Allow me."

He turned and ran toward the fighting. He moved straight for the knight, the crossbow hidden behind his back. When he was no more than three paces away, he stumbled to a stop.

"Hoi," he shouted.

The knight was busy fending off repeated blows from Katerina and Jack, blows that were raising showers of sparks along his arms. He quickly turned, ready to strike out. But when he saw Wren, he hesitated, his raised arm faltering.

That was all Wren needed. He stepped forward, raised the crossbow, and fired it directly into the eye slit in the knight's helmet.

The knight's head jerked back from the force of the blow. He slowly straightened up again, then tilted his head to the side, as if confused about something.

Then he fell apart.

At least, that's what it seemed like to Emily. A cloud of oily smoke wafted into the air, and then the armor simply dropped away, clattering to the ground and forming an untidy pile of metal. Of the Black Knight, there was absolutely nothing left.

Emily and Corrigan hurried forward to join them. Jack

was pushing the armor aside with his foot, but there was no sign of the body.

Wren handed the crossbow back to Emily and smiled weakly. "I think you saved our lives there, young lady."

"I didn't shoot him," said Emily. "You did."

"I pulled the trigger. You came up with the idea."

"Not me," said Emily, looking at Will.

Wren shivered and looked around. "Cavanagh has a house just around the corner. We should take him there and tend to his wounds."

"And then?" asked Katerina, pulling the piece of rowan wood from inside the knight's helmet and handing it back to Emily.

"And then you all explain to me everything that is happening. And I do mean everything."

⚜ Chapter Ten ⚜

*Revelations and mysteries. In which Emily and Co.
learn the legends of the Raven King.*

Wren and Jack carried Cavanagh between them as they hurried out of the college grounds in search of Cavanagh's house. It really wasn't too far. In fact, it was only one street over in Shoreditch Street. Which made sense, thought Emily, if you considered that the college had been the headquarters of the Invisible Order. Cavanagh obviously wanted to be close.

As they hurried along the street, Emily did her best to fill Wren in on what had been going on. The history of the Invisible Order (what she knew of it, anyway), and all that had happened back in 1861.

He took it rather well, thought Emily. No outbursts. No refusal to believe what she was saying. No accusations of her being a liar. Maybe all that would come later. It was a lot to take in at once.

"This is it," said Wren, shifting Cavanagh's weight and pushing a gate open into an unkempt garden. Emily fumbled around inside the satchel and pulled out the key she had seen when Wren had emptied out the bag.

She inserted it into the lock on the front door.

Or at least, she tried to. The key didn't fit.

Emily stared at the key. Now what? Cavanagh had been very clear. Go to his house. There were things there they had to see. Notes of some kind. Had he been delirious?

Wren interrupted her thoughts by reaching around her and testing the latch. The door swung silently open, revealing a dim, shadowy room. Squares of pale silver lay across the carpet, the light of the moon cut into neat segments by the lead window frames.

"How did you know it was unlocked?" asked Emily.

"I didn't," replied Wren. "But I thought it was worth a try."

Wren and Jack entered the house first, carrying Cavanagh over to a musty couch in the front room. They laid him down while Emily, Katerina, and William followed them in.

Katerina looked around the sparse room. "Wasn't much for ornaments, was he?"

Wren looked up from where he was placing a cushion beneath Cavanagh's head.

"Cavanagh spent most of his time at the college. Most of his belongings are in his rooms."

"Then shouldn't we be searching there?" asked Katerina.

"No," said Emily firmly. "He said his house. Not his rooms." She glanced at Katerina. "He was specific." She looked around, realizing something was missing. "Where's Corrigan?"

The piskie was nowhere to be seen.

"He was with me a minute ago," said William. "Outside."

Emily hurried back outside to find the piskie sitting on the grass of Cavanagh's garden. He looked ill. His skin color, usually a deep, walnut brown, was now washed out, closer in color to the bark of a silver birch.

"Corrigan?"

Corrigan opened his eyes.

"What's wrong?" she asked.

Corrigan jerked his head at the house. "Iron," he said. "Lots of it. I felt it when I stepped inside. Nearly fainted dead away."

"I didn't see any."

"It was underneath us. Trust me, Snow. I know iron when I feel it."

"Are you going to be all right?"

Corrigan waved his hand irritably at her. "I'll survive. As long as I don't go back in there. Just need to get my breath back. Go. Look for whatever it is we're supposed to find."

Emily nodded and hurried back inside. The others were standing around Cavanagh's still form. "Corrigan said there's a lot of iron underneath the house," she said. "Maybe that's where we need to look . . ." Emily trailed off when she realized no one was paying attention to her. "What's wrong?"

Jack looked over at her. "Cavanagh's dead."

Wren straightened up from his crouch. "I didn't think he would survive. Not with those injuries."

"Then why did we carry him all the way here?" asked Jack.

"Because I thought he would want to die in his own home," said Wren quietly. "I know I would."

⊹≕ ≕⊹

They observed a few minutes of silence while Wren said good-bye to his friend, but once those minutes were up, Wren was like a man possessed. Cavanagh's death had presented him with a purpose, giving him something to grasp hold of, to focus his anger on. He quickly rounded up all the lanterns in the house and handed them out, instructing everyone to search for a trapdoor of some kind.

It was Jack who eventually found it. He spotted the keyhole first, hidden beneath a heavy set of drawers in the kitchen. The keyhole was formed into a natural knot in the wood, so cunningly fashioned that Emily found it hard to make out even after Jack showed it to her.

121

Wren was impressed. "Lord, boy. You must have the eyes of a hawk."

"Even better," said Jack proudly. "The eyes of a thief."

Emily inserted the key from the rucksack. This time it fit. She turned it in the lock, and Wren heaved the trapdoor open, revealing a set of wooden stairs leading into the darkness. Jack lowered his lantern through the hole. The light glinted on something on the floor, dull highlights striking off metal.

"Must be the iron," Emily said, straightening up. "Should we go down—?"

William didn't wait for her to finish the sentence. He clattered down the steps before anyone could stop him. The others followed after and found themselves in a low room that ran the length of the house. The light from their lanterns revealed piles of books stacked neatly against the walls, largest at the bottom, smallest at the top. Tables filled almost every available space, all of them covered with parchment and scrolls, half-opened books, used-up quills, and empty ink bottles.

The light also revealed the iron that had affected Corrigan so badly. Candelabras, candlesticks, cutlery, plates. All of it tossed randomly around the room.

Emily examined the books closest to her. *The Anatomy of the Cornwall Sprite,* said one. *The Wars of the Irish Tuatha,* was another. Emily moved to another pile. *The Influx of Russian Trolls into France. Scottish Dryads. Battle for the Twilight Court.*

"These are all about the fey," she said. "Every one of them."

They spread out and searched through the clutter, looking for anything that might give them a clue as to what was going on.

It was William who found what they were looking for.

He was standing by a long, crudely built table, paging through a small book, squinting at the pages by the light of his lantern.

"What's that?" asked Jack.

"Looks like a diary. There's an inkpot and a quill here as well."

"Is it Cavanagh's?" asked Wren.

"Seems to be," said William. He handed the diary across to Wren.

Wren took the book and held it close to the lantern. He paged through for a moment, scanning the words. "It's his. I should probably just start at the beginning," he said.

He turned back to the first page and cleared his throat.

"'I'm not sure if anyone is reading this,'" began Wren. "'I can only hope so. If not, then all is lost. Because I'm the last. The last member of the Invisible Order. And if I fall, then there is no one left to carry the fight against the fey.

"'Events have taken a dark turn. For a long time now,

Queen Titania has kept our two races from descending into war. But I fear those days are over. There is a faction among the fey who want mankind wiped out, and it seems the first move in their game plan was to kill off the Invisible Order, one of the few groups who could stop them.

"It has been happening for some time now. Members of the Order disappearing over the past six or seven years. But we thought it nothing more than the natural course of events. A natural attrition caused by the dangers of what we do. But as more and more of our members vanished and our numbers were reduced by half, we began to suspect a conspiracy. Of course, we suspected the fey. We approached Queen Titania with our suspicions, but . . . how can I put this? She was rather offended at our accusations and banished us from her court. I suppose she had a right to be upset. Titania had always been keen to keep our races on, if not friendly terms, then at least *civil* terms, so her taking offense was not unexpected. Regrettable, but not unexpected.

"'But I think she knew we were right. We had been hearing rumors that she was losing control, that factions were developing within the fey who were not happy with her rule, not happy with the uneasy peace she had ordered between our races. I think she realized, as we did, that our problems were one and the same.

"'It wasn't until one snowy night in February sixteen

sixty-three that we began to fathom the scale of these problems, when a member of the Order, a man called Septimus Peel, escaped capture and managed to return to us. How he did so, with the extent of the injuries he carried, is a testament to the man's character and loyalty to the human race.

"'He told us he had been kidnapped from his home by the fey and taken deep into the countryside. Here he was tortured and beaten, and all the while the fey asked him only one question. One question over and over.

"'Where is the Raven King?

"'Obviously, he didn't know. None of us did. Not me, not Septimus, and not any of those who had been taken before him. It was the first any of us had heard of this mysterious figure.

"'But the fey did not believe this. They thought we knew, that we were protecting our secrets, protecting this . . . Raven King, whoever he may be.

"'Septimus died soon after. His wounds were too serious. But he had accomplished what he set out to do. He had brought us information. Information on what the fey were after.

"'I should rather say he brought *me* information. I knew this was important. I also knew that the fey had ways of prying the truth out of us. So I kept the information to myself and resolved to do my own research into this Raven

King, praying all the while that I was not one of the unlucky ones who would be taken. I withdrew from the Order—not attending meetings, not taking part in any activities—hoping that these precautions would keep me from being noticed.

"'And then one day I came back from my travels to Europe and discovered that there were no more of us left. I was the last member of the Invisible Order. I wasted no time. I moved all of our books and manuscripts out of Gresham College.

"'Once I had secured our archives I carried on with my research into the Raven King. I searched through our own files but could find no proof of his existence anywhere. I'm sure it exists, though. There have always been rumors that there is a second library, a library hidden away and stocked with books handpicked by Merlin the Enchanter. But no one knows where that library is.

"'Having exhausted our own archives and finding absolutely nothing, I had to use other means of finding out about the Raven King. It was a dangerous year for me. Through magic, I became that which I had spent my life fighting. I allied myself with fey who cared not for the politics of Titania and her enemies, but who were only interested in gold and trinkets. I traveled far and wide, all in my search for this elusive Raven King. I found . . . hints and whispers. Nothing more than legends, really, all things that the fey already knew.

"'To put it simply, the Raven King is the soul of London.

The holder of the city's dreams and nightmares. He is the King of Dreams, the protector of the bones of the city. As long as the Raven King lives, then London, and by extension Britain, is protected from the fey. This is why they want to find him. They are terrified of him. They have all sorts of legends and folktales about him. They think that if they make a move that will put London under threat, then this Raven King will awaken into his power and destroy them all.

"'But according to these legends, the Raven King doesn't even know who he is. Like King Arthur, who is supposed to return to Britain in her hour of need, so the Raven King will only awaken into his power when Britain is in desperate danger. But no one knows *how* that power will be woken. For all I know, *I* could be the Raven King. It could be anyone. That is why they search for him. They fear this unknown man, fear his power, power he does not even know he has.

"'But I think I am close to finding something out about our elusive King. I have a contact who has set up an appointment with a fey called Croth. I see him tomorrow night. My contact says there is a chance someone called the Prophet may be able to help, and that this Croth can put me in contact with him. I only hope this is true. Because after this, all my leads are finished. If this fails, the only thing to do is sit back and wait for the fey to make their move, hoping this Raven King will wake up. But I fear by then it will be too late.'"

Wren stopped reading. He paged forward, then looked at the others. "That is all. The last entry was dated yesterday."

The lantern light guttered slightly, as if blown on a breeze. Katerina shifted her weight, leaning against a table. "So Kelindria and the others want to kill this Raven King before they make their move? Before he wakes into his power. So that he can't do anything to stop them?"

"According to Cavanagh, yes," said Wren. "And from what's written in this book, that's the last thing that must happen," said Wren. "It seems as though the fate of Britain lies in the hands of someone who does not even know of his potential."

"Probably safer that way," said Jack. "If he doesn't know who he is, there's less chance the fey will know. He should just be left to do whatever it is he does."

"No," said William sharply. Everyone turned to look at him. "Think about it. *We* need to find him. Before the fey do. If he's as powerful as these legends say, he could help us. He could stop the fey. Stop the *fire*. And maybe we could take him back to our time. He could get rid of the Faerie Queen there as well. He could be the answer to all our troubles."

"I don't think that's the best path, Will," said Emily.

Will glared at her. "Why am I not surprised? Come on then, O great leader. What do you think we should do?"

"We should find Merlin."

"Oh, yes. Simple," said Will sarcastically. "Except for the fact that no one knows where he is."

"No one knows where the Raven King is, either," Emily pointed out.

"But Cavanagh had *leads*. We can meet with this Croth, find out who this Prophet is."

"And then what? Even if this Croth knows where the Prophet is, we still have to find him. And then we have to ask him for help. Which he might not give. And we would still be no closer to finding the Raven King. And even if we *do* find him, how are we supposed to 'awaken his power' or whatever Cavanagh said? Do you know how? Because I certainly don't." Emily paused and took a deep breath to calm herself.

"But if we focus on finding Merlin, we can find out where he hid those books Cavanagh mentioned. Actually, I doubt we'd even *need* the books. Merlin will probably know how to track down the Raven King using his magic. We find Merlin, he finds the Raven King, we stop the fey. Remember, Will, Merlin said that I helped him, that we had met before. That means we *must* have found him, must have rescued him from wherever he's being held prisoner."

"You can't just jump to that kind of conclusion!" protested Will. "Who knows *when* Merlin turns up? Right now we are two hundred years in the past. And this happened just because we traveled through a fey gate. Who's to say what will happen if we use one again? Who's to say you don't meet Merlin a thousand years ago? Or five hundred? Why do you think it has to be now?"

Emily paused. She hadn't thought about that. If they skipped back through centuries once before, who's to say it *wouldn't* happen again. In fact . . . hadn't Merlin said something about her meeting King Arthur? She'd thought he was playing a joke on her, but . . .

What if he wasn't?

She thought about it some more. And what *if* he wasn't? It didn't change anything right now. They didn't know enough about this Raven King to go seeking him out. He might not even exist. They had no proof.

On the other hand, they *did* know that Merlin existed. She had met him, after all.

She looked at the others. Will was sullenly rooting about in Cavanagh's desk. Jack was idly inspecting an old candlestick. Wren was paging through the diary, perhaps searching for some other clues. Katerina looked at her but simply shrugged. There was no help here.

Nobody here was going to be any help.

She needed to speak to Corrigan. Emily headed for the stairs, and William shouted after her.

"Why do you have to be right all the time? Can't you

accept the fact that someone else might have a good idea besides you? It doesn't make you any weaker you know."

Emily ignored him and kept on walking.

⊱ ⊰

After Emily had explained what they had found in Cavanagh's diary, the piskie folded his arms thoughtfully, leaned back, and stared up at the night sky.

"So have you ever heard of this Raven King?" Emily prompted.

"No," Corrigan replied. "Not a thing."

"So do you think we should concentrate on finding Merlin?"

"I didn't say that, either. Merlin is a pain in the backside. A silly old man who allowed himself to get tricked by a pretty face. He should have known better."

"Maybe he really loved her," said Emily softly.

Corrigan made a disgusted sound that admirably conveyed his feelings about love.

"I don't suppose you happen to know where he is?" Emily asked hopefully. After all, it was the fey who had captured Merlin in the first place.

"No," said Corrigan, quashing Emily's hopes. "And even if I did, how do you think you'd go about rescuing him? You wouldn't be able to stroll in and open the door. He'll be hidden away. There will be guardians, magical traps, all kinds of fail-safes."

Emily felt her hopes fading. "We have to do *something*. This Fire King is going to try to destroy London. And you said there will be a war. A . . . a war of the races. We can't have that knowledge and simply do nothing! Maybe we can stop it! Stop the war from happening. Stop the fire."

"And you think finding Merlin is the answer to all that?"

"It's a start!" Emily snapped. "Didn't you lose anyone you knew during this war? Don't you want to try and stop that?"

A cloud passed briefly across Corrigan's face. He sighed, then glanced around the nighttime streets. "Fine," he said. "I'm not saying it will work, but if you're set on finding the old fool, then we should start by tracking down Nimue."

"Who's that?"

"She's the fey who trapped him in the first place."

"The one he fell in love with?" asked Emily excitedly. "Do you know where she is?"

"No. But I know someone who might. A fey called Beezle. He's what you might call an information broker. Lives out on London Bridge."

"And he'll help us?"

"Depends on his mood. He's a bit on the . . . dishonest side, so you'll have to let me deal with him."

"I'm sure the two of you must get on splendidly," said Emily.

Corrigan opened his mouth to reply, then frowned angrily. "What's that supposed to mean?"

"Nothing at all."

"Hmm."

A thought suddenly occurred to Emily. "How can you know about this Beezle?" she asked. "I thought the you in the past wasn't here right now." Emily ran the sentence back through her head to make sure it made sense.

"I wasn't. But he was. And still is. In your time, I mean. He comes and goes, but he always ends up back at his shop on London Bridge. Can't leave it behind. Let's just hope this is one of the times he's there."

"When should we go? How do we get there?"

"Same way everyone gets there. Head out to the gate and say the password: *Ansible Cru.*" Corrigan squinted up at the moon. "The bridge only picks up after midnight. So there's more chance he'll be there then. I suggest you try and catch a few winks of sleep while you can."

Emily nodded and stood up. William wasn't going to like any of this, but he'd just have to understand it was the most logical decision to make. Finding Merlin was the answer. She was sure of it.

After all, she'd done it before. She was sure she could do it again.

ᐊCHAPTER ELEVENᐅ
In which Kelindria summons the Fire King.
The Second War of the races is set in motion.

The Morrigan's ravens were restless.

They picked up on Kelindria's pensive mood, ruffling their feathers and cawing softly in the dimness. Kelindria sat on her throne, listening to the birds and staring absently at the flames as they burned in the fire pit in the center of the room. Something had changed. A new element had entered the picture, and it was in danger of unraveling all her plans. Plans she had been nurturing and tending for years. *Decades*. It all seemed connected to the appearance of this girl. Who was she? Where had she come from? It was as if she had simply appeared out of thin air, intent on causing havoc.

The second key was what bothered Kelindria. It simply should not exist. There was only one key. Everyone knew that. And the Queen of the Faeries (whoever it was that currently held the title) controlled it. It was the way it had always been.

Kelindria's thoughts circled back to her first suspicions regarding this supposed key. Was it, after all, a trap? Had Titania finally grown a backbone and decided to put a stop to Kelindria, proof or no proof?

But no, Kelindria's instinct told her this wasn't so. It wasn't Titania's style.

So back to the question at hand. Who was this . . . this *girl*? And what did she want?

She sensed the Sluagh shifting in the garden outside. She closed her eyes and concentrated, looking through the creature's eyes. It was that idiot Barnaby again. She sighed and briefly toyed with the idea of letting the Sluagh take him, but she resisted the temptation. He may still have some uses.

She ordered the Sluagh to let him enter.

She didn't have to wait long. Barnaby came running into her presence, disheveled and sweating. His eyes were wide and darting as he stumbled to a stop in front of her.

"He's dead. They . . . they killed him! Shot him—"

"Stop talking!" thundered Kelindria.

Barnaby started, then visibly tried to calm himself down.

"Now begin again. Who is dead?"

"The Black Knight."

Kelindria thought for a moment that she had heard wrong. "The Black Knight? The Morrigan's warrior?"

Barnaby gulped down a breath and nodded.

"How?"

"It was Wren. And the children. And Cavanagh."

"Talk sense!" Kelindria shouted.

Barnaby drew a deep breath. "I took the Black Knight to Wren, as you ordered. But Cavanagh was with him."

"Who is this Cavanagh?"

"Someone from the college. I never suspected him of being a member of the Invisible Order. I didn't see his name anywhere, and he was always away . . . But he was there with Wren. He helped him escape. He wounded the knight in a fight, and then Wren and the children finished him off. He's gone."

"These children. Was the girl there again?"

"Yes. And . . . and that's not all."

Kelindria knew that whatever she was about to hear would be bad. "Speak," she ordered.

"I heard them talk about the Raven King. I couldn't hear what was said, but I definitely heard them mention it. More than once."

Kelindria sat back in her throne. This was . . . distressing news. Most distressing. Catastrophic, one might say.

"Is that all?"

"I think so, milady. What should I do?"

"What do I care?" she snapped. "Just leave me to think."

Barnaby scurried from the room while Kelindria sank deeper into thought. Her plans were in very real danger of coming undone. If she didn't do something drastic, her window of opportunity would be gone. Did these children have something to do with the Raven King? What about this Christopher Wren? Was *he* perhaps the Raven King?

Kelindria slapped the arms of her throne in frustration. She wasn't ready for this right now! Her plans were supposed to carry on for another decade or so. Only then had she intended on making her move. She didn't have enough followers. She *certainly* didn't have enough allies.

Unless . . .

She stood up and slowly approached the fire in the center of the room, staring deep into the flames. Dare she?

But no, such a thing was madness. When she had raised the subject to the Dagda, he had told her in no uncertain terms that to do such a thing would incur his wrath and break their partnership.

But maybe she wouldn't need him anymore. If she did this, she would have the power all to herself.

Say it, she told herself. Say what you are thinking of doing.

To summon the Fire King.

The wood shifted in the pit, the flames dancing higher as if in response to her thoughts.

It was the Morrigan who had first told her about him. An elemental lord. Not from here. Not from Faerie. But from somewhere in between. A place of molten rocks and fierce heat. An elemental being that hungered to devour.

She'd had many dreams about this being. To scour the whole of Britain clean. To wipe everything away and start again. And this time *she* could lay the first stone that claimed London. It wouldn't be Merlin and his Invisible Order. It wouldn't be like the last time. No, this time round it would be the *humans* hiding away in their little groups, living underground like animals. Not the fey. The fey would rule from above. The fey would rule the whole land.

And she, Kelindria, would be Queen.

The flames mesmerized her, drew her in. She could feel the heat on her face. Should she just do it? She had the power. After the Morrigan had told her about the Fire King, Kelindria had searched through the ancient lore until she found out how to do the summoning.

But some fey would die as well. She could tell the Fire King not to harm them, but from what the Morrigan had said, he was hard to control. Once he started feeding, once the flames started spreading, would he hold true to their agreement?

But not *all* the fey would die. Most of them would head

underground. And besides, when she was Queen, she would control the key. She could open the gates and allow more fey to come from Faerie. Most of the humans, on the other hand, would perish.

Almost of its own volition, Kelindria's hand slipped into a pouch and withdrew a small, round stone. It was a dull black in color, surprisingly heavy for something so small. When the light shifted, tiny red sparks shimmered across its surface.

Afterward, she was never really sure if she had made a conscious choice, or if the stone had simply slipped from her hand. Either way, it dropped heavily into the flames, sending a shower of sparks drifting up into the air.

At first, nothing happened. But then Kelindria saw that the flames were drawn to the stone, wrapping around it like nurturing hands.

Kelindria waited. After a while, a sharp crack echoed through the room, and the stone split in two. Kelindria leaned closer and saw a lizardlike creature curled up inside one of the halves. Flames crawled across its skin. It flickered orange and red, like the embers in the fire. Then it jerked, and unfurled, crawling sluggishly out of the stone.

A salamander, thought Kelindria, watching the little lizard burrow deep into the flames. It lay basking in the heat, then it burrowed deeper into the ash and embers and simply disappeared.

Kelindria frowned. She used her dagger to push the wood around in the fire pit, but the salamander had vanished. She straightened up and looked around her chamber. Where had it gone?

There was a sudden roaring sound, and Kelindria felt a flare of intense heat against her face. She stumbled back and turned around to find the flames in the fire pit soaring high up to the roof. The flames were brighter now, almost white hot. She raised a hand to shield herself, squinting against the glare and the heat. The flames were rushing upward as if blown by a terrific wind, and in the center of this maelstrom was the outline of a fiery figure.

It was humanoid. But only just. Its face was long, its eyes dark pits of red heat that stared silently at Kelindria.

The heat was intense. Kelindria opened her mouth to speak, but the air was burned from her lungs. She had to step farther away from the fire.

"Greetings, Fire King," she began. "I've summoned—"

You have not summoned me. I came of my own volition, said the Fire King. The words crackled and roared, as if the flames themselves were doing the talking. The words sent heat shimmers into the air between herself and the Fire King.

"Of course," Kelindria said. "May I present my offer to you?"

I know of your offer. You wish me to burn this city from the earth. You want to be rid of the human animals.

Kelindria didn't ask how he knew such things.

The question I ask, is what can you offer me?

Kelindria frowned. "I offer you food, I offer you London. I offer you Britain. To wipe all clean so that a new growth can begin through the ashes."

You misunderstand. That is my prize. But what I am asking now is what you *offer me. I desire something from* you.

"What? What do you desire?"

Something precious. I demand a tithe. You must sacrifice that which is most precious to you.

"But why? I am giving you Britain. You can only come through if I summon you. Why should you need anything more?"

Because I am the Fire King! Because it is my whim. Now. Do you agree?

Kelindria stared at the flames thoughtfully. What choice did she have? It seemed that to complete this transaction she would have to hand over extra payment. Unexpected, but not something she was about to let deter her. Not now she had gone so far.

"What do you require? Gold? Sacrifices?"

Just tell me whether you agree to my terms.

"Fine. I agree."

Kelindria thought she saw the mouth on the Fire King part in a smile. A glowing red hole gaped in the white hot mass.

Good.

And then Kelindria felt a prickling in her hands. She looked down and for a moment saw nothing unusual. Then a faint cobweb of lines appeared on her fingers. She lifted her hands to her eyes. As she did so, the faint lines grew deeper, wider, the pale flawlessness of her skin sucked away and replaced by wrinkles.

"No!" Not that. Anything else, but not that.

She turned and staggered back to her throne. The white ravens flew away from her in a panic, roosting high in the rafters. Kelindria fumbled for her looking glass, almost dropping it when she saw her nails growing long and yellow, her fingers shrinking to withered twigs.

She lifted the looking glass to her face. Except it wasn't her face anymore. As she watched, her hair lost its lustrous red sheen and faded to dull white. Her face caved in before her eyes, her cheeks becoming dark hollows, her once glowing eyes becoming tired, surrounded by wrinkles and black shadows.

The Fire King had taken the one thing she treasured more than anything else.

He had taken her beauty.

Her screech of fury was heard far and wide. The white

ravens took to the air in a panic, flying madly around the room in an attempt to escape the horrific, pain-filled scream.

The Fire King smiled and reached upward, plucking the white ravens one by one from the air.

⊹⇒ ⇐⊹

All was quiet on Pudding Lane in the early hours of Sunday morning. Inside the bakery of Thomas Faryner, the bread ovens were banked for the night, checked by both Faryner and his maids.

The fires were out.

But in one of the five ovens, in the far corner, an old, still-warm coal shifted. It rolled over, revealing an orange ember. The orange glowed brighter, then a tiny claw appeared, poking out from the coal. The claw reached out, grasping blindly, and touched a second coal. This second coal flared to life, and the orange head of a salamander pushed slowly out, its fiery tongue flicking into the air.

It could smell food. Lots of it. And nearby.

The salamander paused to gather its strength, then pulled itself out of the coal. It crawled sluggishly to the door of the oven. There was wood nearby. It could sense it. Fuel to gain strength.

It crawled over the edge and dropped to the floor. A small stool stood not far away. The salamander pattered across

143

the cobbles, leaving red-hot footprints behind that quickly cooled to black ash. It reached the stool and climbed slowly up the leg.

The wood started to smoke. Then there was a small puff, and a flame appeared beneath the salamander. The lizard settled down while the flame grew bigger, letting the heat wash over its body.

It tasted the air with its tongue again. There was so much food nearby. It tasted oil. Pitch. Resin. Tar. Hay. Paper. Everything its master could possibly want.

Once the flames had taken hold of the stool, the sala-mander hopped to the wooden table. Behind it, a second salamander crawled from the flames it had just left behind in the wood. This second salamander looked around, then crawled in the direction of the wooden door.

The Great Fire of London had begun.

⇥CHAPTER TWELVE⇤
In which Corrigan faces something wholly unfamiliar to himself—
to whit, his conscience—and wrestles it into submission.

Corrigan didn't like introspection. It distracted him from the moment, called his attention away from what was really important in life (i.e., enjoying himself). But sometimes he couldn't help it. Sometimes, his thoughts demanded to be attended to; otherwise, they would itch away at him like an insect bite.

And right now was one of those times.

He stalked up the street, then turned around, glared at Cavanagh's house, and stalked back to the front gate once again, where he stood glaring at the house with his hands on his hips.

He was muttering to himself.

The source of his current bout of introspection was Emily

Snow. Specifically, the events that he had taken part in since meeting her, and the changes she had brought about in someone who had been perfectly happy the way he was before she came along, thank you very much.

She was turning him into someone who . . . *cared*. (Even thinking the word caused his lips to curl with distaste.) She was turning him into someone who wanted to . . . *do the right thing*.

What was this unholy power this little dark-haired girl possessed? Why did he feel so guilty every time he had a thought she would disapprove of, thoughts that—only a few days ago—he wouldn't have even batted an eyelid over?

She was trouble, that one. It would all end in tears. Nothing good could come of it. And . . . and many more such sayings, which he was too upset at the moment even to think of.

And now there was this latest idea to come out of that too-adult mind. Finding Merlin the Enchanter! Fine, it was a good idea. *If* they could pull it off, a number of fey might survive the coming days, fey who would otherwise die in the fire or the war.

Corrigan paused at this thought. Could they even do that? Could they change history in such a way? Wouldn't they get into some kind of trouble? Surely there was someone who watched over that kind of thing? Changing the course of history had to be frowned upon in polite society.

Now there was a thought. Corrigan straightened his back. That actually made him feel a bit better about the whole thing. It probably went against a whole number of natural laws. Corrigan carefully explored this new line of reasoning, the same way one would tentatively probe a loose tooth. So ... by helping Emily do this, even if *her* reasons were good ones, Corrigan was probably breaking the biggest law out there. He was breaking the laws of Nature. Surely that made him the biggest criminal mastermind of *all eternity*!

Corrigan liked the sound of that. It had a nice ring to it. Course, he wouldn't tell Emily that. She could just carry on as normal, smug and happy in the mistaken knowledge that she had managed to make Corrigan a *better piskie*.

Hah! Just shows what you know, my lass, thought Corrigan gleefully. *I'm not helping you because it's the right thing to do. I'm breaking the laws of Nature! Beat that, Spring-Heeled Jack.*

Now that he had wrestled his conscience to the ground and beaten it into submission, Corrigan checked his surroundings with renewed interest. He wondered where the nearest alley was that would take him through to the fey side of London. He felt like a tankard of real Faerie mead, and he still had a couple of hours till midnight came around and they headed out to the bridge.

He wandered along the street, whistling softly to himself. He hadn't gone far before he heard the click of a door latch.

He turned around and saw the front door to Cavanagh's house opening. Corrigan thought it must be Emily, coming to berate him about something, or lecture him about some crude comment he had made hours ago.

But he was wrong. Because stepping through the doorway, casting a nervous glance over his shoulder, was Emily's brother, William.

"Hello," mused Corrigan. "What have we here?"

William closed the door softly and moved silently along the garden path. Corrigan trotted along the road and stopped directly in front of the gate, his arms folded across his chest.

"You're up to no good," he said as the gate opened.

William breathed in sharply and froze. Corrigan smiled to himself as William struggled to recover.

"And please don't insult me by denying it," said the piskie. "I know the look. You can't fool someone who's . . . fooled . . . others." Corrigan winced. "Sorry. That didn't come out as dramatic as I thought it would. What are you up to?"

"Nothing," said William.

"What did I just say, boy? I said, 'don't insult me.' You want I should shout for your sister?" Corrigan nodded with satisfaction at the look of panic that flashed across William's face. "Thought not. Now tell me what you're doing. And if I think you're lying, I shout. Got it?"

William hesitated for a moment, then shrugged. "Emily's

fixed on finding Merlin," he said. "I think she's wrong. I think we should track down this Raven King."

"Ah, I see. Your plan is to track down the Raven King all by yourself? Showing your big sister that her little brother isn't so little after all? That maybe she should listen to his opinion once in a while. Is that it?"

"That's it exactly," said William quietly.

Corrigan hesitated. "Oh," he said. He had expected some sort of denial, some sort of argument. Truth to tell, he was rather taken aback by the determination in the boy's voice. "And is there anything I can say that will talk you out of it?"

"Not a thing."

"And do you have a plan? Or were you just thinking of wandering around aimlessly in the vain hope of bumping into this Raven King?"

William held up a piece of paper. "I found this on Cavanagh's desk. It has the address of the fey he was going to see. The one called Croth." William then held up a small purse. It jingled. "This was sitting on top of the paper. I take it to be payment."

"Oh," said Corrigan again. "That's actually quite logical. Well done. And what do you think your sister will say about this?"

William snorted, halfway between a laugh and a curse. "I'm not going to tell her. Why should I? She's made her feelings clear enough. She doesn't think I'm old enough to make my own decisions. She had her chance, Corrigan. She can look for Merlin, and I'll look for the Raven King."

"You're playing a dangerous game, boy. Thousands of lives are at stake here. The fate of London, even."

"Exactly. And this way we double our chances. Emily looks for Merlin; I look for the Raven King. If we both succeed, great. If only one of us does, then that's fine as well. But if we all just follow Emily, we're ignoring another avenue. We'd be foolish to do so."

William stepped around Corrigan, then paused and crouched down so he was face-to-face with the piskie. "I hope we all see each other after this is finished. But if not . . . If something happens . . . then it's been a pleasure knowing you."

William straightened up and hurried away into the night.

Corrigan hesitated. He couldn't just leave the boy to wander around London on his own, could he? He'd get himself captured. Or killed. Or both. And Corrigan just *knew* that Emily would blame him for that.

And besides, thought Corrigan. The boy actually had a point. Why not double their chances by following two clues instead of one? He'd told Emily how to contact Beezle. She had brains. She'd been into fey London before.

But William, no matter how sure he was that he could

look after himself, needed someone to watch over him. Someone wise, someone knowledgeable in the ways of the world. Someone to teach the boy, to guide him, to pass on centuries of experience.

Someone like Corrigan.

The piskie broke into a run, a grin spreading across his pointed face. Besides, he reckoned William would be a lot more fun than his sister.

⊰⊱ ⊰⊱

A few moments later, the door to Cavanagh's house opened again. Someone truly observant may have noticed that there was no sound of the latch clicking this time. Someone with a bit of intelligence may deduce that this was because the door hadn't actually been closed. That it had remained slightly ajar so that whoever was hiding on the other side could hear the conversation taking place outside the gate.

That someone would be right.

A dark figure slipped out of Cavanagh's house and followed after Corrigan. The figure kept to the shadows, but every now and then the moonlight would shine on the determined face of Katerina Francesca as she trailed the piskie and William through the streets of London.

151

⊰ CHAPTER THIRTEEN ⊱

*In which Emily and Co. travel to London Bridge
and learn some bad news about Beezle.*

Emily felt as though she had been dozing for only a few minutes before someone roughly shook her awake. She squinted into the lantern light to find Christopher Wren peering down at her, his face lined with worry.

"Is it midnight already?" she asked, struggling into a sitting position.

"Nearly. But that's not why I woke you. It's your brother, I'm afraid."

"Will?" Emily looked around the cellar. Jack was a dark shape curled up on the floor, but she couldn't see Will anywhere. Or Katerina, for that matter. "Where is he?"

"That's the problem. He's gone. And so has the girl."

"Gone?" Emily quickly stood up, wondering if Wren was playing a prank on her. "He can't be gone."

Jack stirred and sat up. He looked around blearily. "What's going on?" he asked, stifling a yawn.

"Will's gone, Jack. And so has Katerina."

Jack sprang to his feet and scanned the room. "If she's done anything to him, I'll kill her!"

"Maybe he's upstairs?" said Emily hopefully.

Wren shook his head. "I've searched the entire house. Plus . . ." Wren hesitated. "He's taken Cavanagh's diary."

It was at that moment that Emily realized what Will had done. She locked gazes with Jack and saw him arrive at the same conclusion.

"He's gone to look for the Raven King," said Emily flatly.

"It would appear so," agreed Wren.

Emily could scarcely believe it. After all they had been through, after everything that had happened. For him to just . . . leave like that. It felt as though he had simply walked out of her life forever without even saying good-bye. That was how betrayed Emily felt. Didn't he realize how important all this was? It had nothing to do with his needing to prove himself. It was about saving lives. For him to just . . . go off on his own like this was so incredibly irresponsible that Emily struggled to take it in.

"Maybe he's outside. Speaking to Corrigan," suggested Jack, although there was no real conviction in his voice.

They checked anyway. The street was silent and empty. Very empty.

There was no sign of the piskie either.

"Corrigan?" she called out, but there was no answer.

"You think Katerina and Corrigan have gone with him?" asked Jack.

"They must have."

"Do you think they planned this?" asked Wren.

Emily shook her head. "No, I don't think so. Corrigan would have told me if he thought we should look for the Raven King. I think Will tried to slip away and Corrigan saw him."

"Then why didn't he tell us? And what about Katerina?"

Emily shrugged. "I don't know." Well, at least it meant that Will wasn't alone. That he was with people who knew their way around, who knew the ins and outs of fey London.

"We have to go after him," Jack said. "Maybe there's time—"

"No," said Emily heavily.

Wren and Jack stared at her.

"But he may not have gone far."

Emily shook her head. "Doesn't matter. He made his choice. We carry on with our plan. We look for Merlin."

"But Snow—"

"No, Jack. We don't have time to run around searching for Will. And what if we do find him? What do we do? Tie him to a piece of rope and pull him along after us? He's my brother, and I love him, but he's made his choice. Let him look for the Raven King. Corrigan and Katerina will watch over him."

"And who's going to watch over them?" asked Jack.

Emily didn't answer.

"So what is our plan?" asked Wren.

"Same as before," said Emily. "We go to London Bridge."

⊹

In Emily's time London Bridge was exactly that. A bridge people used to get from one side of the River Thames to the other.

But here it was rather different.

Here, the bridge was an extension of London. Shops and houses had been built along the massive structure as if it were a city street, the buildings on the edges actually hanging out over the fiercely churning river, held up by wooden struts that had been hammered against the bridge supports. A narrow lane about two meters across was all that was left for pedestrians and carts that wanted to actually cross the river, and even that was allowed grudgingly by those who lived on the bridge. The path was more like a tunnel cutting through the businesses and homes, a slowly eroding walkway that was being swallowed by structures the same way a forest path was gradually swallowed up by trees and weeds. It seemed to Emily that another bridge would soon have to be built so that those who actually wanted to *cross* the river would have a means of doing so.

All the while, as Emily, Christopher Wren, and Jack made their way toward the bridge, she wondered if she had made the right decision. Maybe they *should* have gone looking for William. Maybe she should have listened to what he had to say about the Raven King. Was he right? Were they following the wrong course, searching for Merlin?

She searched inside herself, trying to see past the guilt, the anger, the confusion of conflicting emotions she felt when she thought about her brother.

Had she done the right thing?

After her parents had vanished, one of the first things Emily realized was that being an adult meant making hard decisions that no one else would make. But she was constantly terrified that she was making the wrong choices. Emily was well aware she was only twelve years old. That there was every possibility she was doing everything wrong. But she knew that if she let that thought take hold, it would mean the end of both her and William, so she fought it off with bossiness and bluster. It was the only way she could keep the fear at bay.

Emily stared up at the massive gates that led onto the bridge. She was feeling a lot of fear right now, but she still felt that her decision had been the correct one.

William would have to find his own path.

The gates were locked tight for the night. Emily could just make out small, roundish shapes mounted on spikes at the very top of the gates. She had an uneasy feeling that she knew what they were, but it was too dark to see for sure. Now, what was the word Corrigan had said would gain them entry? *Annabalish?* No, that wasn't it. It sounded like a name of some kind. *Anna Cru?* That wasn't it. It was longer. *Ansible Cru.* That was it.

"Ansible Cru," she said loudly.

For a moment nothing happened. Emily wondered if she had maybe got the words wrong, but then a red glow shone from above the gate. To be more precise, the glow came from inside one of the roundish shapes mounted on spikes. Emily's suspicions had been right. They were human skulls. The red glow shone through the empty eye sockets and nose hole, pulsing like a heartbeat, growing stronger and stronger, brighter and brighter, lighting the other skulls and the metal gates with a lurid, fiery glow.

Emily, Jack, and Wren took a fearful step backward, wondering what Emily's words had summoned.

Then came a fit of coughing, which the red light kept pace with, growing frantically brighter, then subsiding, brighter, then subsiding, with each hacking splutter.

The coughing stopped, and the light died with it.

Emily glanced uncertainly at the others, but before they could do anything, the glow flared up again, and a tiny creature flew from one of the skull's eye sockets and landed with a grunt on a ledge just above her head. It took Emily a moment to realize that the creature was a fairy, because he looked nothing like the ones she had seen when Corrigan had taken her beneath London. This faerie was male, he was old, and he was fat. He was wearing a leather jerkin that was too small for his body. His hairy stomach bulged out from beneath the stained material. The red glow coming from his rather tattered wings was sickly, pulsing with his heaving breath.

"Sorry," he said in a rough, gravelly voice. He pounded himself in the chest. "Heartburn. Can't seem to shift it. Think it's all the snails." He looked at Emily, then glanced over her shoulder at the others. He closed one eye and leaned forward, squinting at them. "You're humes," he said.

"If by 'humes' you mean humans, then yes, we are," said Emily.

"Then what you want? You can't come here. Get out. Go away."

"No. I knew the password, didn't I? You have to let us in."

"We'll see about that. Where'd you hear it, anyways?"

"Corrigan told me. He's a friend."

"Corrigan? The piskie? The thief? The vagabond? The gambler?"

"Uh . . . possibly." Emily thought about it for a second. "Actually, that sounds about right. Yes."

"Why'd he give you the password?"

"He wants us to get something for him. From Beezle."

"That a fact. From Beezle, eh?"

"Yes, now are you going to let us in?"

The faerie peered over Emily's shoulder. "What's wrong with him?"

Emily turned around to find that Wren had crept forward and was staring at the faerie with a look of rapt fascination on his face. He reached out a trembling hand toward the suddenly nervous creature.

"What's he doin'? Get off. No touching." The faerie flapped his wings and lifted into the air, his weight causing him to rise incredibly slowly. He glared suspiciously at Wren.

Emily slapped the man's hand down from where he was trying to reach up to the faerie, his finger held out as if trying to catch a bird.

Wren snapped out of his reverie. "Oh. So sorry. Got a bit distracted by . . ." He looked up at the faerie again. "Fascinating," he said. "Absolutely fascinating."

"Are you going to let us in or not?" demanded Jack.

The faerie flew higher. He didn't answer until he was perched on top of the skull again. "Aye, I suppose so," he said. "But you'd better keep an eye on the tall one. Tell him not to prod anyone."

Wren bowed. "Of course. My most humblest apologies, good sir."

"Well . . . fine. Just don't let it happen again."

There was a deep grinding sound, and a second, round door opened within the gates of London Bridge, a door that hadn't been there a moment ago. Light and sounds spilled out: the hubbub of voices, raucous cries, the music of fiddles and flutes, laughter, shouting, crying. Emily could see figures moving on the other side of the door, figures that were not visible on the London Bridge she could see through the iron bars of the gates.

Emily stepped forward. The others followed, and the small door slammed shut behind them. Emily glanced over her shoulder and saw a fey creature about the same size as her turning a heavy brass wheel that moved a series of cogs and gears, locking the door tight. Once she had finished, the fey stepped back. The wheels and gears and cogs flared white then vanished, leaving behind a blank wall.

The bridge extended before them, and like the real version, it was lined with shops and buildings. But that was where the similarity ended. On the real London Bridge, there was some semblance of order, but here it seemed that every shop and house had simply been dropped from the sky and then left wherever it landed. Structures were piled haphazardly one atop the other, stilts and poles used to stop them from falling over. Emily was sure she could see some of them swaying in the warm night breeze. The buildings were painted every conceivable color. Red, purple, bright green, faded yellow. Everything combined to give the bridge the vibrancy of a carnival.

Fey of all descriptions went about their business: tall, short, fat, thin, flying, or crawling. Three huge, shaggy men lumbered out of a building ahead of Emily, and judging by their raucous laughter and unsteady walking, Emily assumed the building was an inn. The door opened as another fey entered, and Emily was surprised to see a group of human men and women playing music. All but one had their eyes closed as if asleep, and the one who was awake looked desperately afraid as he played his fiddle, his eyes darting around as if searching for escape.

The bridge reminded Emily of market day back home,

when the wives bought the food for the coming week and the afternoon was coming to an end. All the serious business was taken care of, and now was the time for the fun to start. Except, knowing what she now knew about the fey, she thought there probably never *was* any serious business. That the bridge always felt as it did now, barely restrained, overcrowded, too noisy, and very confusing.

"So where do we find this Beezle fellow?" asked Wren, unable to take his eyes off the scene before him.

"I'm not sure," Emily replied. "I suppose we could ask?"

But who? Who could they ask? Emily didn't trust the fey. They were sneaky and conniving, so she had no idea who would offer them genuine help and who would hinder them simply because they thought it a funny joke.

She took a step forward, only to feel a firm hand grab her and stop her from moving. It was Wren. He was staring down at her feet. Emily followed his gaze to find what looked like a family of tiny fey with snail shells on their backs crossing in front of her. One of the tiny fey shook his fist at Emily.

Emily carefully lowered her foot to the side of the tiny creature. "Sorry," she said.

The fey cast a disgusted look at her, then moved slowly on.

They set off again, this time Emily being more careful where she trod. They moved off to the side of the thoroughfare so they could get a look inside the shops as they walked.

The problem was, Emily had no idea what kind of shop Beezle owned. She didn't even have a clue what type of fey Beezle was. He could have been one of those creatures she had nearly squashed.

Emily stopped walking. "This is ridiculous. We'll have to just ask someone." If they didn't, they'd be wandering around the bridge all night. She looked around. They had stopped next to a bookshop. That would do, surely? If any fey shop was going to be harmless, then surely a bookshop would be the one?

Emily pushed open the door. A bell jingled as she entered into a musty, dimly lit interior. She peered into the shadowy interior of the shop, but there didn't seem to be anyone around. She was just about to leave when what had to be the untidiest, most unruly head of hair Emily had ever seen popped up from behind the counter. About half a yard below this bird's nest a face appeared, blinking owlishly from behind thick, round spectacles.

There was a moment of silence while she turned her magnified eyes onto each of them. Then her face broke into a huge smile, revealing overlarge, but perfectly formed teeth. "Good *eventide* to you all. And welcome to Bansho and Co., purveyors of ethereal books, dream texts, and various other knicks and knacks. 'Even if it hasn't been written, I can most likely still get hold of it for you.' That's my motto. Although it needs some work. Not very catchy, is it? I'm Bansho, by the way. In case that wasn't clear."

"We're not really after a book," began Emily apologetically.

"Sorry," said Wren. "Can I just clarify something? Did you say you can get books that haven't been written yet?"

"Oh, yessir. We pluck them from the dream space. One of our best lines of business." Bansho picked up a leather-bound book from the counter. "Take this one, fer instance. Won't be written for almost four hundred years. Got a collector after this one."

Emily tried to catch a glimpse of the title. *Preludes and ...* but she couldn't see the rest, as the fey had put the book down again and picked up another. This time Emily could see it clearly: *The Hound of the Baskervilles,* by Arthur Conan Doyle.

Wren stepped forward, his hands eagerly outstretched.

"Mr. Wren," said Emily. "We are here for another reason."

Wren stopped and forced his hands down to his sides. "Of course. I'm so sorry." But he couldn't help casting a sad look at the shelves of books that surrounded them.

"We're actually looking for someone called Beezle," said Emily.

Bansho's face creased into a frown. "Oh, no, no. No, you don't want to look for him. Oh, no."

"Uh, I'm afraid we do," Emily said.

Bansho shook her head. "Oh, no. No, no, no. You don't want him. Trust me. Think of someone else. Anyone. I'll help you with someone else."

"We really need to find Beezle," pressed Emily.

"No. You don't. Trust me on this."

"Is there any reason why we *shouldn't* be looking for this Beezle?" asked Jack.

"He's a crook," said the fey promptly. "And he's not nice."

"Be that as it may, I'm afraid we still need to see him," Emily said.

"Oh. That's a shame. And nothing I say will change your mind?"

"I'm afraid not."

Bansho sighed. "Fine. But don't say I didn't warn you. What time is it?"

Emily stared for a moment, then shook her head in puzzlement. "Sometime after midnight?"

"Then you'll find Beezle at the Regent. It's a theater about halfway down the bridge. You can't miss it."

"Theater? Is he an actor?" Jack asked.

"Actor? Oh, bless you, no. The Regent is where we hold our trials. The guards arrested Beezle yesterday. He's facing charges of theft, forgery, lying, bamboozling, sneakiness, staying up too late, and all-round naughtiness. Reckon he'll be put to death this time."

"Put to death?" said Jack. "That's a bit extreme, isn't it? From what I've seen, nearly all you fey are guilty of those charges."

Bansho smiled brightly. "Bless you, young sir, and you've hit a nail on the proverbial head there. But Beezle is even more guilty than most."

"How so?" asked Emily.

"He tried to bamboozle the Queen."

⊹═ ═⊹

Silence lay like a shroud over Bishopsgate Street. It was as if the heat of the day had leeched all life from the stones and bones of the city, leaving behind a desiccated husk. A hint of what used to be.

Two red eyes lit up the darkness at the end of the street. They were joined a moment later by another pair and then another. They blinked and wavered, shifting as the owners looked this way and that, sniffing the air, searching for a scent.

The Crimson Knight followed his hounds, waiting for the sign he knew would eventually come. They had already been to the college. The trail there had been confused, both old and new trails crossing over each other. But the hounds had finally fixed upon a scent they recognized, leading him here.

The hounds stopped before a small house. A low growl crawled from their throats, low and menacing.

A fresh trail.

The Crimson Knight issued a sharp command, then followed after the hounds as they loped along the street.

The ravens kept pace above him, a burst of white through the night sky.

⊱ Chapter Fourteen ⊰

In which Emily and Co. must rescue a scoundrel from a sneak.

It was impossible to miss the Regent. About halfway across the bridge was a large section where the shops and houses suddenly stopped, as if they had been swept away into the raging waters by an enormous hand. In their place, built up against the left side of the bridge, stood a huge, sprawling, open-air theater of an incredibly flamboyant design.

Emily stared at it critically as they approached. It was far too overdone for her tastes. She got the impression that whoever had built it had been trying to show how artful he was by filling every available surface with carvings and frescoes. Everywhere she looked, stone faces peered out at her, or cavorting fey danced around trees and stone circles.

The stage was raised from the ground by wooden supports

carved in the shape of odd-looking animals. The two closest to her were a lion with the head of an eagle and a monkey with the head of a dog. She couldn't see the others as the space beneath the floor was cloaked in darkness.

A wooden cage sat on the stage in front of a backdrop that had been painted to resemble a prison cell. Inside the cage sat a fey slightly shorter than Emily. He was slim and looked to be middle-aged (as far as Emily could judge such things), and could probably pass as a human if he had wanted to. He wore a floppy hat similar to the one Katerina wore, pulled down to one side at a rakish angle.

A crowd of fey were jostling one another in an attempt to get a seat in the tiers of benches that faced the stage. The fey lucky enough to have their seats already were having a good time, laughing, booing the fey in the cage, eating (and throwing) food.

"Why am I not surprised that someone Corrigan knows is a criminal on trial?" Jack said as they drew level with the theater. "What are we supposed to do now, Snow?"

Emily studied the creature in the cage. He was doing his best to look forlorn and sad, but Emily could see it was all an act. His eyes were shrewd and calculating, weighing everything for its value and use. "I suppose we wait till this is over and try to talk to him. Maybe he can still help us."

A tall, thin figure swept imperiously onto the stage, his

arms raised into the air. The figure wore a green frock coat that trailed along the floorboards and a red top hat that was ludicrously high. At his appearance, the assembled fey burst into enthusiastic applause. The man twirled his hands and bowed.

"Thank you, thank you," he said. "Munifus the Magnificent has returned."

The applause grew even louder. Munifus allowed it to continue for some moments more before raising his hands.

"Please, please. You are too kind. I don't deserve it." He paused for dramatic effect, then smiled, showing star-tlingly white teeth. Emily wondered if he had done some magic on them, because they really did appear . . . strangely bright. It was just possible that they would light up a dark-ened room.

"Actually, that's a lie," continued Munifus. "We all know I *do* deserve it. Because I really am just *that* amazing. But now, back to the business at hand. Because as you know, I stand before you here not as one of the greatest actors of all time, but as my alter ego—the greatest *lawyer* of all time. I put the 'prose' into prosecution. I put the 'dance' into evidence. I put the 'ooh' into proof. For I am the one, the only . . . *Munifus the Magnificent*."

This got another round of cheers from the fey.

"So to conclude the proceedings before us. To cap them

off. To tie the final knot. To lower the curtain, so to speak, I shall finish up reading the tally of charges."

Munifus lifted his hat, revealing a startled-looking rabbit. It blinked as Munifus took a scroll from inside the hat before placing it back on his head.

"Ahem. Now, where were we? Had we done 'blowing a raspberry at the King and Queen?'"

The crowd responded with an enthusiastic "YES!"

"Ah. What about 'charming the maids of the visiting Spinster Queen and stealing the crown jewels?'"

Again, a loud "YES!" swept through the crowd.

"What about 'trying to sell the aforementioned crown jewels *back* to the Spinster Queen at double their value?'"

Another "YES!"

Munifus rolled the scroll up as he read farther down the list. "Ah, yes, here we are. The final charges leveled against Beezle. 'Smuggling goods out of Faerie.'" Munifus turned to Beezle and shook his head sadly. "For shame, Beezle. For shame." He resumed his reading of the list. "'Supplying fake invisibility potion to the Queen's secret service.'" Munifus shook his head. "Very embarrassing for them when they tried to sneak into Queen Mab's castle in Eire. Very embarrassing, indeed. And of course, let us not forget the main charge, the one that convinced me to take up this case in the first place. That of enticing the attentions of my wife! Now, to the good fey gathered before me, what say you? Guilty or not guilty?"

The crowd erupted into a frenzy. "Guilty! Guilty!" The roars swept around the benches. Munifus spread his arms wide and moved in a slow circle, letting the shouts and screams wash over him as if they were personal adulations.

"Good to see they have a fair legal system," muttered Jack sarcastically.

After a full minute of basking, Munifus finally lowered his hands, bringing the shouting and screaming to a reluctant end. He turned to face Beezle. "And so you hear your judgment, foul creature. The people of fey find you guilty of all—" Munifus paused and turned to the crowd. "Was it *all* charges?" The crowd shouted their agreement. Munifus smiled and nodded, turning back to Beezle. "*All* charges. The sentence is death, to be carried out by me at a future date when I can clear enough time in my diary to enjoy . . . uh, I mean, to properly give my full attention to such a serious and burdensome task. Take him away!"

Munifus swept his hands into the air again. This was the signal for more cheering, and the cage Beezle was locked in started to descend shakily through the floor.

"Now's our chance," said Emily. "Come on."

"What are you planning on doing?" asked Wren nervously.

"I'm gong to sneak under the stage. Maybe we can get close enough to speak to him."

"And you think that will work, do you?" asked Jack. "You think he's just going to tell you what you need to know?"

"Hopefully. Unless you have a better idea?" Emily paused and looked expectantly at Jack.

He didn't say anything, so Emily led the way beneath the benches, stepping around the litter that had been dropped by the fey above them. When they arrived at the edge of the stage, one of the wooden creatures—the lion with the head of an eagle—turned its head and stared at Emily.

"Um . . . hello," she said hesitantly.

"Hello," said the creature.

"Can we come in?"

"Come in where?"

"Under the stage?"

"Why would you want to do that?"

Emily glanced over the creature's shoulder. In the dim light beneath the theater's floor she could just make out the cage that imprisoned Beezle. It had lowered through a trapdoor into another, much larger cage. This one had wooden wheels attached to it.

"I . . . I lost something. It fell through the floorboards. Please? I'll only be a second."

"I'm not sure." The eagle-headed lion turned to the next pillar, which was the monkey with the head of a dog. "What do you think, Walter? Should we let her in?"

The dog's head turned to look at Emily and the others. "Don't know. They look a *bit* shifty to me. Why does she want in?"

"Said she dropped something through the floorboards."

"Bloomin' careless, if you ask me."

"My thoughts exactly."

"What does Barglehun say?"

"Haven't asked her yet."

"Well what are you waiting for? Ask her."

The eagle turned its wooden head so that it was looking into the shadows beneath the stage. "Barglehun?"

"What?" shouted a rough voice.

"Girl here wants to come under the stage. Says she dropped something."

"She sounds silly. Send her away."

The eagle-headed lion turned back to Emily. "Sorry. You heard Barglehun. No entry. She says you're sill—Hey! Where are you going?"

Emily had grown tired of listening to the wooden creatures. *They* were the ones who were silly. Very silly indeed. She strode past the pillar and headed toward the cage. Jack and Wren hurried after her.

"Are you sure it's wise to go against their wishes?" asked Wren.

Jack grinned. "What are they going to do, Mr. Wren? Throw splinters at us?"

Emily stopped before the cage. The lights from above filtered down through gaps in the flooring, tracing thin lines across the cobbles of the bridge.

Beezle sat on the floor, his legs stretched out before him and his hat pushed down over his eyes.

"Hello?" Emily called.

Emily tried the door of the second cage, but it was locked with a bronze padlock. The bars themselves were about as thick as her arm. Emily didn't think they'd be breaking them apart anytime soon.

Jack bent down to inspect the lock, peering inside the mechanism. He straightened up after only a moment. "There's something in there," he said. "It stuck its tongue out at me."

Emily looked inside. Sure enough, a tiny beetle with a curiously human face blocked the keyhole. There was a hole all the way through its body the same shape as a key. Its legs were all stretched out to—Emily assumed—hold the lock mechanism in place.

The beetle stuck its tongue out at her and made a rude noise. "You're very rude," Emily said, then straightened up.

"Excuse me," she said. "Hello? I wonder if you could help us? It's really rather urgent."

Beezle didn't respond for a moment. Then he let out a heavy sigh, uncrossed his arms, and slowly lifted the hat up over his eyes.

"What?"

"Um . . . we're friends of Corrigan. He said we were to find you—that you could help us with something."

"Sorry. Can't even help myself at the moment. Nothing I can do for you."

He lowered his hat and made himself comfy once again.

"Please," said Emily. "It's urgent. Lives are at stake!"

The hat lifted quickly. "Lives are at stake?" asked Beezle. "Madam, why didn't you say so in the first place?"

"Then you'll help?"

"No." Beezle dropped the hat back in place.

Jack stepped forward. "What if we get you out of here?"

Emily grabbed Jack's arm. "What are you doing?" she whispered.

"Getting the information we need. Come on, Snow. You saw that trial up there. The whole thing was a sham."

"You've got that right," said Beezle's voice right next to Emily's ear. Emily took a hasty step backward. As did Jack. Beezle was now lounging against the bars only an arm's reach away. Neither of them had heard him approach. "Munifus has got it in for me. He's the one who turned me in, led the guards to my shop."

"Then how did he come to be the prosecutor in the case?" asked Wren. "Surely that's a conflict of interest."

Beezle laughed. "Conflict of interest. That's the most

polite way I've heard it put. But aye, you're right. That's what it is. Thing is, the prosecutor who was supposed to be hearing the evidence 'mysteriously' disappeared. He was last seen going out to dinner with Munifus. Hasn't been sighted since."

Jack cast an annoyingly knowing look in Emily's direction.

"Now, what were you saying, young lordling? About getting me out of here?"

"If you agree to help us."

"Oh, I agree."

"You don't even know what we're asking," Wren pointed out.

Beezle cracked a smile at Wren. "Very true, good sir. What do you want, then?"

"We're looking for a fey—a creature called Nimue."

"There're lots of fey called that."

"This is the one who trapped Merlin—Ow!"

Emily glared at Jack, who was rubbing his arm where Emily had just punched him.

Beezle cast a slow look across the three of them. "I see," he said. "*That* Nimue."

"Do you know where she is?" asked Emily.

"Might do, might do."

"Stop playing around," ordered Emily. "Do you or don't you?"

"Not sure." Beezle knocked on the bars. "Believe it's this cage. Makes it hard for me to think, if you know what I mean."

"How are we even supposed to get you out?" Emily asked. "I assume this lock is magical?"

"Of course. But Munifus has the keys. He'll be up in his changing room now. At the back of the stage. I'm sure someone with your . . . determination will be able to think of something."

Emily glared at the fey. "You're nothing but a scoundrel and a rogue."

Beezle grinned and winked at her. "And proud of it," he said.

After speaking to Beezle, Emily, Jack, and Wren had come up with a hasty course of action. They left the area beneath the stage and found a set of stairs behind the canvas backdrop that descended into a warren of tunnels and rooms that were built beneath the actual bridge itself. They found Munifus's dressing room, and Jack slipped away, leaving Emily and Wren standing before a bright green door. The words *Munifus the Magnificent* were painted on the wood in a childlike scrawl.

"Are you ready, Mr. Wren?"

Wren smiled at Emily. "It's not exactly a challenging part to play, is it? Yes, I'm ready."

Emily swallowed nervously and nodded. She wasn't

exactly sure if *she* was ready. At some point she had become the leader, the most experienced in all things fey, and she wasn't sure she liked it. She missed having Corrigan along, having someone to turn to for advice. Now that he was (hopefully) watching William, all she had to rely on was her own instinct. Oh, she was used to it. It was what she'd been doing since her parents went missing. But it was easier in London. She *knew* London. She'd grown up there.

Here, she was simply bluffing, hoping nobody noticed that she didn't know what she was doing.

Wren laid a friendly hand on her shoulder. "Shall we?" he asked gently.

Emily squared her shoulders and knocked hard on the door.

"Leave me be!" shouted Munifus in an aggrieved tone.

Emily knocked again.

"I said, 'Leave me be!'"

This time Emily kept knocking until the door was yanked open to reveal Munifus the Magnificent, standing in the opening, his jacket unbuttoned to reveal an old, stained vest.

"Gods, girl! Don't you know a genius must unwind after a performance of such magnitude? Otherwise, he's a danger to those around him. A drawn weapon, a raised hand, a . . . a . . ." He waved his hand in the air, clutching for inspiration.

"A sharpened quill?" suggested Emily.

Munifus froze. "Sharpened quill. Sharpened quill. I like that." He whirled around and stepped back into his extremely cramped dressing room to scribble something down on a piece of parchment. Once he had finished, he turned around to face Emily once more. He looked her up and down, his upper lip curling with distaste. Then his eyes flicked across to Wren, who hadn't moved a muscle since the door first opened.

"You're a human child."

"Correct."

Munifus stepped closer. He bent forward, almost folding himself in half so that he could peer into Emily's eyes. Emily did her best not to flinch.

"Stand on one leg," he ordered.

"No!"

"You can resist my orders? You're not bewitched? Bedazzled? You're not under a spell?"

"No."

"You're here under your own free will?"

"Correct."

"How did you get on the bridge?"

"Not telling."

"How did you find out about us?"

Emily shook her head but didn't say anything.

Munifus's long nose twitched. He stared at Emily for

some time, before exhaling loudly. "You . . . *fascinate* me, girl."

"That's nice," said Emily. She grabbed hold of Wren's arm. He still didn't move. "This man, on the other hand, is. Bewitched, I mean. And bedazzled."

Munifus barely gave Wren a glance. "Mmm."

"And he's from the circus. In his real life. Very sought after. A tumbler."

Munifus's face finally showed a flicker of interest. He straightened up and peered at Wren. "Doesn't look like much."

"That's what I thought. Till I saw him, that is. Do you want to see?"

"Are you selling him?" asked Munifus, surprised.

Emily shrugged. "Why not? I'm due my pay. Had to get a special potion and everything to get him here."

"Oh? And where did you get such a potion?"

Emily almost froze. She hadn't thought of that. But then a name jumped out at her. "Merrian. He's a friend. He gave it to me."

"Merrian?" Munifus sounded amazed. "Are we talking about the same Merrian? Half-giant? Big, heaving lout?"

"Careful there," said Emily. "Merrian's a friend. Don't think he'd take too kindly to being called a heaving lout."

"No. No, quite. Good call." Munifus squinted at Wren again, then stepped forward and lifted Wren's lips, peering at his teeth as if checking a horse's condition. "Come on then. He can give me a demonstration topside."

Munifus buttoned up his jacket and stepped from his changing room, pulling the door closed behind him. Emily and Wren followed him back through the tunnels, Emily praying with all her might that there wasn't some kind of magical lock on the door.

Jack could pick a lot of things, but magical locks were where his talents would let him down.

⊶ ⊷

It was Emily's job to make sure Jack had enough time to search for the keys. The problem was, she hadn't really thought past getting Munifus out of his changing room. She, Munifus, and Wren climbed the stairs and emerged from the tunnels into the open air.

Munifus led them onto the stage. Emily looked around curiously. She'd never been on this side of a theater before. The seats were almost empty now, the fey all heading back to their own business now that the show was over.

"Right," said Munifus. "Show me what he can do."

Emily turned to face Wren with some trepidation. His eyes had a slightly panicked look about them. "Come on then," she said. "Show Munifus what you can do. I order you."

Wren swallowed nervously, then he turned and started to

jog across the stage. For a brief second, Emily was worried he was going to make a run for it. But she needn't have worried. When he reached the edge of the stage, he turned and jogged back toward them.

When he was about ten feet away, he tripped. At least, that's what it looked like to Emily. He threw his right shoulder down, lifted one foot from the floor, pushed back with the other, and flew through the air. He landed on his shoulder, and it was at that moment that Emily realized he was trying to do a roll. Unfortunately, all he did was bang his shoulder into the wooden planks, tumble head over heels, and land flat on his back with a painful *Oof!*

"What," said Munifus slowly, "was that?"

"Uh . . . that's his act," said Emily, desperately seeking inspiration. "He's a sort of tumbler clown. That may have looked extremely clumsy and painful to you, but he's spent hours and hours practicing that move."

"Is he alive? He's not moving."

"All part of the act." Emily hurried forward and pulled on Wren's arm. He groaned. "Come on. Up you get. Show us another. I order you to." She stared into Wren's eyes. "You're *bewitched*. You *have* to do what I say. Now come on. Up you get."

Wren climbed slowly to his feet. He put his hands in the air, then lowered them to the ground and tried to do a handstand. It took him a few tries to actually get his legs past the halfway point, but when he did finally manage it, he overbalanced and fell all the way, landing on his back once again.

"What do you think?" asked Emily. "You can put him on the bill as the comedy acrobat."

"Noooo, I don't think so," Munifus said. "We don't have an apothecary traveling with us, and I fear he may need one quite frequently."

He turned toward the stairs. Emily hurried after him. "Wait!"

Munifus paused, but at that moment, Emily saw Jack and Beezle slipping out from beneath the stage and darting into the crowd.

"Well?" snapped Munifus.

"Nothing," said Emily. "You can go now. I'm finished with you."

Munifus stared at Emily in amazement as she turned and led a rather shaky Wren from the stage. As soon as her feet touched the bridge she put on an extra burst of speed in an attempt to put as much distance between themselves and the Regent as possible.

She didn't want to be anywhere close by when Munifus found out that Beezle had escaped.

⊰ CHAPTER FIFTEEN ⊱

Stolen memories. An unexpected companion.

The street was called Gutter Lane, a name that William thought wholly fitting with his surroundings. He glanced around with distaste, noting the rubbish piled up against the buildings, the huge rats that scurried through the shadows, fighting one another for whatever scraps they could find.

"Are you sure this is the place?" he asked Corrigan. They were standing before an abandoned shop. The windows had been boarded up, a huge red cross painted onto the thick planks. William glanced nervously to either side. He'd always hated the dark.

"Course I'm sure," said Corrigan. "You said Gutter Lane. And this is the only fey building on the street."

"How do you know?"

"I just do."

"So . . . what now?"

Corrigan shrugged. "Why are you asking me? You're the man with the plan. I'm just along for the fun of it. I defer to your experience," he added with a bow.

William bit his lip. The only plan he had was to pretend to be Cavanagh. And if this Croth had already met the man, then obviously everything would go badly wrong. But he wasn't about to admit that to Corrigan, especially when the piskie was being so sarcastic.

Instead, he leaned forward and knocked on the door. He did it louder than he intended to, the sound echoing up and down the street. A dog started barking.

"Why don't you just shout?" said Corrigan. "Wake everyone else up as well."

A small hatch in the door slid open. Two yellow eyes glared at William.

"Yes? What?" snapped the unseen figure.

"Uh, we're here to see Croth?"

"Why?"

"Because we have an appointment," said William, praying his ruse would work.

"What's your name?"

"Cavanagh."

There was a pause. The eyes flicked downward. "Do you know you've got a piskie stuck to your boot?"

"Oh, most amusing," snapped Corrigan. "Yes, quite the comedian, aren't you? Do you want this gold or not?"

The hatch slammed shut, and the door was pulled open by what William had no hesitation in labeling the ugliest creatures he had ever seen. Croth—if this was, in fact, Croth—had a face that was a mass of warts and flaking skin. His yellow eyes flicked around constantly, shivering in their eye sockets as if he couldn't seem to keep them still. He had long, thick arms that trailed to the ground, and his knuckles were covered in calluses from the constant rubbing as he walked. William swallowed nervously, resisting the urge to back away.

"Ugly beggar, aren't you?" asked Corrigan.

"Speak for yourself, runt. I'm considered quite the catch among a certain type of female."

"What type is that? The blind?"

Corrigan strolled past the creature's knobby legs as he said this. The creature glared down at him but didn't try to stop the piskie from entering. William took this as an encouraging sign.

"Are you Croth?" asked William.

"Maybe. Let's see the color of your purse and we'll know for sure."

William held up the small pouch he had found on Cavanagh's desk. Croth snatched it from his hand and brought it up to his bulbous nose, sniffing deeply.

"Good enough. Come on."

He stood aside, and William stepped into the shop. He hesitated and looked around. You couldn't really call it a shop. Not anymore. The room was a ruin. Broken shelves lay in pieces across the dusty floor. What had once been a shop counter was now lying on the floor split in two. Rather worryingly, an axe was buried deep in the wood right where the break was. Shards of glass crunched underfoot as William turned in a slow circle.

"What happened in here?" he asked.

"Hmm?" Croth looked puzzled for a moment, then his brow cleared and he smiled, revealing green and black teeth. "Oh, the mess. Nah, that was just a bit of a party, that was. Come on. Follow me."

Croth turned and disappeared through a door at the back of the shop. William hurried over to Corrigan, who was testing the edge of the axe.

"Do you think we can trust him?" whispered William.

Corrigan looked up. "No. But then I'm a cynical soul, me. Let's just see what Cavanagh thought he'd found and get out of here. I don't like the smell."

William and Corrigan followed Croth through the door,

finding themselves in a short corridor. Strange lights emanated from the room at the end of the passage, flickering over the walls in constantly shifting patterns. They cautiously approached the doorway. Corrigan pulled himself up William's clothes to sit on his shoulder. William wondered if the piskie was scared. *He* certainly was.

No, he corrected himself. That was the William Emily thought she knew. This was the brave William, the William who didn't need anyone or anything. *This* William wasn't afraid of some flickering lights.

He squared his shoulders and stepped through the door.

His steps faltered immediately. William's eyes widened, and he stared around in amazement.

They were in a huge space, a warehouse of some kind. The vast floor was lined with shelves that receded into the far distance. On these shelves, crammed in as tightly as possible, were thousands of strange, bulbous creatures about the same size as William's head. His face wrinkled in disgust. They looked like fat gray ticks. Their tiny legs waved uselessly in the air, lifted from the ground by their bulbous, stretched bodies.

"Nostalgae," whispered Corrigan.

"What?"

"Nostalgae. They feed on memories, hold them inside their bodies. But I've never seen so many of them. . . ."

Frowning, William stepped forward to investigate the closest of the creatures. Sure enough, the flickering light came from moving images that were somehow on the *inside* of the nostalgae. The one closest to William showed a young woman and a small child in a park. The woman smiled at William, but he realized that if these were memories, then she was actually smiling at whoever's memory this *was*. He moved to the next one. It showed a street littered with corpses. The bodies were covered in black pustules that wept blood and pus. The image was from low to the ground, and William realized that whoever this memory was taken from was probably dying, crawling along the ground because he or she was too weak to stand up.

He looked away. "This is disgusting," he said angrily.

"You'll hear no argument from me," muttered Corrigan.

"Over here," called Croth.

William looked over to see that Croth had brought a nostalgae over to a small table in the center of the huge room.

William moved over to the table and stared into the body of the creature.

The image before him was that of a forest. The owner of the memory was walking along a path through the trees. The image shifted as he looked upward, and William could see the full moon between the tree branches. The owner of the memory entered a clearing, and inside the clearing was a large, grass-covered mound. He approached it—

The image froze, then started from the beginning once again.

William looked at Croth, confused. "Is that it?"

"That's it. A memory from the Prophet."

William frowned. This wasn't what Cavanagh had talked about in his diary. His contact had said the Prophet could maybe help him in his search for the Raven King, but Croth seemed to think that Cavanagh just wanted to see one of the Prophet's memories. That didn't help them at all. How were they supposed to find out who the Prophet was from this?

"This isn't what I asked for," said William.

Croth frowned. "Your representative said you wanted to see something taken from the Prophet. That's exactly what this is."

"That's not good enough," said William. "Bring us another one."

"But you've already seen this one," complained Croth.

"That could have been taken from anybody. Show us something that proves it's from the Prophet. Something specific to him."

Croth muttered under his breath, but he grabbed the nostalgae and disappeared between the shelves.

"What are you doing?" whispered Corrigan.

"We have to find out who this Prophet is. I think that's what Cavanagh was going to do."

"And how was he going to get the information?"

"I have no idea."

Croth appeared from the shadows and dropped another nostalgae onto the table. "Here you go. This one is from inside Elfhame. So you know I'm not tricking you."

William and Corrigan both leaned forward. The pictures inside the nostalgae showed some kind of royal court. An elegant fey woman sat on a dark wooden throne that was carved into the wall behind her. She looked down at the owner of the memory and said something. The image shifted as the person turned to look out over a sea of assembled fey creatures. The expressions on the fey changed, some of them laughing, some of them nodding, and Will realized this was because the Prophet must be speaking. The fey burst into silent applause, then the image restarted again.

"Happy?"

Far from it, thought William. The memory still didn't bring them any closer to finding out who this Prophet was.

"I'll be truthful with you," said Corrigan. "We actually need to speak to the Prophet himself, not sniff through his memories like scavengers."

"You want to meet him? Don't be ridiculous. He's my best supplier. I can't just tell you where he is. How do I know you won't poach him from me? I'd go out of business."

"Your best supplier?" William glanced around the room once again. "How many of these are his?" asked William.

"About a third."

"A third? How long have you been . . ." William hesitated, unsure how to put it.

"Harvesting his memories? A few hundred years. Give or take a decade."

"A few hundred?" asked Corrigan in surprise. "Then he's fey?"

Croth frowned. "Enough talking. I've given you what you paid for. Now get out."

"We just need to speak to him," said William. "He might know something that could help us."

"You're wasting your breath. I don't even know where he is. I always deal with his handler."

"His handler? You make him sound like an animal," said William angrily.

"You're not far off it, boy. Now get out. Before I eat you."

"Is that supposed to scare us?" snapped William.

"No. But this is," said Croth. He opened his mouth, baring his teeth at them. But to William's horror, Croth's mouth kept on opening, revealing a darkened maw that gave off the stench of rotten meat. William stumbled back in fear as Croth's lower jaw dropped to his chest.

"Now get out!" he shouted, and his voice was so loud the floorboards vibrated under William's feet.

"I think we should go now," whispered Corrigan.

"I was thinking the same thing," said William, backing slowly away.

⌁ ⌁

Croth watched them go. He gave his head a violent shake, causing his jaw to swing to and fro like a pendulum. Then he jerked his neck back, and the jaw snapped into its normal position.

When Will reached the corridor leading to the front shop, he put some speed into his steps. He pulled the door open and stumbled gratefully into the warm night air. He listened for a second to make sure Croth wasn't about to come charging after them, then flopped down onto the pavement.

"Well, that was a waste of time," he said.

"Let me see that piece of paper you took from Cavanagh's desk," ordered Corrigan.

William fished around in his jacket for the piece of paper he had found and handed it Corrigan.

"'*Got an appointment with a fey called Croth,*'" Corrigan read. "'*(Or to give him his full name, Second Pardoned Lord Bataus Croth of the Everleaning Scry.) Gutter Lane. Vitay has told Croth I want to see something by the Prophet. He tells me*

194

that if I use his name, Croth will talk to me and that I will find what I'm after. I hope this is so.'"

Corrigan stopped reading and looked at William.

"You really are a fool, you know that?"

"What?"

"If you'd just shown me this, instead of trying to do everything yourself—" Corrigan broke off, muttering beneath his breath. He hopped down from William's shoulder and turned back to the shop.

"Where are you going?"

"Wait here. I'll be back in a minute."

Corrigan disappeared inside the shop.

William waited, scuffing at the cobbles with his feet.

"Hello again," said an amused voice.

William surged to his feet and spun around, twisting his feet together and falling onto his backside in the middle of the street. He was rather taken aback to find Katerina standing above him, shaking with silent laughter.

"Sorry," she said. "I didn't mean to give you such a scare."

"You didn't," snapped William, pushing himself to his feet. He looked around for the others, wondering what Emily would have to say about his sneaking off on his own.

"It's just me," said Katerina.

William frowned. "Just you? What? How did you find me?"

"I saw you sneak out and decided to follow you."

195

"But . . . why?" William repeated. "Why didn't you just wake the others?"

Katerina shrugged. "One of my hunches," she said. "I get them every now and then. I know better than to ignore them." She smiled. "They usually take me to where the action is."

A terrific roar of anger spilled out of the shop. William and Katerina whirled around just in time to see Corrigan come sprinting through the door, a large pouch clutched tightly to his chest. He didn't even pause when he saw Katerina. He just threw the pouch to William and then carried on straight past them.

William caught the small bag. He and Katerina glanced at each other, then turned and ran after the piskie as he sprinted along Gutter Lane and turned onto the next street. As they drew level with him, William scooped him up.

"Keep running," panted the piskie.

William did as he was told. They kept going until they saw the dark waters of the Thames glinting in the night up ahead. Only then did they slow down for breath. William collapsed against a building, breathing deeply. "What . . . what was all that about?"

Corrigan glared at Katerina. "What's she doing here?"

"*She* is making sure you don't get *him* into any trouble," said Katerina, indicating William with a nod of her head.

"Oh, is that right, is it?"

"Yes."

William cleared his throat. "Corrigan? What happened?"

Corrigan tore his gaze away from Katerina. "That note you found on Cavanagh's desk. His contact had supplied him with Croth's real name. His fey name."

"So?"

"So, if you know a fey's true name you can force him to tell you the truth."

William straightened up. "Really?"

"Aye, really."

"So did you ask him about the Prophet?"

"Aye."

"And did he tell you who he was?"

"No. He really doesn't know."

William deflated. "Oh."

Corrigan broke into a sly grin. "But he *did* tell me where to find his handler."

⊹═CHAPTER SIXTEEN═⊹

In which Beezle makes a deal,
and the Hounds of the Hunt are on their trail.

Emily and Wren would have run straight past Jack and Beezle's hiding place if Jack hadn't leaned out of the alley and grabbed hold of Emily's arm. He yanked her into the lane where Beezle was lounging against a wall, grinning.

"You got the keys then," Emily said to Jack.

"As if there was ever any doubt," said Jack. "Actually, they were just sitting on his desk. Not much of a challenge, if I'm honest." He looked at Wren, who was wincing and rubbing his back. "What's wrong with him?"

"Sore back. Seems Mr. Wren isn't exactly athletic."

"Yes, thank you," he snapped. "A little warning would have been nice. So I could prepare."

"Would it have made a difference?" Emily asked.

Wren hesitated, then sighed. "No, probably not," he admitted.

"Right," said Emily, turning her attention to Beezle. "We did our part. Now, where's Nimue?"

Jack looked uncomfortable. "Ah," he said.

Emily frowned. "What do you mean 'ah'?"

"Seems we have a bit of a problem there."

Beezle straightened up. "I think 'problem' is a bit too strong a word. I simply need to get my notebook from my shop. It's the only way I can be certain of her location."

"That doesn't make any sense," said Emily. "Why would you have her location written in a book?"

"It's a timetable of sorts. A shift rota."

"Then what's the problem?" she asked. "Let's just go and get it."

"Love to," said Beezle awkwardly. "Great idea. But that's where we *do* have a bit of a problem. My shop will be watched by guards. It's where I was arrested. You'll have to sneak in somehow."

"We're not sneaking in," said Emily. "You do it."

"I'm not risking getting caught again. If you want the book, you'll have to do it."

"If I may make so bold," said Wren, casting a distasteful glance at Beezle, "I have a feeling we are being used here."

"Funny," said Jack. "I have the same feeling."

Beezle raised his hands in the air. "Look, I'm just telling you what needs to be done. If you don't trust me, you can walk away now, and we'll never see each other again. But if you want to know where Nimue is, I need that book."

Emily and Jack exchanged glances. He shrugged in resignation.

"It's not as if I'm an amateur," he said. "Although I never thought I'd see the day when Emily Snow encouraged me to thievery."

"I'm not encouraging you. And anyway, it's not thievery. It's his property. We're just getting it back for him."

"Yes, I seem to recall your using that same argument when you asked for my help to get that seeing stone. And look at the trouble *that* got us in."

"I would advise you to make your mind up swiftly," said Beezle. "Once Munifus finds out I'm gone, my shop is the first place he'll look."

"Fine," said Emily. "Lead the way."

+═ ═+

Beezle's shop wasn't far, but it was, as Beezle had said it would be, watched by guards. They weren't much to look at, just two goblin-type creatures with old, mismatched armor and helms that were too big for their heads. They would actually look quite comical if it weren't for the spears they were holding, the only things about the pair that looked menacing. The sharpened heads glinted in the torchlight.

"There's two more round the back," said Beezle from their hiding place outside a busy tavern about five shops away.

"So how are we supposed to get in?" Emily asked.

"The same way thieves always get into houses like that," said Jack. "The roof."

He pointed. Emily followed the direction of his finger and saw a small window on the rooftop of a shop about seven buildings down from Beezle's. It looked like an attic room of some sort. Then he pointed to Beezle's shop. There was a similar window set into his roof.

"How are we going to get up there?" asked Emily doubtfully. "Do we just walk in and ask if we can climb out their window?"

"You're half right," said Jack. He grinned at her. "Relax, Snow. This is what I do best, remember? Who got you into Somerset House? Who got that safe open for you? Spring-Heeled Jack, that's who. You concentrate on all the thinking and leave the lawbreaking to me."

"We're not *technically* breaking the law," interjected Beezle. "It's my shop, and I'm giving you permission to enter."

"Yes, but the fact that we just broke you out of prison *does* mean we're breaking the law," Emily pointed out.

"Mmm, good point," said Beezle.

"So where is this book of yours?" Jack asked.

"Hidden. When you get into the shop, go to the back room. You'll see a painting on the wall. Take the painting out of the frame, then stick it back on the wall where the painting originally hung."

Emily and Jack waited.

"And?" Emily prompted.

"And nothing. The painting *is* the safe. It will open once it's mounted on the wall."

"Ah," said Jack. "Magic. Come on, then, Snow."

"Should I come?" Wren asked.

"Um . . . no. Better not, eh? With that back? You might fall off the roof and kill yourself. Terrible tragedy and all that."

If it was at all possible for a person to look both crestfallen and happy at the same time, Wren managed it.

Jack jogged across the street to the building he had pointed out with the attic room. Emily followed after and discovered that it was, in fact, a restaurant. Heavily laden trays floated through the air and dropped onto cramped tables, where fey of all kinds tucked into their food.

Jack walked purposefully, acting as if he belonged there. Emily tried to imitate his style, but it wasn't something that came naturally to her. She *knew* she didn't belong here. And so, apparently, did everyone else.

"You. You there." A creature with a man's body and the head

of a goat waved at her from behind the counter. Emily hesitated, which was probably a mistake. If she had just carried on, maybe she would have gotten away with it. But the goat-headed fey saw her hesitation and started to make his way toward her.

Jack saw this and quickly headed him off. "Don't worry about it. She's with me." He winked at the creature. "New on the job. You know how it is." He grabbed Emily by the arm and led her through a door into a room filled with wooden casks. A set of stairs led upward. "Hurry up. Before he uses whatever brain he has and comes after us."

Jack hurried up the stairs to the top floor and opened doors until he found the attic room. He opened the window and leaned out.

"It's fine," he said over his shoulder. "Lots of footholds. Come on."

Jack hopped out onto the window ledge and straightened up, so Emily could see only his legs framed against the night sky. Then the legs disappeared as Jack pulled himself up onto the roof. Emily could hear him just above her as he walked across the tiles. The roof didn't sound very thick at all. A worrying thought, considering they were both putting their weight on it.

Jack's head appeared at the top of the window, upside down. "What are you waiting for? We haven't got all day." He hesitated. "You're not scared, are you?"

"Of course I'm not scared."

Jack grinned. "Then get a move on," he said, and vanished.

Emily climbed carefully onto the windowsill. She peered up to find Jack lying on the roof with his hands dangling over the eaves, waiting to help her. She ignored him and pulled herself up, then climbed to the peak of the roof and set off in the direction of Beezle's shop.

"Hey," complained Jack from behind her, "*I'm* supposed to be leading the way."

"Oh," said Emily. "I do apologize. You're welcome to go past if you think you can." She waited, but Jack didn't try to get past her, so she carried on until they reached the window to Beezle's shop.

They pushed it open and Jack was about to climb through when Emily grabbed him by the arm and dug her nails in.

"Ow. What?"

Emily didn't answer straightaway. She was peering upward, searching the night sky.

"What's wrong?" asked Jack nervously.

Emily wasn't sure. She thought she had heard something, something that brought dread to her heart.

The flapping of many wings.

"Snow?"

Emily waited a moment longer, but she couldn't see

anything and the sound didn't repeat itself. Perhaps it had just been a fey creature with wings.

"It's nothing," she said. "Come on. Let's get this over with."

Jack cast a last distrustful look at the sky, then ducked through the window. Emily followed after, breathing a sigh of relief when her feet touched the flat wooden floor. She would never admit it to Jack, but walking across the sloping roof had actually been quite terrifying.

Emily's relief was short-lived. She looked around their surroundings, her nose crinkling in distaste.

They were in a bedroom—Beezle's, Emily assumed. And the fey certainly didn't know how to keep things tidy. A small, unmade bed was pushed up against the wall and the floor was littered with all sorts of rubbish. Clothes, empty bottles, old news sheets, and unwashed plates.

Jack opened the door that led down to the shop. He waited for a few moments, listening to make sure there weren't any guards inside the building. When he was satisfied that everything was clear, he slipped through the door and moved carefully down the stairs, making sure to keep to the edge of the steps. Emily recalled Jack's telling her that there was less chance of creaking that way.

Emily followed Jack down the stairs. The shop was dark. The only light came from the bridge outside, struggling to make it through the dirty window. Emily supposed that was a good thing. It meant the two guards standing outside wouldn't be able to see much unless they put their heads right against the glass.

"Make sure I'm not interrupted," Jack whispered, his mouth close to her ear. "I'll get the book."

Emily wasn't very happy with being left alone but nodded anyway, and Jack disappeared into the dark room behind the counter.

Emily waited. The only sound in the shop was her frightened breathing. It was so loud she was surprised the guards couldn't hear it. She swallowed and tried to force herself to calm down.

What was Will doing now? Her best hope was that Corrigan had taken him back to Cavanagh's house, but she doubted very much Will would let him do that. Which meant he was out there somewhere, with only Katerina and Corrigan to watch over him. And that was only if Katerina hadn't just deserted them. Emily had no proof she had gone after William. She may have returned to Puck.

Emily sat down on the stairs. She supposed it was her own fault. Maybe she should have taken him seriously, paid more attention to what he had to say. But he had been so . . . so *pushy*. So *arrogant*. As if only his opinion mattered, and everyone else was too stupid not to see he was right.

Emily frowned. Wasn't that exactly what William had

said about Emily back in Cavanagh's cellar? But she'd always thought it was best to act decisive. That was what adults did, wasn't it?

Maybe that's what Will was trying to do. Exactly what *she* had done when their parents had vanished. To act more like a grown-up.

Emily pushed the thought away for the moment. What was taking Jack so long? The shop was making her nervous. It was filled with strange smells: spices, meat, bread, fruit. But there were other scents as well. An odd, acidic stench that was starting to hurt her nostrils. A peculiar, cloying, sickly sweet odor that stuck at the back of her throat. What *did* Beezle sell in here?

The guards moved position outside, so that they were now standing directly in front of the window. Their shadows stretched across the wooden floor, their helms touching Emily's toes.

She moved her feet away, then stood up, planning on finding her way to the back room to see what Jack was doing.

But a noise stopped her.

She held her breath, every fiber of her being attuned to the sound. It was like a sheet rippling in the wind.

Or wings. Many, many wings.

Emily whirled around and banged into Jack, who was just coming out of the back room. He held the book triumphantly.

"Got it. But listen, I had a glance . . ." He trailed off when he saw the look on Emily's face. "What's wrong?" he whispered.

But Emily said nothing. The sound was growing louder, the sound of hundreds, thousands of birds. She turned slowly toward the window. The guards' shadows were no longer there, but she could just see them standing in the middle of the bridge, staring up into the sky.

Then they dropped to the ground and flung their arms over their heads as the white ravens dived out of the sky and swept along the bridge. It was as if a white cloud was tearing past the window. The ravens' shadows flickered madly across the floor and walls of the shop. It felt like she and Jack were trapped in the center of an unholy storm.

And all the while Emily could hear the *click-click, click-click* of their snapping beaks.

A moment later they were gone. Emily could hear screams and surprised shouts as the ravens moved along the bridge.

"Do you think they're looking for us?" asked Jack.

Emily gave Jack what he often referred to as "her look." He raised his hands in the air. "Fine. They're looking for us. So what do we do?"

Emily peered through the glass door. The guards had disappeared.

"Come on," she said, and opened the door. She and Jack moved outside into the warm night and hurried to where

Wren and Beezle were hiding on the other side of the bridge.

"Thank goodness you're all right," said Wren. "What were those birds? Was that normal?"

"No. They were looking for us."

"They're looking for you?" Beezle looked worried. "Then this is where we part ways."

"Why are you so nervous?" asked Emily. "They don't have anything to do with you."

"No, but those things are the Morrigan's eyes. What they see, she sees." He licked his lips nervously. "Did you get the book?"

Jack held it up. Beezle tried to grab it, but Jack yanked it out of reach.

"We need to talk about that," said Jack.

"What's to talk about? Just give it to me."

"Jack?" said Emily. "What's wrong?"

"I had a quick look inside. This isn't a book of shift rotas or anything like that. It's a blackmail book. Isn't that right?"

"How dare you, sir! I take offense at that."

"It lists payments made to him by people he's blackmailing. Plus, what it is he's blackmailing them with. That's why he wanted the book so badly."

Emily struggled to take this in. If it was true, then it meant . . . She turned to Beezle in dismay. "So you don't even know where Nimue is? You just used us?"

"No! Well, yes. I may have used you a little bit. But I *do* know where Nimue is."

"Where?"

"Can I have my book back?"

"No. Tell us where she is. Otherwise, we throw the book in the Thames."

Beezle's face twisted with uncertainty. He looked nervously at the sky, then threw his hands up in defeat. "*Fine.* Nimue is part of Queen Titania's consort. There. Are you happy now?"

"What do you mean, her consort? Where are they?"

"Are you dense? She's part of the Queen's court. She lives in Underlondon. In the tree."

Emily hadn't thought it was possible to feel any more despair. She was wrong. "In the tree? The Faerie Tree?"

"Yes, the Faerie Tree! What other tree would I be talking about?"

Emily turned away from the others, staring blankly across the bridge. The Faerie Tree! There was no way they could gain access to that! Not without someone like Corrigan to guide them. It couldn't be done.

And yet, it had to be done. If they wanted to find Merlin, they had to find Nimue. And if she was in Underlondon, then that was where they had to go.

Emily glanced back at the gate they had used to come

onto the bridge. They had to get away from here. Before the ravens came back.

But then Emily froze. Too late. As she watched, the Crimson Knight came through the gate on his charger, his massive hounds straining against their chains as they sniffed the ground. A split second later they lifted their heads to the sky and howled.

The hounds had their scent.

Emily whirled back to the others. "Beezle, you will get us off this bridge, and you will do it now. Otherwise, you will never see your precious book again. Is that understood?"

Beezle stared over Emily's shoulder. The hounds were baying wildly, straining against the knight's grip.

"Beezle!" Emily shouted.

The fey jumped, then fixed his attention on the book, then on Emily. "Yes," he snapped. "Fine."

"*Can* you get us off the bridge?" asked Jack.

"You think I don't have escape routes planned? What am I, an amateur? Of course I can get you off the bridge."

"Good. Then let's go."

⤐ Chapter Seventeen ⤏
The hounds catch up. A watery grave beckons.

Beezle didn't wait around. He turned and ran across the street to the other side of the bridge. Emily, Jack, and Wren followed, dodging around confused fey who had seen the ravens and were milling about, wondering what was going on.

As she reached the center of the street, Emily glanced over her shoulder and saw the Crimson Knight release the chains, the massive hounds leaping forward with bloodthirsty snarls and barks. Emily quickly pushed through the crowd and caught up with Beezle.

"The hounds are coming!" she shouted.

Beezle nodded, a frantic, panicked look on his face. "Follow me," he said, and ran straight into a shop, darting around the startled shopkeeper, slipping around the counter into a back room, then pushing open a back door and darting out into a narrow alley that ran between the line of shops and the low walls of the bridge.

Emily, Jack, and Wren followed him into the alley, Jack pulling the door shut behind him. A plate thrown by the owner of the shop smashed into the wood on the other side.

"This way," said Beezle, hurrying along the lane.

Emily moved forward to keep pace with the fey. "Where are we going?"

"To my shop. I've got an escape route there."

"Then why didn't you use it before?" asked Jack.

"I was caught by surprise," said Beezle bitterly. "Didn't have time."

The sound of the hounds howling in anger reached them from the other side of the shops.

"Sounds like the wolves are too big to get through," said Wren.

"Don't worry," said Beezle. "They'll find a way. No one escapes the Hounds of the Great Hunt when they have your scent."

"How do you know what they are?"

"Everyone knows." Beezle glanced at Emily and shook his head. "I don't know what you did to get the Phantom Queen so angry, but you'd better do something to fix it if you want to last the night."

"Believe me, we're working on it," said Emily grimly.

They arrived at the rear of Beezle's shop. It was hard to see anything in the dim light, but Beezle seemed to know what he was looking for. He leaned over the bridge wall and felt around for a few moments before turning to them with a smile.

"It's still here. I was worried the guards would find it."

Emily stood on her tiptoes and peered over the wall. The water of the Thames roared and thundered far below, the small spaces between bridge supports causing the water to build up against the structure in a white-foamed frenzy before shooting out in a ferocious torrent on the other side. Because of this buildup, the river was actually higher on this side of the bridge than the other.

It took her a moment, but Emily finally spotted what Beezle was talking about. A rope had been tied to the bridge wall; attached to this rope was a tiny row boat that swayed alarmingly about twenty feet above the raging waters.

She turned to Beezle. "Please tell me you are not suggesting we use that boat. We'll smash against the bridge!"

"Rubbish. All we have to do is hold on. With a bit of luck we'll be through in no time."

Jack and Wren both leaned over to get a look.

"A bit of luck?" exclaimed Jack. "We'll need more than a bit of luck to survive that!"

"Well, here's the thing," said Beezle. "You won't *actually* have to worry about it."

Jack frowned. "Why?"

Beezle lunged forward and grabbed Emily by the arm. He yanked her around and pressed a bronze knife against her throat.

"Because you're not going. It's nothing personal. I prefer my own company is all." Beezle grinned. "That way I can make sure the conversation stays interesting. Now hand the book over."

"Don't you dare, Jack," snapped Emily.

"I mean it! Hand it over; otherwise, I stick her."

Jack looked uncertainly between Emily and Beezle.

"I think you should give it to him," said Wren quietly.

Jack stared at the knife, then hesitantly took the book from his coat pocket.

"Jack. I order you not to give that book to him. He won't do anything."

"Oh? And what makes you so sure, little miss?" snapped Beezle.

"I just am. Jack, hold the book over the wall."

Jack licked his lips, obviously wondering what to do. "Jack!"

Jack thrust his arm out, holding the book above the thundering waters. Emily could feel Beezle tense up. She smiled.

"Now," she said. "Please let me go. Otherwise, Jack drops the book and we take your boat while you stay here to face the hounds. There are three of us and only one of you."

Beezle didn't move.

"You have until I count to three. One . . ."

Still he didn't move. Emily experienced a moment of doubt. Had she been wrong? The way he had looked at the book when they had left the shop, Emily had been sure he would do anything to keep it safe. But what if she had misjudged him?

"Two . . ."

"Just give it to me!" Beezle screamed.

"Three."

Even before she had finished saying the word, Beezle let go of her and stepped back. Emily hurried forward to stand next to Jack and Wren.

"Are you insane?" he hissed. "He could have killed you."

"He could have. But he didn't."

"That was a very dangerous gamble, Miss Snow," said Wren sternly. "Anything could have happened."

Emily was about to answer, but it was at that moment that she realized it wasn't so dark in the alley anymore. Their surroundings had a slight red tinge to them.

A low, rumbling growl came from above them, barely heard over the sounds of the river.

All eyes turned upward. One of the hounds was on the roof of Beezle's shop, front paws braced against the gutters as it glared down at them with its glowing red eyes. It darted glances between them, leaving lines of red in the darkness every time it moved.

Emily reached slowly into her jacket, fumbling with shaking hands for the sharpened branch of rowan wood Katerina had given her.

"Nobody make any sudden movements," whispered Jack.

Too late. Beezle leapt forward, scrabbling toward the bridge wall. As soon as he moved, the huge dog pushed itself from the roof, landing so that Emily, Wren, and Jack were on one side of the beast, and Beezle on the other.

The hound's back stood higher than Emily's head. It glared at them, then its muscles bulged and rippled beneath shaggy fur as it turned and lunged toward Beezle.

The fey screamed and dropped to the ground. This was all that saved him, as the beast's slavering jaws snapped closed where his head had been only moments before. Beezle scrabbled backward as fast as he could go. The dog padded toward him, but a moment later it stopped. Its ears pricked up, as if listening to someone. The hound bared its teeth, then pivoted to face Emily. She held the stick of rowan wood out, but it looked pathetic when compared to the size of the dog. She wondered whether it would even penetrate its hide.

Emily could just see Beezle past the dog's shoulder. He was creeping toward the wall. Jack saw him as well.

"If he gets on that boat, we're finished," he whispered.

"I know," Emily replied, not taking her eyes from the dog. "Try and shuffle around."

Jack put one foot to the side, but even that slight movement caused the hound to jerk its head around and snap at him. Jack froze. The hound watched him for a second, then turned its smoldering gaze back to Emily.

"It's keeping us here," Emily realized. "Holding us for the knight."

"We can't let that happen, Snow."

"I *am* aware of that, Jack," said Emily, not taking her eyes from the dog. "If you have some kind of idea about how to get out of this, then now would be the time to tell me."

"Use the witchbane. But be quick."

"What? I can't—"

Emily didn't get a chance to finish, because at that moment Jack threw himself into a somersault that took him rolling between the hound's front legs.

"Jack!"

The hound dropped its head and snapped at Jack, but he was already rolling to the side, out from beneath the dog and up against the bridge wall. He pushed himself to his feet and whipped out his old dagger. The dog turned to face him, snapping at his hand. Jack darted to the side and sliced his hand through the air. The blade caught the dog across the muzzle, leaving a thin line of red. The hound didn't even notice.

Emily gripped the rowan stake in both hands and braced the back end against her stomach. Then she ran forward with all the speed she could muster, aiming straight for the hound's ribs.

She hit the creature at full speed, the shock of the collision making it feel like she had been smacked in the stomach. The stake slammed into its side, punching through the hound's thick hide and sliding between its ribs.

The hound stiffened, then released a long, plaintive howl of pain.

The sound froze Emily where she stood. She stared in horror at the blood on her hands, at the stake sticking out of the hound's shivering side.

What had she done?

Then Jack grabbed her and yanked her back. She fell to the ground as the hound's huge teeth snapped together where she had been standing. Jack pulled Emily to her feet, but she couldn't take her eyes off the wounded dog. It turned haltingly in their direction. It tried to snarl, but all that came out was a low whimper. It limped forward, but its legs couldn't support its weight and it collapsed to the ground.

Emily stared. This wasn't the creature that had chased

them. This was a creature in pain. Dying. Something she had killed with her own hands.

Emily felt tears trickling down her cheeks as she watched the hound's crimson eyes slowly dim. She shook Jack off.

"Snow! Come on."

Beezle was just disappearing over the wall. Wren was sitting next to the rope, ready to follow. Jack was waiting, casting anxious glances at Emily.

But she ignored them. For the moment, there were only two things that existed in Emily's world. Herself and the hound. She knelt down on the cobbles, just out of reach of the creature's jaws. It was still alive, but it didn't move, only whimpered softly.

"I'm sorry," whispered Emily. She had never killed anything before. Not even a spider. What had made her think she had the right? The hound's life hadn't been hers to take. Yes, it had turned on Jack, yes, but surely they could have found another way out of the situation?

She hesitantly reached out her hand. The hound sniffed it. Then its tongue came out and licked her fingers, just like any other dog's would.

A moment later it was dead.

Emily blinked through her tears as the hound's body melted into a dark smoke that whirled up into the sky and drifted away on the warm wind.

Howls of anguish erupted from the other side of the shops as the remaining hounds sensed their brother's death. Through eyes blurry with tears, Emily saw one of them come loping around the corner at the far end of the alley, its eyes flaring red with hatred.

Jack grabbed Emily and pulled her to the wall. She hoisted herself up and grabbed hold of the rope with numb fingers. She looked down and could just see Beezle dropping the last few feet into the boat, the water roaring and thundering past just below him. Wren was about halfway down.

"Hurry up!" snapped Jack, giving her a shove.

Emily dropped the first few feet, then looked up and saw Jack peering anxiously over the wall. He glanced over his shoulder, stiffened, then threw himself over the wall, just managing to grab hold of the rope as he fell. His legs slammed into Emily's head, causing her to lose her grip. She cried out in pain and slid down the rope. She tightened her fingers, feeling the rough rope tear the skin from her palms. Jack was lowering himself as fast as he could, and a second later Emily saw why. A hound appeared over the lip of the wall, growling and snapping at them.

"Move!" Jack shouted.

Emily tried to move faster. She glanced down to see how far they had to go, but something else caught her attention.

Beezle was busy sawing at the rope, casting frantic glances up toward the bridge.

"Beezle!" Emily screamed. "Don't you dare!"

Beezle ignored her and carried on sawing through the rope. The strands were already parting.

Emily half slid, half climbed down the rope, moving as fast as she could. She caught up with Wren, her feet banging into his shoulders. He picked up speed. They were almost close enough to let go . . .

They nearly made it. When they were only a few arm spans away from Beezle, the rope parted with a loud snap. The boat dropped through the air and slammed into the water.

But Emily wasn't about to let Beezle get away. As soon as she saw the rope separate, she let go. As did Wren.

A split second after the boat hit the Thames, Emily landed feetfirst at the back end of the vessel, falling onto her knees. The craft was already moving forward, swirling around in circles and heading toward the spaces between the bridge struts. Wren landed next to her, banging his head on the wood. He didn't move.

Emily looked up just in time to see Jack miss the boat altogether and disappear into the water.

"Jack!" she screamed, frantically searching for some sign of him amidst the rapids. She saw him pop up out of the water a few feet away. They were already being pulled in separate directions. She searched for something that he could grab hold of and spotted the oars lying beneath a foot of water at the bottom of the boat. She grabbed one and heaved it over the side, keeping a tight grip on one end. Jack had vanished again. Emily wasn't even sure if he could swim.

"Jack! *Jack!*"

Nothing. And they were heading straight for the bridge supports. The boat bucked and lurched. The water swirled and thundered in violent whirlpools as it strained to push its way through the narrow gaps.

Then she saw him. His head bobbed to the surface behind the boat. Emily struggled with the oar and heaved it toward Jack, almost smacking him in the head with the heavy wood. He grabbed hold of the oar and pulled himself toward her. Emily leaned out and grabbed his shirt, pulling him into the boat. He collapsed next to Wren, coughing and spluttering, vomiting up the water he had swallowed.

They hit the rapids. The front of the boat shot straight into the air, sending Emily staggering backward. The backs of her feet smacked against the seat and she felt herself falling. The night sky flew past above her. A hand grabbed hers just as she was about to fall into the water. A second later the boat slammed back onto the river and Emily and Jack were thrown to the deck. Jack wrapped Emily's hand around the seat, then grabbed the still form of Wren and did the same, just as the boat smashed up against the stone pilings of the bridge.

The breath exploded from Emily as the boat swirled around and around, smacking up against the supports with every turn. She heard wood cracking, the roar of the river, someone screaming, cursing into the night. Water poured over them, thundered into the boat. There was a brief moment of weightlessness—

—and then they were through, the boat skimming away over the river. Emily took a deep, shuddering breath. She turned and peered over the edge of the boat and saw the bridge receding into the darkness behind them. Emily collapsed onto her back and let out a shaky laugh.

They had made it. Somehow they had made it.

⇥ CHAPTER EIGHTEEN ⇤

In which William and Co. meet the Abbot.

S o what's *your* true name?" asked William, as he, Katerina, and Corrigan moved through the dark streets, leaving the neighborhood of Cheapside far behind them.

"You really want to know?"

"Yes!"

"Can I trust you never to use it?"

"Of course!"

"*Really* trust? I mean, you realize the power I'm giving you? Knowing a fey's true name is deep magic. It's bone magic, boy. It goes right back to ancient times."

"I promise you. You can trust me."

"And what about her?" Corrigan nodded at Katerina.

Katerina simply raised her hands in the air and shook her head. "Leave me out of this," she said.

Corrigan appeared to think about it, then he nodded. "Fine." He was sitting on William's shoulder and leaned to his ear. "Can you hear me?" he whispered.

William nodded.

"My true name is Lord High Banzilum of the First Degree, Adept of the Order of the Second Suppers and Second Shin-Kicker in Service to the Queen."

There was a pause. William turned to look at the piskie. "That's not your true name, is it?"

"No."

"You're not going to tell me, are you?"

"Nope."

"Then why didn't you just say so?"

"More fun this way."

William sighed and checked the darkened houses that surrounded them. It was quiet. He reckoned it had to be a couple of hours past midnight by now. Nearly everyone would be asleep. Except for them. They were wandering around the dark streets of seventeenth-century London searching for a so-called Prophet in the hope that they could find someone called the Raven King and stop the Great Fire of London. It sounded like some kinds of children's story that his ma would have read to him before she vanished. He felt a wave of sadness at the thought. He wished it *was* just a story. "Do you know where we're going?" asked Katerina.

"To Blackfriars. Seems Croth deals with an abbot who lives in the district."

"Priests?" Katerina almost spat the word out.

"Aye."

Katerina's face clouded with disgust. "Then I'll wait outside. I have no time for priests."

Corrigan shrugged. "Do what you like. Feel free to go away, if you really want to. It's not like we asked you to come along."

Katerina glared at him.

"There's a Blackfriars district back in our time," said William, trying to distract the two of them.

"Here as well. Got its name from the Dominican friars who used to have a monastery here."

"How are we going to cover such a large area?"

"We're not. There's a church in Blackfriars where Croth told us to go. Croth supplies this abbot with the nostalgae and the Abbot returns them to Croth filled with the Prophet's visions. They fetch a pretty price to collectors. They sift through them looking for any information they can use, any foretellings."

William thought about this. "So this Abbot is using the Prophet? Making money from him?"

"That's what it looks like."

"But . . . that's not fair."

Corrigan snorted. He leapt down from William's shoulder, then turned and stared up at him incredulously. "Not fair? Are you being serious? You're not, are you? You're being funny, yes?"

William flushed, confused. "What? No. I . . . It's not, is it? Fair, I mean."

Corrigan stared hard at William, then shook his head. "Dear, oh dear," he muttered. "You and your sister are not as different from each other as you'd like to think, you know that?"

"What are you talking about?"

"'That's not fair,'" Corrigan mimicked. "That's exactly what Emily would say. How on earth did you both manage to hold on to that kind of thinking living the kind of life you did?"

"What kind of thinking?" said William, *really* not liking Corrigan's comment about him and Emily being similar.

"So . . ." Corrigan waved his hands in the air. "So *naïve*. So bloomin' innocent. It's disgusting."

"Leave him alone, piskie," snapped Katerina. "Let them hold on to that as long as they can. We both know it won't last."

"No, it won't." Corrigan turned away and stalked a few paces down the street. Then he whirled around and pointed up at William. "Because I'm making it my solemn duty to knock it out of you. You hear me? It's dangerous walking around with that kind of attitude. Now come on. We're here."

Corrigan pointed across the street to a church surrounded by a low, stone wall. William hadn't seen many churches that were as big as the ones back in his time, but this one was pretty close. By the light of the moon he could see it was fronted by two heavy arched doors. Above the doors was a stained-glass window, although William couldn't see what the picture was in the glass. Behind and towering above the church was a square bell tower totally covered in dark ivy.

"Come on, then," said Corrigan. "Let's go wake up this Abbot."

"I'm waiting here," said Katerina. She hesitated. "In case there's any . . . you know. Problems." She looked apologetically at William. "I don't talk to priests," she explained. "Long story, but any God that allows what happened to me and my family has no place in my life. I'll keep watch."

"Fine. You do that," said Corrigan. "Come on, boy. Let's go."

They moved through the churchyard and approached the front doors. They towered above them, the old heavy wood reinforced by black metal hinges as thick as William's arm. Corrigan eyed them nervously.

"Hope there's not too much of that inside."

"What? Oh." William realized the hinges were made

from iron. He looked anxiously at Corrigan. "Will you be all right?"

"Should be. Let's just get this over with. Knock."

"Do we have a plan?"

"Of course we have a plan. What do you take me for? Now knock."

William knocked on the heavy, wooden door. But his hands hit the solid wood with barely a sound. He tried again, hitting the door harder. Again, there was barely an echo.

"Maybe we should look round the back?" suggested William.

"Fine. Come on, then."

They followed a dirt path that led around the side of the church. William's steps faltered when he saw that they were walking through a graveyard.

"What's wrong?" snapped Corrigan from up ahead. "They're already dead. They can't hurt you."

Will steeled himself and carried on walking, trying to ignore how the moonlight lit the gravestones, casting dark shadows that stretched across the ground. It didn't make a bit of difference telling himself they couldn't hurt him. It was still unsettling, being in a graveyard at night.

The path led them to a much smaller door at the back of the building. This one had a door knocker. Will lifted it and slammed it down as hard as he could. The crack of metal on wood split the air like a gun shot, echoing inside the building. Even Corrigan jumped.

"Bones, boy. What are you trying to do? Stop my heart?"

"Sorry."

They waited, and a few minutes later the door swung open to reveal a tall, thin man. He was holding a candle and glaring at them.

"What are you doing, boy? It's after midnight! How dare—"

He stopped talking when he saw Corrigan standing. His eyes widened, all traces of sleep leaving him in an instant.

"What's going on?" he snapped. "What do you want?"

"I see we've found the right man," said Corrigan. "Will? The bag."

William had almost forgotten about the bag Corrigan had thrown at him. He untied it from his belt.

"Give it to the nice Abbot," said Corrigan.

William handed it over. The Abbot nervously reached out and snatched it away, opening it up and peering inside. He locked eyes with Corrigan.

"I don't understand."

"Croth sent us. He has—how did he put it?—'an order to fill for a rich fey duke with more gold than sense.' He wants it done right away."

The Abbot reached into the bag and pulled something

231

out. William saw they were small, bulbous insects. They looked like—

Nostalgae. They were nostalgae, but before they had been filled with memories.

"This is most irregular," said the Abbot, eyeing them suspiciously.

"Irregular or not, Croth wants them filled. Before the night is out. We're to wait for them."

"What nonsense. How will you carry them all?"

Corrigan pointed at Will. "Why do you think he's here? A bit slow in the head, but a good worker. He'll make a few trips."

The Abbot glared at them, but he obviously didn't want to threaten his relationship with Croth, because he finally stood aside.

"Come on then. We'd best get started."

William and Corrigan entered the church, finding themselves in a small, carpeted corridor. There was an open door just to their right. Will peered inside, but it was only a bedchamber.

The Abbot led them along the passage and unlocked a door that opened into darkness. They followed him through, and although William couldn't see anything, he could tell they were in a large room from the echo his footsteps made.

A scraping sound made him jump. A small flame flickered

to life as the Abbot lit a lantern. He trimmed the wick and lifted it from the small table next to the door, raising it high into the air so they could get a proper look where they were going.

Will glanced around. They were in the actual church now. Pews were arranged neatly all the way back to the arched doors and the stained-glass window. To their right were a raised area and a pulpit from which the priest would deliver his sermons.

"Follow me," said the Abbot, heading past the first line of benches and toward another door in the wall opposite. He took a key from his belt and unlocked the door, pushing it open and standing to the side.

"After you," he said. "I have to keep it locked."

William hesitated, but stepped through the door, followed closely by Corrigan. What choice did they have?

The door opened onto a short landing. At the end of the landing a flight of stone stairs led downward.

"Hold this," said the Abbot, handing William the lantern. William took it, holding it up so the priest could lock the door once again. He turned to William and gave him a brittle smile. "Down we go."

The stairs were worn smooth and dipped slightly in the middle due to years of use. William didn't like it at all. It reminded him of Kelindria's cells, where he had been locked away in the darkness, not knowing if anyone would ever come to let him out.

The stairs stopped at another door. The Abbot squeezed past William and unlocked it. It led into a stone passage, but this one was brightly lit by lanterns placed inside small niches in the walls.

"He doesn't like the dark," explained the Abbot. "Have to keep these lit all the time or he throws up such a fuss. It's very expensive," he said disapprovingly.

"I'm sure you can afford it," said Corrigan coldly. "What with all the money you make from him."

The Abbot glared at Corrigan, but said nothing. Instead, he walked briskly across the large flagstones and stopped before a thick, black door.

"You keep him in a cell?" asked William.

"It's not a cell. It used to be a wine cellar. And where else am I *supposed* to keep him? The man's mad. If I had him upstairs, my congregation would hear him. Besides, he's happier down here. He likes his privacy."

"As I'm sure you keep telling yourself," muttered Corrigan.

The Abbot slid a small panel to the side and peered through the hole. He nodded, then slammed it shut again and lifted the heavy latch that kept the door locked. He pulled open the door and raised the lantern.

"Hello, Tom. It's only me. I've got some work for you. Are you up to it?"

There was a low mumbling from inside the cell.

"I've also got some guests. Can we come in?"

More mumbling.

The Abbot glanced back at William. "Follow me. But please, no sudden moves. He's easily startled."

The Abbot stepped through the door and moved to the side to allow William and Corrigan to enter. They stepped into a large stone room. The walls were dotted with dark, empty niches, presumably where the wine had once been kept. Against the far wall was a row of wall torches. They cast their illumination over a bed, a chair, and a table. A thin man was seated on the bed, rocking backward and forward as he stared at the floor.

He stopped rocking, then slowly looked up at them, studying their faces. Finally, he nodded.

"It is time," he mumbled. "Time to die. Time to war. Time to burn."

William felt a rush of air behind him, and he turned just in time to see the door slam closed. He heard the latch fall into place, then the panel slid aside.

"Most dreadfully sorry," said the Abbot. "But don't worry. I just want to check with Croth that your story is true. I should be back in an hour or so. If it turns out you've been lying to me"—here he smiled, the light from his lantern glinting off his teeth—"then I'll hand you back to Croth to dispose of you as he sees fit." He pushed the pouch of nostalgae through the small hole. "But if you *are* telling the truth, you might as well get started on these. Just give them to Tom. He knows what to do."

The panel slammed shut. William stared around in despair. Corrigan was glaring at the door, so furious that he was actually shaking with anger.

"I'll get him," muttered the piskie. "I'll see him fall for this."

William heard a noise. He turned around to find the Prophet had quietly approached and was now standing directly behind him.

"The flames know our names," he said. "They'll sniff you out. Eat you up. Burn you to a crisp. They're coming, William Snow, and nothing can stop them."

⊰ CHAPTER NINETEEN ⊱

In which Emily and Co. find out about magical disguises.
A statue speaks.

I've done my part!" complained Beezle as they hurried through the dark streets, putting as much distance between themselves and the bridge as possible. "I got you off the bridge. Now it's your turn. Hand over my book."

"You were going to leave us there!" said Emily.

Beezle looked shamefaced. "I panicked," he said. "I just wanted to get away."

"By leaving us hanging over the River Thames," said Wren dubiously. He had regained consciousness when Beezle grounded the boat on the banks of the river. He had a massive bump on the head, but otherwise seemed to be suffering no ill effects.

"I wasn't thinking straight."

"It doesn't matter if you were thinking straight or not," said Emily. "We still need your help."

"This isn't fair!"

"Hey," snapped Jack. "If it wasn't for us, you'd still be stuck in that cage back on the bridge. We saved your life, remember?"

"Yes, I remember! You're not likely to let me forget, are you?" Beezle stomped ahead of them, then stopped and whirled around. "Fine! What do you want this time?"

"We need to get into the Faerie Tree," said Emily simply.

Beezle burst out laughing. "Impossible. No humans are allowed."

"I've been there before," Emily pointed out. "With Corrigan."

"Yes. With Corrigan. Let me rephrase that. *Unaccompanied* humans are not allowed."

"Then you can take us in," said Jack.

"Afraid not. Some of that stuff Munifus said was true. I really am wanted by Titania for . . . causing mischief. I'll be arrested on sight."

"Then we need some kind of disguise," Emily said. "Something that will get us in so we can speak to Nimue."

"You're insane, you know that? She is part of the Queen's court. You think you can just walk into the throne room and say to Nimue, 'Oh, excuse us, where exactly did you trap

Merlin? We'd like to have a word with him, if you don't mind.'"

"Something like that."

"And when she asks you why you want to know? What are you going to say? 'Oh, he owed me some money, that's all.' Or, 'I need to return a book I borrowed.' Yes, I'm sure that will work."

"Let us worry about that." She held up the book. "The question is, can you find us disguises?"

Beezle eyed the book hungrily. "And if I do, then that's us quits?"

"You'll never see us again," Emily said.

Beezle licked his lip. "Fine! I'll have to call in a favor, but if it will get you off my back, then it will be worth it. Follow me."

⤙ ⤚

He led them eastward, moving through the side streets and back lanes of the city. They never strayed far from the river, though. Emily could always smell the stink of it, hovering on the warm air. It got worse as they walked, and it took Emily a few minutes to realize this was because they were approaching Billingsgate Market. The stench of rotting fish was heavy and cloying, causing her stomach to heave unpleasantly.

"This way," called Beezle cheerfully, leading them down toward the river, then onto a wooden walkway that traveled along the waterfront. Emily eyed the planks beneath their feet. Some of them seemed to be rotting away.

The walkway turned and extended out over the water, leading to a squat, brightly lid building about halfway across the river. Emily frowned, confused. That couldn't be right, surely? Wouldn't the boats and ships crash into it?

Unless they had crossed over into fey London again.

"What is this place?" Jack asked.

"It's Lady Steel's Coffeehouse," said Beezle.

This brought a snort of laughter from Jack. "A coffeehouse? Really? Aren't you lot more suited to taverns?"

Beezle stopped walking and turned to face Jack. "You shouldn't make assumptions, boy. I don't drink. Never have. It clouds the mind, right? I like to stay clearheaded. What's wrong with that?"

"Nothing," said Emily hastily. "Nothing at all. Very admirable, actually."

"Hmmph. And for your information, there are a lot of fey like me. Lady Steel saw an opening in the market and took advantage. She runs a whole chain of coffee shops and eateries across fey London." As they drew closer, Emily could hear the sounds of merriment coming from inside. The lilt and squeak of a badly played fiddle, the clink of glasses, the shouts of laughter. A coffeehouse it may be, but the fey were certainly having a good time inside. The door opened, and

Emily found herself staring at a pair of legs that disappeared up past the top of the door. The legs folded up and a huge head peered out at them.

"'Scuse me," said the giant. "Comin' thru."

Emily, Beezle, Wren, and Jack stood aside while the large fey wriggled through the doorway. He pushed himself to his feet with a sigh and brushed himself down.

"Not exactly a giant-friendly establishment," he said. He turned and stomped away, the whole walkway shaking with his footfalls.

Beezle led them inside. Fey of every kind filled the coffee-house. Squat, yellow-skinned goblins; tall creatures with white skin and white hair; faeries flitting through the air, casting colorful glows wherever they went. There was a table filled with fish-headed creatures. Emily wondered how they could breathe, but they seemed perfectly content to sit there eating . . . Emily peered closer. Eating frogs! She looked away in disgust, hurrying after Beezle as he made his way to the front of house. Over in a corner Emily saw a fey similar to one she had seen back in Merrian's shop, a tall creature with a hollowed-out back. But this fey had hooks attached to the inside of the hollowed-out area, and other fey were taking turns trying to throw little wooden circles over the hooks. As Emily watched, a broad-shouldered dwarf, his beard tied around his waist, took his turn. He missed, the wooden circle falling inside the hollow fey's body. The dwarf cursed as the fey turned around with a grin, holding out his hand. The dwarf handed over some coins and stomped away in anger.

The serving area of the coffeehouse was a huge circular bartop that looped around a stand-alone wall covered with clear jars. Inside the jars were various brands of coffee beans. Emily had no idea there were so many different types. Beezle pushed his way through the crowds and hauled himself up onto a barstool. After a moment's hesitation, Emily, Jack, and Wren followed suit.

"Service!" Beezle called, smacking the stained wood.

Emily looked around; there was no sign of anyone serving behind the bar. But a moment later she heard a squeaking sound, and a small platform came whizzing around the circular bar from the other side of the drinks wall. Sitting in the platform was an ancient fey woman who would probably come up only to Emily's knees if they were to stand side by side. The woman's face was a mass of such deep wrinkles that her features were hard to make out. What Emily *could* see, however, were two tiny black eyes that glared at them as her platform jerked to a squeaky halt in front of Beezle.

"Evening, Lady Steel," said Beezle.

"Beezle."

"I've come to call in my favor."

"Is that so?" asked Lady Steel. "You sure?"

"Aye."

"'Bout time. How long has it been? Fifty years?"

"Sixty."

"So what do you want?"

"Disguises. For these three."

The woman glanced at them. "What kind?"

"Fey," said Beezle. "And they have to pass muster. So none of the cheap potions."

The fey woman drew herself up. "Cheap potions? How dare you? All my products are of the finest quality."

"Aye," Beezle said wryly. "That's why I was sniffed out the moment I stepped into Queen Caelia's castle. They were actually watching me from across the field. Knew who I was the whole time."

"Pah. The Irish fey are a paranoid lot. Anyway, I've adapted my work since then. Learned from your mistakes."

"*Your* mistakes."

"Whatever. Take them through the back. I'll join you in a moment."

Beezle slid off his stool and motioned for them to follow. He moved through the crowds and opened a door at the far end of the coffeehouse. It led into what looked like a private dining area. A long table dominated the room, but it was empty at the moment.

A few minutes later, Lady Steel entered the room carrying

a small wooden box. She climbed up a small set of stairs that Emily hadn't even noticed and put the box on the tabletop, flicking it open with a sharp click of her fingers.

"Right," she said, eyeing Emily. "What are you after? Big or small? Goblin? Faerie?"

"What?" Emily looked uncertainly at Beezle.

"Your disguise," the fey said. "What do you want to be?" He saw the look on her face. "It's not permanent, you idiot. It'll last ... what?" He glanced at the old fey. "Five? Six hours?"

"About that."

"Enough to get you where you're going without being discovered."

"So. What'll it be?"

Emily thought back to her time in the Faerie Tree. What had been the most common fey she had seen? What stood out in her mind were the tall, graceful fey. But the very fact that they stood out meant that they were too visible. She thought harder. As she and Corrigan had walked through the branches, there had been lots of smaller fey going about their business. She had seen quite a few piskies, she recalled.

"A piskie?"

"Ah, the rats of the fey world," said Beezle.

"Good choice," said Steel. "Common as mud, piskies. You'll blend right in."

She fished around in the box and took out two small

vials, handing one to Emily and one to Jack. She rummaged around a bit more.

"Sorry, only have two piskie potions." She handed Wren a third vial. "This will do you, though."

Wren took the vial. Jack looked at his uncertainly, then pulled Emily aside so they could talk without being overheard.

"I'm not sure about this, Snow."

"Neither am I. But we need to track down this Nimue if we want to find Merlin."

"Maybe your brother was right. Maybe we should look for the Raven King instead."

Emily frowned. "It's a bit late to change your mind now, Jack! We agreed that finding Merlin was the best way to stop the fire and get us home. We just have to follow this through to the end."

Jack sighed. "Fine," he said reluctantly. "Let's get this over with, then."

Jack took the cork out of his vial and drank the contents. For a moment, nothing happened. Then a ripple spread across his face, like water lapping against a riverbank. Jack tentatively prodded his skin, then a grimace crossed his features and he convulsed, falling to his knees as if in pain. Emily hurried forward to help, but he waved her away.

"'M all right," he mumbled. He waited a few moments, then pushed himself to his feet again.

What Emily saw made her step back in alarm. It wasn't Jack who stood before her anymore. His skin had turned dark brown and was covered with fine hair. His eyes were large and black, his ears long and pointed.

And not to mention the fact that he had shrunk as well, to the same height as Corrigan.

The thing was, although to all intents and purposes a piskie now stood before her, Emily could still see Jack in the disguise. The shape of his face, the curve of the mouth, the slant of the eyes—all that was Jack, but his features had been placed on a piskie.

He stared at his hands in amazement, patting down his body. "My clothes . . ." He looked at Steel, because Emily noticed for the first time that his clothes had shrunk with him so that they still fitted his smaller frame.

"Part of the magic," she said smugly. She looked over at Beezle. "You won't find that kind of attention to detail any-where else."

"Does it . . . does it hurt?" Emily asked.

"No. It was just . . . uncomfortable. Very uncomfortable."

There was a gasp from Wren. Emily turned around to find he had already taken his potion. Except that instead of a piskie, he now looked like a goblin. His face was the color of mustard. A long, sharp nose dominated his face, over-shadowing his tiny black eyes. He was staring at his hands, turning them this way and that. He looked up at Emily and grinned, showing serrated teeth.

"Amazing," he said delightedly.

Her turn. Emily pulled the cork out of her bottle, took a deep breath, then swallowed the contents. It tasted sickly sweet, like sugar syrup. Not unpleasant, but not pleasant, either. Emily put the vial down on the table and waited.

She felt it on her face first. A persistent tickling, like ants were crawling across her skin. The feeling grew stronger and stronger, until it no longer felt like an ant, but more like a mouse. Her fingers tingled. Her feet itched. A strange bubbling sound came from her stomach. She burped and lifted a hand to cover her mouth. A hand that no longer looked like her own. It was the same color as tree bark. Her nails were yellow and slightly pointed.

She looked at the others. Jack was staring at her, a half grin playing over his new mouth. "At least it's made you better looking," he said.

"Very funny."

Steel was holding a small mirror out. Emily took it and lifted it to her face. She half knew what to expect after seeing Jack and Wren, but the transformation still took her breath away. It looked like her, but a fey version of herself. The structure of her face was the same, just smaller. Her eyes were much bigger than before, and her nose was tiny, a mere bump. She stuck out her tongue, using it to probe her tiny teeth.

"Right," said Beezle, smacking his hands together. "That's me done here. If you'll just hand over my property, then we can part ways and never have to see each other again. I like the sound of that. Ever again. It has a very permanent ring to it."

"Actually, we *do* need one more thing," Emily said.

Beezle said nothing for a few moments. He breathed in deeply, then exhaled loudly. "Lady Steel," he said, "could you please give me and my *friends* some privacy?"

"Of course. Just . . . don't break anything."

Beezle waited till the old fey had left and closed the door behind her. "You're breaking the deal," he said. "You wanted a disguise, I got you a disguise."

"I know. But we need you to get us into the Faerie Tree."

Beezle shook his head. "No. Can't be done. I already told you. There's a reward on my head. If I'm seen down there, my life is over."

Emily thought about this. "Fine. What about to the market outside the lift?"

Beezle frowned suspiciously at Emily. "What lift?"

"Mr. and Mrs. Stintle."

"You know about them?"

"I've met them. So how about that? You take us to the lift, and we'll find our own way in."

Beezle stared thoughtfully at the ceiling. "And then you'll leave me alone?"

"You'll never see us again," said Emily.

"Swear. Swear on your mother or father's life."

Emily hesitated, then nodded. "I swear. On my mother's life."

"Fine then. Let's get this finished."

"Suits me," said Emily. "But first, I need a blanket."

"What for?"

"Doesn't matter. Can you get one from your friend?"

Beezle sighed. "I'll see what I can do."

⊣⊱ ⊰⊢

It took them an hour to reach their destination, and every minute that passed had Emily ruing the fact that they had already drunk the disguise potion instead of keeping it until they were closer to the Faerie Tree.

But what was done was done, she supposed. There was no point in complaining.

Beezle didn't take them down through any route Emily had already used. Once away from the riverfront, he led them through the city and finally stopped before an abandoned house.

"It's through here," he said, entering the garden and following the path to the rear of the building. The others

249

followed after, finding themselves in a wildly overgrown garden.

Creepers and bushes pushed up against the wood of a large rickety shed, weeds and small trees taller than Emily (when she was normal-sized) clogging up the rest of the space.

Beezle led them into a huge patch of bushes, where Emily was rather surprised to find a large metal statue. It was of a man on a horse, and it was easily over six feet tall. "You should bow," said Beezle. "This used to be your King."

Emily looked at the statue, confused. "What are you talking about?"

"It's Charles I. His statues were destroyed during the civil war, but the Royalists took what they could and hid them. Some of them still lie around London. Forgotten." He patted the flank of the horse. "Ain't that right, your Kingship."

"It's a liberty, if you ask me," said the statue.

Emily jumped back, startled. She stared up to find the metal King leaning over his horse, watching her curiously.

"What's wrong with the piskie?"

"Uh . . . nothing. Easily scared. That's all. Can we get in?"

"What's the password?"

Beezle frowned. "I wasn't aware there was a password."

"New rules."

"*Whose* new rules?"

"Mine."

"So how are we supposed to know the password if you haven't told us?"

"Mmm. Good point. It's Charles."

"What?"

"Charles."

"I know who you are."

"No. The password is Charles. Wanted to make sure I remembered it, y'see."

"Ah." Beezle nodded. "Very wise." He waited. "So . . . can we come in?"

"You haven't said the password yet."

"Oh. Sorry. Charles."

"Yes? What can I do for you?"

Beezle opened his mouth to probably say something rude, but the statue cackled with laughter.

"Sorry. Just my little joke. You may enter."

He flicked the reigns on his horse. It neighed and stepped aside, pulling creepers of ivy and large clumps of grass aside to reveal a dark hole in the ground with a set of wooden stairs leading into the earth. Muttering under his breath, Beezle disappeared through the hole, Emily, Jack, and Wren following quickly after.

Beezle led them through old earthen tunnels and fey-built passages, descending deeper and deeper until Emily found herself back in the huge tunnel with the market outside the Stintles' little shop.

"And this is where I really say good-bye," said Beezle. "I'd like to say it's been fun, and that I'm sad to see you go, but I'm not, so I won't. Good riddance, and if I ever see you again, I'll be sure to run in the other direction. Good-bye." Beezle saluted, turned on his heels, and vanished back into the darkness.

Emily watched him step back into the tunnel. His sudden departure made her feel incredibly exposed. They were alone now. Really alone.

It was all up to them.

⊰⊱ CHAPTER TWENTY ⊰⊱
Locked in. Riddles. The Great Fire is sighted.

I can't believe him!" said Corrigan, for about the twentieth time. "Locking us in here like this. Who does he think he is?

"The Abbot, the Abbot, fast as a rabbit," said the Prophet.

"Yes, thank you, Thomas," said Corrigan.

William watched the man as he sat on his bed, playing with the threads of his blanket.

"You called him Thomas. Do you know who he is?"

"Hmm?" Corrigan glanced up from where he was pushing against the wood of the door, testing for any weak spots. "Him? Aye. I think so, anyway."

"And?" prompted William.

"Thomas of Ercildoune."

"Is that supposed to make sense to me?"

"You must have heard the story of Thomas the Rhymer."

The name rang a vague bell in his head, but he wasn't sure why. William shook his head.

"He was taken to Faerie by the Faerie Queen a few centuries ago. He became something of a favorite of hers. But she thought his life would be in danger during one of the wars, so she sent him back home. With a special gift."

"What was the gift?"

"That he could never lie again. That everything out of his mouth from that moment on would be the utter truth."

William thought about this. "Doesn't seem much of a gift to me."

"I know. I think the Queen had gone a bit funny in the head. She was quite old at that time."

William stared at Thomas in pity. "And this is what her gift has done? Turned him into some kind of Prophet? Kept prisoner so others can use him?"

"Looks that way, doesn't it?" said Corrigan cheerfully.

"But . . . doesn't that bother you?"

"Boy, the only thing that is bothering me right now is getting out of here before that priest comes back."

William sighed and pushed himself to his feet. The wine cellar was quite large, although the Prophet used only a small section against one wall. There were two torches lighting his living area. William approached him.

"May I borrow one of your torches?" he asked. "I'll bring it right back, I promise."

"Promises, promises, sow what you reap. Easy to give, and hard to keep."

"Uh . . . all right," said William, unsure if that was a yes or no. "I'll really bring it back. I'm just going to search the room for a way out. Maybe we can get you out of here as well, yes?"

"Out, out, Thomas does doubt. In, in, away from the din."

William straightened up. He was having serious doubts regarding Thomas the Rhymer's sanity. How were they supposed to get anything of use out of him if he just kept speaking gibberish?

William carefully took one of the torches out of its wall sconce. Thomas shifted on his bed, moving closer to the remaining torch, but otherwise, he didn't seem to mind.

William took the torch deeper into the wine cellar, passing stone pillars that supported the low roof. He did a complete circuit of the room, peering into the small niches in the walls, but there was no other door. No other way out.

He moved into the center of the room and lifted the torch above his head. Nothing in the ceiling, either.

He lowered the torch once again, but as he did so, he noticed something odd. The shadow cast by one of the pillars was slightly skew. The other three pillars cast shadows that were perfectly straight, but the shadow for the center pillar seemed to bend slightly.

William hurried forward and saw this was because the shadow fell across a slight dip in the floor. He got down on his hands and knees, holding the torch low to the floor. The dip leapt out in stark relief thanks to the flames. It traveled in a straight line directly into one of the wall niches.

William crawled forward and got down onto his stomach, using the torch to peer into the niche. Inside, instead of a small nook used to hold wine, he saw a hole that ended at a metal grill. It had to be some kind of drainage system, in case of flooding.

"Corrigan," he called. "Over here."

Corrigan stopped trying to slide his bronze dagger between the door and the doorframe and hurried over to join William. He peered into the hole.

"Can you fit?" asked William.

"Reckon so."

He got down onto his belly and wriggled into the opening. William couldn't see what he was doing because he was blocking the light, but he could hear the piskie banging on the metal, trying to dislodge it. He eventually stopped and retreated back into their cell.

"It's loose. Need more leverage, though," said Corrigan,

then pulled himself back into the hole feetfirst. It only took a few hard kicks to dislodge the grate.

"I'll find my way round to the door," he called. "You see if you can get any sense from Mr. Rhymer over there, preferably something not in verse."

Corrigan pulled himself through the opening and disappeared from sight. William straightened up and returned the torch to its wall sconce. He stared at Thomas, uncertain how to start, uncertain if the man was even sane.

He sat down at the bottom of the bed. "I'm supposed to ask you some stuff," he said after a while. "But I think you must be pretty sick of that, yes? Questions all the time." He smiled awkwardly at Thomas. "I thought *I* had a tough life. My mother always used to say that no matter how bad things were, there was always someone worse off than you. I never believed it until today."

Thomas's rocking slowed as William spoke.

"I wonder what Em is doing?" mused Will, more to hear the sound of his own voice than anything else. The silence was oppressive. "If I know her, she's probably already found Merlin and stopped the Fire King. Then I'll look like a fool, as usual." Which was the problem with having a sister who was so smart. He knew he could never be as clever as her— he knew that in the pit of his being. But Emily didn't. She thought he was just as clever and was simply not applying himself. That he was lazy. In fact, Will reckoned she thought that about everybody. That everyone could be smart if they just applied themselves. Was that a bad trait or a good trait? Will couldn't decide. It was certainly an *infuriating* trait.

"See, she thinks we should find Merlin. That he'll be the answer to all our problems. Me, I'm not so sure. I mean, he could be anywhere. That's why I wanted to search for the Raven King. Cavanagh had a lead, you see. That gave us something we could aim for. But try telling Em that. Oh, no. She knows her own mind, and you'd better not dare to disagree with her." William shifted on the bed, noting that Thomas had stopped rocking altogether. William sighed. "I know she means well. But she's not my ma. She never will be." William tried not to think about what Emily had said back at Somerset House. That their parents were still alive, held captive somewhere. He wasn't sure he believed it. After all, it was the Dagda who had told Emily, and he had been trying to get the key to the Faerie Gate. They couldn't believe what he said.

Could they?

"If only she'd stop ordering me around," he said quietly. "If she stopped treating me like I was five years old, things would be better. I know they would."

He trailed into silence and cast a sideways glance at Thomas. He smiled ruefully. "This is what it's come to. The only person who listens to me is a half-mad Prophet. No offense."

William got up and walked over to the door, trying the handle just in case it had miraculously unlocked itself. It hadn't. He supposed he should ask Thomas about the Raven King now. That was why they came here, after all.

"Oranges and lemons," said Thomas.

William turned around to find the man sitting on the edge of the bed. He was staring intently at him.

"I'm . . . sorry?"

Thomas stood up. "Here comes a candle to light you to bed," he said, taking a slow step forward. "Here comes a chopper to chop off your head." Thomas lunged forward and grabbed him by the arms. William tried to pull away, but Thomas held him tight, his fingers digging into his skin. "Chip chop, chip chop—the Last Man's *dead*!"

As he said these last words William heard a loud *click* from the door behind him. Thomas released his grip, and William whirled around and yanked open the door, almost tripping over Corrigan in his haste to get away.

"Hey," snapped the piskie. "Easy there, tiger. What's the problem?"

"Him," said William, nodding his head at Thomas, who now stood in the doorway.

"All you that in the condemned hole do lie," said Thomas

softly. "Prepare you for tomorrow you shall die; Watch all and pray: the hour is drawing near, That you before the almighty must appear—"

"Stop speaking like that!" shouted William. "Why is he saying that? Is he saying we're going to die? Is that what he's saying?"

Corrigan was staring thoughtfully at Thomas, who stepped through the door and looked around the corridor with interest.

"I'm not sure," said the piskie.

"Oranges and lemons," said Thomas, moving toward the stairs. He paused at the bottom, then turned to look at them expectantly. "Oranges and lemons?" he said, a questioning tone to his voice.

"I'm not sure if he's hungry, or if he's trying to tell us something," said Corrigan. "But he's going in our direction, so get a move on. Before that Abbot comes back with Croth."

They followed Thomas up the stairs and out into the dark interior of the church. William started moving toward the front doors, thinking they could unlock them from this side and escape. But he had only gone two steps before Thomas was dragging at his shirt.

"No go, you come; he comes, we go."

"What?"

Thomas pointed urgently at the door. "He comes. We go."

He released William's shirt and moved off a few paces, then stopped and waited, staring expectantly at William and Corrigan.

"Seems he doesn't want us using the front door," said Corrigan.

"Then we go out the same way we came in," replied William, heading for the door that led to the Abbot's rooms.

As he pulled it open he heard guttural voices coming from somewhere up ahead. He froze. The sounds were coming from outside the church. The handle on the door leading out into the cemetery started to move. William closed the door.

"Someone's coming," he hissed.

"Who?" asked Corrigan.

"I don't know, but it doesn't sound like the Abbot."

"Croth. He must have gathered up some of his heavies."

"What do we do?" asked William.

"The only thing we can do. Follow our new friend."

William turned. Thomas was disappearing through a door that was hidden behind a wall covering. He and Corrigan hurried after him. William had only just pulled the covering back into place when he heard the main doors of the church heave open to admit a babble of eager voices.

"Oranges and lemons," whispered a voice.

Thomas was waiting at the end of a short corridor. When

he saw he had their attention, he turned and disappeared up a flight of stairs.

The voices in the church grew louder.

"Please," William heard the Abbot say. "If you will just follow me. I have them downstairs. You can take them away and do what you wish with them."

"Oh, we've got something planned," said a voice William recognized as Croth's. "Don't we, lads?" A loud, bloodthirsty cheer greeted these words.

"And you can guarantee I'll be left alone?" asked the Abbot. "If things get ugly. *Out there*. You'll tell them I'm on your side?"

"I'll try," said Croth. "But my advice is to hide for the next few days. Things could get ugly."

What did he mean by that? William turned away from the door and hurried after Thomas. Corrigan had already gone on ahead. The stairs wound around and around in a spiral, and Will realized they were climbing the tower he had seen when they first approached the church. His steps faltered with this thought. Weren't they trapping themselves? If the fey came up the stairs looking for them, there would be nowhere to go.

William sprinted up the rest of the stairs and arrived in the bell tower. He slowed. Corrigan was standing on the wall that surrounded the top of the tower. Thomas was leaning next to him. They were both staring out into the city.

William hesitated. Something about the way their attention was fixed outward filled him with dread. He approached slowly, and with each step, more of the night sky was revealed. But instead of the blackness he should have seen, he saw orange-tinted clouds.

Another step. The orange grew brighter. William thought he could hear distant screams, people shouting.

Another step. The first of London's buildings came into view. Another step, then another, and William was out on the battlement.

Corrigan glanced at him. "It's begun," he said bleakly.

William leaned on the wall. As he did so, he saw that it wasn't clouds he was looking at. It was smoke.

From their position high up in the bell tower they could clearly see the fire devouring a small section of the city close to the London Bridge. The flames roared high into the sky, the hot wind fanning the fire and spreading it through the wooden buildings and dry thatch.

They could see small figures running around as people struggled to contain the flames. Bucket lines had been formed from the nearby Thames, but they had as much effect as spitting into the fire would.

"Water's not going to do anything," said Corrigan. "The only thing that can stop that fire is sending the Fire King back to where he came from."

"Then we have to move!"

"Move where?" Corrigan nodded at Thomas the Rhymer, who was gazing in rapt fascination at the orange and red light pulsing against the clouds of smoke. "Did you ask him about the Raven King? Did he tell you anything?"

"No. Well, nothing except all that stuff about the condemned man dying."

"But did he say it in response to a question? Prophecies and foretellings are never straightforward. They always come in riddles."

William thought back. What was he doing before Tom spoke? He had just been sitting on the bed prattling on about his life. He *had* mentioned the Raven King, but he didn't think he asked a specific question.

"Regardless, we need to find another way out of here," said Corrigan. He hopped up onto the wall and peered over the edge. While he did this, William moved to stand next to Thomas.

"Thomas?" he said softly. The man's face moved slightly, but he still stared out at the flames. "Tom, do you see the fire down there? It was started by a fey called Kelindria. We want to stop it. Because if we don't do something, then the whole city is going to fall. Thousands of people will die. But to do that we need to find the Raven King. Do you know who that is? Because someone thought you did. A man called Cavanagh. He is in a society called the Invisible Order. They want to protect us from the fey. Thomas? Can you help us?" William waited, but Tom didn't move. William sighed. Maybe Cavanagh had been wrong. Maybe Thomas couldn't help them.

"I think it will hold," said Corrigan.

William turned to Corrigan. He was pulling at the ivy that grew up the tower wall.

"I'm not climbing down that," he said, horrified.

"You're more than welcome to stay here," said Corrigan, swinging around and grabbing hold of a stem. "See you at the bottom," he said. Then he disappeared from view.

William leaned over the wall. Corrigan was almost halfway down the wall already, dropping hand over hand at an incredible speed. He heard a rustle behind him and turned to see Thomas climbing slowly down as well. That left just him.

He sighed. Looked as though he didn't have a choice.

William pulled himself up onto the wall and lowered himself until his feet found a grip in the branches. Then he let go with one hand and grabbed hold of a thick vine. He yanked it. He pushed down. The branch felt strong. He let go with one hand and grabbed a thick clump of the ivy. Then he started to drop slowly downward, moving hand over hand, shifting his feet around until they found solid purchase in the vegetation.

"Come on," said a voice from beneath him. "You can drop the rest of the way."

William finally looked down to see Katerina waiting about six feet below. He let go and dropped onto the grass.

"I saw that fey and his friends arrive," she explained. "Came in here to hide till I could figure out what to do and saw the other two climbing down the tower."

William looked around, but couldn't see Thomas or Corrigan anywhere.

"They jumped over the wall at the back," said Katerina softly. She held up a hand for silence. William could hear the sounds of raised voices coming from the other side of the church. "And I think we should join them. Rather quickly."

William agreed, and they both ran through the graveyard and climbed over the wall to the street outside the church grounds. William could smell the fire now. Even though it was far away, the smell of burning wood and smoke hung in the air, scratching at the back of his throat.

"Over here," called Corrigan.

William and Katerina hurried over to where the piskie was waiting at the mouth of an alley. He wasn't looking at them. His attention was focused on something else.

William peered over his shoulder to find Thomas sitting hunched on the ground.

"What—?" he started to say, but the words died on his tongue.

There was something crawling from Thomas's mouth.

William stared in horror as spindly legs pulled at the sides of Thomas's mouth. He moaned, then started rocking back and forth as the nostalgae (for William realized this is what was in his mouth), pushed open his jaws. Thomas tilted his head back, then spat the creature out. It dropped onto the ground in front of Corrigan, growing larger as they watched.

"What did you say to him?" William asked Corrigan.

"Nothing. He ran ahead of me. When I caught up, he was stuffing one of those things into his mouth. The question is"—Corrigan glanced up at William—"what did *you* say to him?"

The nostalgae started to flicker and glow, an image forming inside the creature's body. William leaned closer to try to make it out. The picture was that of a dark corridor lit only by a hand holding a candle. The owner of the hand moved along the hallway, passing heavy, forbidding doors. As the image moved and flickered before them, Thomas stood up and started talking in a soft, low voice: "All you that in the condemned hole do lie, Prepare you for tomorrow you shall die; Watch all and pray: the hour is drawing near, That you before the Almighty must appear."

Every now and then, William caught a glimpse of something moving in the person's other hand. It took him a while to realize it was a bell. The owner of the memory was ringing a bell as he moved along the darkened corridor.

Thomas carried on: "Examine well yourselves in time repent, That you may not to eternal flames be sent. And when St. Sepulchre's Bell in the morning tolls, The Lord above have mercy on your soul."

The image stopped before one of the doors. The number 40 had been painted onto it in a neat hand.

The image froze, then restarted again.

"Is that it?" asked Corrigan.

"What does it mean?" asked William, confused.

"*I* know," said Katerina in a low voice.

William and Corrigan turned to face her.

"Every criminal in London knows that verse. It's the death chant. The night before a prisoner is executed at Newgate Prison, the Bellman of St. Sepulchre walks past his cell ringing the execution bell and speaking the verse. It's how you know your time is up."

"Oranges and lemons," said William suddenly, looking at Thomas.

"What?" said Corrigan.

"Oranges and lemons. He's been saying that over and over since you left the wine cellar. I didn't realize until just now, but it's another rhyme. You know the one. Oranges and lemons go the bells of St. Clements?"

"So?"

"So the last lines are of the rhyme are: 'Here comes a candle to light you to bed. Here comes a chopper to chop off your head.'" He nodded at the nostalgae. "It could be about this Bellman of St. Sepulchre. Maybe Thomas is telling us to go to Newgate."

They all turned their gaze to Thomas. He stared back at them, nodding. "Oranges and lemons," he said. He held up a hand and waved it gently, then turned and stepped out of the alley. He turned away from the direction of the flames and started walking.

"Should we stop him?" asked Corrigan.

"No," said William. "He's had enough of people forcing him to do things. Besides, he's already given us an answer."

They all turned their attention to the nostalgae. The image had arrived at the point where the bellman was standing outside the door with the number 40 painted on it.

"We need to get inside Newgate Prison," said Will.

CHAPTER TWENTY-ONE
In which Emily, Jack, and Christopher Wren
infiltrate the Faerie Tree. A nasty surprise arrives.

The little shop that housed the hoist that had taken Emily and Corrigan down to the Faerie Tree looked slightly less run-down than when Emily had come here last. But not by much. Two hundred years didn't seem to change much in the fey world.

"Just follow my lead," Emily said to Jack and Wren. "I've been here before, so there's less chance of us getting caught out if I do the talking."

"No arguments from me," said Jack. "Stealing and sneaking is my thing. In all else I bow to you." Jack sketched an elaborate bow to illustrate his point.

"Be serious," said Emily.

"Why?" asked Jack.

Emily hesitated. "What?"

"Why do we have to be so serious? You're *always* too serious, Snow. You're old before your time. You need to relax a bit. Have fun."

Emily was amazed. The words *Have fun?* were posed incredulously on her lips, but before she could utter them, Jack raised a hand to stop her.

"All right. Maybe 'have fun' isn't quite appropriate. But you *do* need to relax a bit. Stop and smell the flowers." Jack spread his arms wide and turned in a circle. "Look at us, Snow. Look where we are. Look *who* we are. Could you ever in your wildest dreams have imagined something like this happening to us? It's *adventure*. It's escape from the freezing streets. Escape from a life that . . . that was nothing but work and sickness and hunger." He stepped closer to Emily. "No matter what happens to us in the future, even if we go back to our old lives, we'll always have this to look back on. We're different now. Special. Things have happened that can never be taken away. You should appreciate that. I know I do."

Emily was rather taken aback by Jack's outburst. She always thought of him as a bit silly, really. Nice enough, but not really capable of deep thought. But now she would have to rethink that. There was a lot more going on inside his head than she had given him credit for.

Even Wren was looking at Jack with some admiration in his eyes.

She cleared her throat. "Yes. Well. I'll consider your words, Jack Doyle. But later on, when I actually have time, and not when *we're about to sneak into the home of the Faerie Queen magically disguised as the fey*! If that's all right with you?"

Jack grinned. "But of course."

A tiny smile tugged at Emily's mouth. She quickly turned away before he could see it and knocked on the door.

"Come in then!" snapped a voice from inside the shop.

Emily pushed the door open and entered. Wren and Jack followed her, and Jack closed the door quietly behind them. Emily looked around the small room. It was exactly the same as when she had come here with Corrigan.

Mr. and Mrs. Stintle still sat propped up in their bed, their wizened faces peering toward them.

"Who is it?" asked Mr. Stintle.

"Open your eyes, you old fool."

"They are open! I just don't know who they are."

"Well, neither do I!"

"Have they closed the door? It's freezing in here."

"Have you closed the door?" asked Mrs. Stintle. "It's freezing in here."

"We've closed the door," said Emily. "Um . . ." She stepped

forward with the small sack she had been carrying since they left the tavern. "I brought this for you."

Mrs. Stintle straightened up in bed. She fished around the threadbare sheets until she found a massive horn that was almost as big as she was. She held it to Mr. Stintle's ear and spoke into it.

"Did she just say what I thought she said?" she bellowed.

"Bones! No need to shout, woman!"

"Never mind that. Did she say what I thought she said?"

"I don't know, do I? What do you think she said?"

"That she brought us something."

Mr. Stintle almost choked in surprise. "What? When? Never." He glared at Emily suspiciously. "Did you?"

Emily nodded. "Yes. It's . . . not much, I'm afraid. And you might need to give it a wash. But I was here before. I remembered how cold you were." Emily opened the sack and pulled out the thick (but rather musty) quilt she had asked Beezle to get from Lady Steele. She placed it over the bed. Mr. and Mrs. Stintle stared at it in amazement for a few moments. They prodded it hesitantly, as if afraid it was about to burst into flames. But when it didn't, they pulled it closer with ancient fingers and ooh'ed and aah'ed over the material.

Emily smiled. She looked at Jack. He was staring at her with an odd expression on his face. He shook his head wryly.

"Uh . . . can we use the hoist?" Emily asked, turning back

273

to find Mr. Stintle had put the quilt over his head. Mrs. Stintle ignored Emily.

"What's it like? Any drafts?"

The quilt was whipped away. "None! No drafts. No holes. It's warm, Muggins. Warm." He looked at Emily, and she was rather shocked to find tears in his eyes. "No one's ever brought us anything before. We're always cold—"

"We're from the southern fey tribes, you see," interrupted Mrs. Stintle. "Very hot. Can't seem to get used to the chill up here."

"You're the first," said Mr. Stintle. "Thank you."

"It was nothing," said Emily awkwardly. "Honestly. It's just a blanket."

"Not to us," said Mrs. Stintle. "Not to us. Thank you—" she stopped suddenly, staring at them suspiciously. "You didn't bring it because you thought you had to pay, did you? You know the hoist is free to use?"

"I know," said Emily. "As I said, I've been here before. I just thought you'd like it."

Mrs. Stintle nodded. "We do. Don't we, Muggins?"

"We do, indeed, Muggins."

"Now get you away. So we can snuggle and get warm."

Mrs. Stintle pulled the blanket up so that only her head was poking out the top. Mr. Stintle did the same. They both let out contented sighs.

Emily led Jack and Wren to the back wall. "You'd better hold on," she said. She frowned at Jack. "Why are you grinning like that?"

"You're just a big softy," he said.

Emily moved like lightning and punched him as hard as she could on his arm.

"Ow!" he said. "What—?"

That was when Mrs. Stintle pulled the lever. There was an explosion of steam, a horrendous shrieking of gears, and then a circle of floor dropped downward.

Jack and Wren were both thrown onto their backsides. But Jack quickly scrambled to his knees and stared in awe at the earthen walls rushing past them, lit by soft globes of golden light. Wren reached out to touch the wall. Soft earth pattered onto the wood. He smiled at Emily, although the effect was rather discomfiting when seen on the face of the goblin; then they settled down to wait.

Ten minutes later, the lift slipped out of the shaft and entered the vast underground space that housed the Faerie Tree. Both Jack and Wren straightened up, their eyes wide with amazement.

Emily knew how they felt. It was only a few days since she had been here, but that didn't make the sight any less impressive. The sheer size of the tree overwhelmed her, bigger than anything she had ever seen. The lights on the huge branches lit up the cavern with a glow as bright as the afternoon sun. The tree dominated everything, spreading its branches up toward the cavern roof as if supporting it, protecting and sheltering those beneath. There were other platforms rising and descending through shafts in the roof, fey coming and going. Faeries flitted through the air, the glow of their wings washed out by the light from the tree.

As they dropped lower, the details of the tree grew sharper. Emily could make out the small window openings in the branches and trunk. Fey moved around in the rooms beyond, going about their daily business.

The platform slowed down, then came to a standstill at the same branch she and Corrigan had stopped at. Emily hopped onto the wide branch, then turned back to Jack and Wren. Their heads were craned back, mouths hanging open as they tried to take everything in.

"What do you think?" Emily asked.

Jack reluctantly tore his gaze away from the tree. "I think that's a very big tree, that's what I think."

She shifted her gaze to Wren. He swallowed.

"Uh . . . what he said."

They left the platform and headed toward an opening in the tree trunk. As they arrived, a long line of tiny fey riding on the backs of mice streamed outside. Emily, Jack, and

Wren stepped aside while the procession passed them by.

"There must be a hundred of them," whispered Jack, watching the mice hop up onto the platform that Emily and the others had just vacated.

"Come on, you," said Emily, waking Jack out of his reverie. "We should go."

Jack nodded, and he and Wren followed Emily into the tree. Emily paused and took a deep breath, smelling the warm, comforting scent of leaves and rain. A rich golden light suffused the air, striking highlights against the dark wood. It reminded Emily of a time she'd been in Hyde Park. It was autumn, and the late-afternoon sun had peeked out from behind the clouds, throwing hazy streamers of gold into the trees and fallen leaves.

"So what's the plan?" asked Jack.

Emily blinked. "Sorry?"

"The plan? You do have one, don't you?"

"Of course I do. You think we came all this way and I didn't have a plan?"

"I'm just asking. So what is it?"

Emily caught the attention of a tall fey who was walking along the corridor with a bored look on his face. "Excuse me. Where's Nimue? I have a message for her."

The fey waved his hand vaguely back along the corridor. "Probably with the Queen, watching the entertainment," he said. "Although why anyone bothers, I don't know. It's the same thing, all the time. Wretched, if you ask me."

"Thank you," said Emily, and she moved along the corridor. Jack and Wren quickly caught up with her.

"That's your plan? 'Excuse me. Where's Nimue?'"

"It worked, didn't it?"

"But if she's with the Queen, how are we supposed to find out where Merlin is?"

"I'm not sure," said Emily. "But we're getting closer. That's all I care about right now."

⊢⇌ ⇌⊣

It took them a bit longer to find the throne room than it had when Emily was with Corrigan. She hadn't been paying too much attention to their route when the piskie had brought her here, so they ended up taking a few wrong turns before they eventually found the corridor leading to the right room. They approached the double doors, taking in the carving of the hill with the seven trees on the top. Emily could hear laughter from the room beyond. Her stomach twisted with fear. The last time she was here, she had been tricked into stealing the seeing stone for Kelindria, something that had started off all these events. She wondered what was going to happen this time.

She paused at the doors. "Are you ready?"

Jack nodded. "Course I am," he said nervously. "I'm Spring-Heeled Jack, remember? I'm ready for anything."

Emily put her hands against the doors. They swung silently open at her touch, revealing the Faerie Queen's throne room to Emily for the second time in her life.

The room was packed tight with fey. They sprawled on the floor, sat at beautifully carved tables, stood around the walls. Some of the smaller fey even hung from small branches that weaved along the ceiling. All their attention was fixed on a small stage that had been set up along the right wall, where a play of some sorts was being acted out.

But Emily didn't care about the play. She moved along the left wall until she found a gap in the crowds. The throne was in the same place, on a raised dais at the opposite end of the room. And on the throne was Queen Titania.

Like Kelindria, she was beautiful. But whereas Kelindria's beauty was fierce and radiant, threatening to burn anyone who came close, Titania's beauty was somehow . . . calmer, less demanding. Her skin was so pure it was almost translucent, and her black hair fell down past her shoulders. She was very thin, with wide eyes that, even from this distance, Emily could see were a startling blue in color.

She sat on the throne, resting her chin on one hand as she watched the play. She looked bored.

There was a familiar-looking fey seated next to her on

a second throne. He looked older than Titania, dressed in robes of white and gold. He was eating nuts from a bowl, taking up huge handfuls and stuffing them in his mouth. It took Emily a while to remember where she had seen him. It was back in Oberon's Court, the alley where she had met Corrigan after she retrieved the key. He was the massively fat fey who was pushed around on the wooden contraption. This was King Oberon, before . . . well, before he fell out of favor, she supposed.

Another fey moved up the steps of the dais to whisper something in Oberon's ear. The King nodded, and the fey turned around to descend the steps again. Emily's heart leapt in her chest.

It was the Dagda.

She watched him as he took his seat at the table directly beneath the King and Queen's dais. He looked exactly the same as he would two hundred years from now.

Emily finally turned her attention to the play. The actors were humans, but not one of them looked worried about the fact that they were performing a play before such strange creatures. And these humans didn't have the blank, half-asleep look of the actors she had seen on London Bridge. These performers seemed perfectly aware of who they were and what they were doing. *Curious,* thought Emily, studying them. The play they were performing seemed familiar to her.

One of Shakespeare's she thought, half remembering it from when she attended school.

"Which one is Nimue?" asked Jack.

Emily leaned in to the fey closest to her, a squat dwarf with long mustaches thrown over his shoulder. "Excuse me, where's Nimue? I've got a message for her."

"Shhh." The dwarf glared at her for a second, then turned his attention back to the play.

"I only asked . . . ," she began, but this time the dwarf's hand moved to grip the handle of a bronze dagger that was stuck through his belt. He turned his eyes slowly in Emily's direction. "Fine," she said. "Don't let me disturb you, I'm sure." She moved around the wall, seeking someone who didn't look like he or she would stab her with a knife if she interrupted them.

She spotted a likely candidate. A young boy, watching the play. He looked harmless enough.

"Excuse me," she said politely. The boy turned to face her, and Emily had to fight the desire to step backward. The boy had yellow-and-black eyes, like a snake's. And when he opened his mouth to respond, Emily could see fangs and a forked tongue inside his mouth. She should have known not to make assumptions based on looks. Not when the fey were involved.

"Yess?" hissed the boy.

"Um, I'm looking for Nimue. I have a message for her?"

"I ssee." The boy craned his neck to get a better look around the throne room. Then he pointed. "Over there. The table by the door."

Emily looked and saw the fey girl he was pointing at. "Thank you," she said. "You're very kind."

"Not a worry, I asssure you," said the boy, turning back to watch the play.

Emily, Jack, and Wren made their way through the crowd. When Emily pointed out Nimue to Jack, he sniggered with laughter.

"What's so funny?"

"Her. She doesn't look like she's over twenty."

"And?"

"And how old is Merlin?"

"I'm sure I don't know what you mean," said Emily primly, putting an extra burst of speed into her step, just in case Jack tried to explain to her exactly what he *did* mean.

As they drew closer to Nimue, Emily could see why someone would fall in love with her. She looked like she belonged to the Tuatha de Danaan branch of fey, as she was tall and regal-looking, very similar to the guards Emily had seen standing at the throne room doors the time she had come here with Corrigan.

Now, here's hoping her story would work.

"Excuse me."

Nimue didn't hear her at first. Either that, or she was ignoring Emily.

"Excuse me," Emily said, rather louder this time.

Nimue finally turned to look at her, and Emily was forced to reassess how old she looked. Her face may have been that of a twenty-year-old, but her eyes told a much different story. They held . . . a lot pain, Emily thought. Many regrets. They were not cruel eyes, like a lot of the other fey had. They weren't distant. These eyes had been affected by the things they had seen.

"Are you Nimue?"

"I am. What do you want, little one?"

"Um. I'm here from the court of the Spinster Queen? In Cornwall?" Emily had heard Corrigan speaking of this before, so she thought it would add a touch of authenticity.

"I know where the Spinster Queen is from," said Nimue wryly.

"Of course. Sorry." Emily hesitated. She had come up with a semblance of a story that involved being an emissary of the Spinster Queen, but as she looked into Nimue's green eyes, Emily changed her mind. There was something there. Nimue didn't seem like the other fey, untouched by life. There was something almost . . . human about Nimue. As if she embraced life, instead of holding herself aloof from it.

"We need to talk to you about Merlin," said Emily, praying that she wasn't making a huge mistake. "There is great danger coming, and we need to release him. He's the only one who can stop it."

"What are you doing?" whispered Jack fiercely.

Emily didn't answer. She was staring into Nimue's eyes. She saw them narrow suspiciously, then clear slightly to show genuine interest.

Nimue glanced around the crowded, noisy throne room. Her gaze came to rest on the Queen, watching the human actors on their small stage. Emily thought she was about to hand them over, but a second later she stood up.

"Follow me," she said.

Nimue led them through a door at the rear of the throne room. She followed a passage that eventually led to a vast open space. Emily leaned over the balcony that circled the pathway, first looking up, then down. *This must be the interior of the actual tree trunk,* she thought. She could see balconies ringing the inner space all the way to the top and all the way to the bottom, each of them filled with fey.

Nimue didn't slow down to take in the view. She walked around the empty space and through another opening that fed onto a set of stairs. At the top of these steps was a smaller passage with doors opening off to either side. Nimue opened one of these doors and stepped inside. Emily, Jack, and Wren followed after, Emily thinking how clever she had been to stick to the truth rather than lie.

So she was rather surprised when Nimue grabbed her by the arm and pressed a sharp bronze blade against her neck.

⊰ CHAPTER TWENTY-TWO ⊱

The Queen is gone. Long live the Queen.

Nimue had led Emily, Jack, and Wren into a sitting room. As they entered, branches that had crisscrossed the wooden walls slowly unfolded and weaved together to form chairs.

"You two," said Nimue, speaking to Wren and Jack, who had frozen just inside the room as soon as the fey had drawn her knife. "Close the door and sit over there." She gestured to two of these newly formed seats. Jack and Wren both hurried across and sat down.

Nimue removed the knife from Emily's neck and gave her a shove. "You, as well."

Emily rubbed her neck and sat down next to Jack.

"Madam," said Wren, "I assure you, we mean you no harm. We are here to avert a tragedy from unfolding, that's all."

Nimue squinted at Wren. "You don't speak like any goblin I've ever seen," she said suspiciously.

Wren straightened up in his chair. "I have to say, I take offense at that. Are you saying that simply because I look like a goblin I can't be intelligent?"

"That's exactly what I'm saying. And what do you mean 'look like' a goblin?"

"Oh. Ah . . ."

Emily sighed. She'd started with the truth. She may as well carry on with it. After all, it couldn't get them into any more trouble, could it?

"We're not actually fey," she said. "These are magical disguises so we could sneak into the tree."

"Explain."

"I already did. So we could ask you for help."

Nimue stared at them for some time. Finally, she shook her head. "I will not lie to you—you have me intrigued."

"We have information that a fey called Kelindria is going to try to take the throne from Queen Titania. She is also going to summon something called the Fire King, and this creature will set fire to London in an attempt to burn it to the ground. We're not sure when this will happen, but definitely within the next few days."

There. That was as simply as Emily could put it.

"How could you possibly know that?" asked Nimue.

"Especially if it hasn't happened yet? And you mentioned Merlin. What does he have to do with anything?"

"Merlin is one of the few people who may be able to stop this creature. There is someone called the Raven King we think can help, but only Merlin knows how to summon him. From the stories we've been told, this Fire King is almost impossible to defeat. Once the fire gets going, he feeds on the flames, getting stronger and stronger as the fire spreads."

"Unless you happen to know how to stop him?" asked Wren.

"No," said Nimue thoughtfully. "But Titania might. I know of this Fire King. It is an elemental being. It doesn't exist on this plane. It would be extremely foolish for anyone to summon such a thing. It won't just stop at London. It will carry on until the whole of Britain is devoured. Why would Kelindria do such a thing? She might want the throne, but what would be the point if she had nothing left to rule over?"

"Are you saying you believe us?" asked Jack.

Nimue waved her hand in the air. "Oh, yes. We've known about Kelindria for a long time."

"Then why hasn't the Queen done anything about her?" asked Wren.

"We have no proof. Kelindria has many followers. If we simply arrested her, or killed her even, it would make her a martyr. She has never done anything to overtly challenge Titania. She is too clever for that."

Nimue sat in silence for a moment. "But why would she make a move now? Even with those who have pledged their allegiance to her, they are not enough. She would need a lot more followers for any attack to be successful. Or some kind of secret weapon."

"Like the Fire King?" asked Wren quietly.

This time Nimue actually looked slightly worried. "We have plans," she insisted. "There's no way she would even get inside the tree."

But Emily had suddenly thought of something else. "The Dagda."

"The Dagda? What of him?"

"He's a traitor. He must help her get into the tree."

"No, not him," said Nimue.

"Yes, him. Don't ask us how we know, we just do."

Emily stood up. "You have to take us to Merlin. He can help. Whatever he did to you all those years ago ... you can't let that stand in the way of stopping Kelindria."

A look of confusion passed across Nimue's face. "What are you talking about? What he did to me—Oh, of course. You are human. You have read the stories, yes? The legends about King Arthur and Merlin and the evil Nimue who stole his power and trapped him in a cave." She cut her hand through the air. "Lies. All of it. There were perfectly good reasons for what happened to Merlin. And

I'm afraid I do not have the authority to order his release."

"Then who does?" asked Wren. "Because whoever has such power is the one we should be speaking to."

Nimue nodded. "Yes, I agree."

"Oh." Wren was surprised. "Really?"

"Yes. So prepare yourself. You are about to meet the Queen."

⊹≕ ≕⊹

Nimue led them along the corridors, heading back in the direction of the throne room. Jack walked next to Emily.

"I really don't like the way this is turning out," he whispered fiercely. "We're handing ourselves over to the enemy."

"Titania is not the enemy. From everything I've heard, she tried to keep the peace between the races. If anything, I think she's the reason the humans and the fey haven't wiped each other out by now. Remember what Cavanagh wrote in his diary? That she wanted things to remain the same. Maybe by telling Titania what we know, it will force her to arrest Kelindria. Have you thought about that? Maybe just by telling Nimue the truth, we can stop the Fire King from even being released."

Jack walked on in silence.

"She has a point," said Wren gently. "Avoidance of conflict is always the preferable solution to a problem."

290

"That's what you say. I prefer the fight myself. Gets the blood pumping."

"You don't really believe that, do you? Think how many people could die."

Jack's shoulders slumped. "*Fine*. No, I don't really believe that." He shook his head bitterly. "Sometimes you're just like my mother, you know that?"

Emily blinked in surprise. Jack had never mentioned his family before, let alone his mother. Emily had always assumed that they were dead, that Jack was an orphan. But the way he spoke, it sounded as though she was still alive.

Any chance of further conversation was cut short when Nimue turned into the passage that led into the throne room. Emily filed the information away, though. She would certainly be asking Jack about it at a later stage. If his parents were still alive—well, to put it mildly, Emily would have a few stern words for Jack Doyle. And if it was only his mother who was still alive, then Emily was going to box his ears for him. She might need his help, and here he was, running around London with his gang, calling himself 'Spring-Heeled Jack' as if he didn't have a care in the world.

Nimue stopped before the door and turned to the others. "Follow me. Don't speak until Titania says so. And be polite. No matter what you humans may think, she is our Queen and you will respect her."

Emily opened her mouth to respond to this statement in the same way she had answered Corrigan when he had told her to respect Merrian. But she managed to bite her tongue. It didn't seem like a good idea to say something like, "I'll not give her respect if she doesn't earn it."

Nimue opened the door and the sounds of laughter and music once again flowed out to them. The play was still in full swing, the assembled fey entranced by the cavorting actors.

The three of them followed Nimue up onto the dais at the back of the room. A few of the fey seated next to the Queen frowned at them, but it seemed that Nimue was well respected, as no one said anything to her. Emily cast a quick eye over the fey seated at the tables below the dais, but the Dagda was no longer there. That was a relief. She was worried about how they would speak to the Queen if he were there to listen. He was sure to interrupt if they accused him of being a traitor.

Nimue leaned forward and whispered into the Queen's ear. Titania turned to hear what was being said, the look of boredom leaving her face in an instant. Nimue talked for a few moments. The Queen's eyes flickered over the three of them. Her flawless face creased with a frown. She muttered something to Nimue, then beckoned the three of them to approach her throne.

She stared at them for some time. "I should have you

arrested on the spot. Who do you think you are, invading our home in this way?"

"Miss . . . Madam." Emily was at a loss as to how to address a Faerie Queen. She settled on the familiar. "Your Highness. We had no choice. We aren't doing this for ourselves. We're trying to stop a terrible tragedy from occurring. And the only way to do that is for you to release Merlin."

"Yes. Nimue already said. The Fire King, you say? I really do find that hard to believe. There are only a few who have the knowledge to summon such a being, and I doubt they would be desperate or stupid enough to pass on such information."

Emily ground her teeth in frustration. She was facing the same problem she always faced when talking to adults. They refused to take her seriously. How could she make the Queen believe she was telling the truth?

"What about the Morrigan," said Jack suddenly. "Would she have the knowledge?"

Titania's eyes focused sharply on Jack. "The Morrigan? What do you know of the Bone Mother?"

"Nothing," said Jack, startled at the intensity of Titania's response.

"Are you saying that she and Kelindria are in league?"

"That's exactly what we are saying," said Emily, wondering if Jack had found a way to get them to believe what they were saying. "We've been chased by the Morrigan and her knights. Attacked by her hounds. *And* hunted by Black Annis and Jenny Greenteeth. All while we've been trying to get this information to you." A slight exaggeration, but under the circumstances, Emily thought it allowable.

Nimue was looking more and more alarmed as Emily talked. She looked around the dais. "Where is the Dagda?" she asked. "They say he is part of the plan. That he is in league with Kelindria."

"No," said Titania. "I won't believe—"

But she didn't get a chance to finish her sentence, because at that moment the double doors of the throne room flew open, banging hard against the walls. All eyes turned in the direction of the sound.

Kelindria was standing in the opening. It was the same Kelindria Emily had seen through the seeing stone, the withered old crone, not the beautiful redheaded queen. The Morrigan stood by her side, and the two of them could have been sisters, so similar did they look.

The White Knight and the Dagda entered behind them, moving to either side.

Titania surged to her feet. "Who dares trespass in my court?"

Kelindria cackled, sending a shiver down Emily's back. There was a touch of madness to her laugh. "Have I changed so much, sweet Titania? It is I, Kelindria. As to trespassing, how can one trespass in one's own throne room?"

"You presume too much, Kelindria. Guards. Take her."

There were ten Tuatha guards standing against the walls of the room. Four of them moved toward Kelindria, but they were stopped by the other six, who quickly moved to block their approach.

Titania stared at the traitors in shock.

"Yes, you haven't really been as attentive as you should have been, have you?" asked Kelindria. The Morrigan chuckled.

Emily had shuffled behind the throne as soon as Kelindria had entered the room, gesturing for the others to follow.

"What do we do?" whispered Jack.

"We have to get to Merlin. It's our only chance now."

"But how?"

Emily saw Titania reach out and take hold of Nimue's hand. The Queen forced something into Nimue's grasp. Nimue closed her fingers around the object and dropped her arm to the side.

"Just stay ready," said Emily.

Kelindria walked forward until she stood in the center of the room. The assembled fey shrank back from her, casting their gaze to the ground. Titania would get no help from them. They would follow the strongest leader, regardless of who it was.

"How was your wine today?" asked Kelindria.

Titania glanced involuntarily at the goblet that sat next to her throne. "Why?"

"Didn't taste odd? Maybe slightly sharp?"

"What have you done?"

"Poisoned you," said Kelindria simply. A ripple of shock swept through the room. Kelindria threw an amused look at the fey. "Oh, don't worry. As long as she obeys me, she will be fine." Kelindria held up a small vial for Titania to inspect. "The antidote. Unless you are given a small amount every day, you will die."

Titania descended from the dais, her pale face furious. "Why not just kill me? Get it over with."

"Oh, you are much more useful to me alive. A guarantee, if you will. In case those of your supporters who survive the war still wish to disobey me."

"War? What war?"

Kelindria held up a hand for silence. In the distance, Emily could hear faint shouting, screams of pain, anger, the clash and clack of weapons. Kelindria waited until all in the throne room had heard it. "*That* war."

Titania staggered, only just managing to stay upright. She glared at Kelindria. "You have brought ruin on us all. Your petty ambitions will be the end of the fey."

"On the contrary. I'm *saving* the fey. You have become too

soft, Titania. London is our city. And after today, humankind will be burned away like the weeds they are. I will sit on a throne under the open air, and all around will bow before Queen Kelindria."

"You're insane."

"No. I am a leader. Unlike you, perfectly willing to live like worms accepting scraps thrown at you by the humans."

Titania slapped Kelindria. The sound was like a pistol shot, echoing throughout the chamber. All eyes turned to Kelindria. A red handprint was clearly visible on her cheek.

Nimue took the opportunity to step backward, glancing down at Emily. She inclined her head slightly. Emily got the message, and they moved slowly toward the door.

Kelindria touched her face and smiled. "You will live to regret that, Titania. I will make sure of it. Now, you will take the Morrigan and her knight to the Gate Room and unlock the Faerie Gate. Then we can move forward with my new rule."

"I'll never give you the key, Kelindria."

Kelindria nodded at one of the Tuatha who had sided with her. He immediately lashed out with his spear and stabbed a courtier who was standing within reach. The courtier fell to the ground without a sound, his body dissolving into a black, bubbling puddle.

"I will say again. You will take my people to the Gate Room, and you will hand over the key. Every time I have to ask, there will be another death. It is up to you."

Emily and the others were at the door. Nimue carefully pulled it open.

"You are too late, Kelindria."

Kelindria frowned. "What do you mean?"

"I've already sent one loyal to me to take the key and hide it where you will never find it." Titania raised her voice when she said this, and Emily realized she was directing the comment at Nimue. "And she will bring someone to stop you, someone who has the power to destroy your Fire King."

Kelindria's eyes narrowed. "How do you know about the Fire King?"

Titania smiled. "I am not as powerless as you think, Kelindria. This is not over. Not by a long way."

Emily just had time to catch a glimpse of Kelindria's furious face, and then Nimue pulled her through the door and closed it quickly behind her. Emily thought that the Morrigan had glanced in their direction just as she did so, but it was hard to tell with all the fey standing between them.

"So," said Wren in a strained voice, "I take it you are going to help us after all?"

Nimue's face was set, her eyes blazing with anger. "Oh, yes," she said. "We're going to stop that evil witch if it's the last thing we do. Follow me."

She turned and sprinted along the corridor. Emily and the others ran as fast as they could, their short legs making it difficult for them to keep up with the fey. They arrived back at the central shaft and the chaos that Kelindria had brought to the Faerie Tree was revealed in its entirety.

Pitched battles were being fought throughout the tree. Emily leaned over the balcony and saw that fey were fighting fey on every level. War had broken out, and nothing would ever be the same again. Friends were battling friends, grappling for weapons that would end years of companionship, simply because they had sworn allegiance to different leaders. The sounds of frantic fighting echoed throughout the Faerie Tree. Grunts of effort, yowls of pain, bellows of anger. The frantic, primitive instinct to kill or be killed.

Emily stared, transfixed by the horror of what was unfolding around her. As she watched, a piskie dropped past her field of vision, screaming as he fell all the way to the bottom of the central shaft of the tree. Emily quickly stood back, feeling sick to her stomach. She had thought they could stop this. She had thought they could change history. But she had been wrong. It was all happening anyway.

There was a shout from behind them. Emily whirled around to see the Morrigan's White Knight appear in the corridor, followed quickly by the Morrigan herself.

"Stop them!" shouted the crone gleefully. "Rip their heads from their bodies. Snap them in half. Just stop them!"

The White Knight pulled his helm off, revealing not a he but a she. A fierce-looking woman with golden skin and cruel eyes. She smiled, revealing teeth as black as oil. She dropped her helm to the ground and pointed at the four of them.

Then she started running.

❧ CHAPTER TWENTY-THREE ❧

In which Emily and Co. flee the wrath of the White Knight.
And a small fey called Cob finally gets his freedom.

Emily and the others had a head start on the White Knight. They leapt down stairs, darted around pitched battles, and avoided the blades of those who thought they were attacking them. The only advantage they had was that the White Knight looked so threatening that she had to stop frequently to fend off attacks herself. Emily didn't think these interruptions would delay her for long, though. Whatever they were going to do, they had to do it quick.

They ran on. Emily's chest was burning, her breath coming in heaving, rasping gasps. Jack and Wren were faring no better. Jack looked as though he was about to be sick, and Wren's goblin face was covered in sweat.

They darted into a corridor that sloped downward.

Identical doors opened off to either side, and Nimue pushed one open and vanished through it. Emily threw a quick look over her shoulder. There was no sign of the knight.

Emily's legs were trembling, but they made it to the door, yanking it open and falling through before the knight could see which one they used. That should at least give them a bit of time. Wren quickly slammed it shut behind them, and they paused for a brief moment to try to catch their breath.

But they couldn't afford to linger. Nimue was disappearing up another set of stairs. Emily set off after her. Nimue led them along more passages and corridors before finally stopping before a single white door.

She glanced quickly at them. "The knight?"

"I think we lost her for the moment."

Nimue nodded and opened her hand. Emily saw that she was holding a pendant on a delicate wooden chain. This was what Titania had pushed into her hand.

"It's a key," said Nimue. She took the pendant off the chain, then placed it in a small hole in the door. The pendant flared to life, illuminating them in a green light. It revolved slowly in the wood. There was a quiet click, then the door opened.

Nimue hurried inside. The others followed her and found themselves in a huge chamber, empty but for an archway of wood that stood in the center of the room.

Nimue approached, the others following after. The wood was still alive. Shoots and leaves grew from archway, writhing in the air like worms seeking moisture.

"This is the main Faerie Gate," said Nimue. She pushed aside some leaves and pulled something from the wood. Emily realized with a jolt that it was the key to the gate. The same key she had in her pocket. She quickly patted her coat. The familiar circle was still there. How odd. They were the same thing from different times, yet here they were existing in the same space.

Nimue pulled and pushed the small branches on the key, fixing it so that it would take them to where she wanted to go.

"Are you ready?" she asked.

Emily nodded. As did Jack and Wren. Nimue placed the key back in the wood. Immediately, the space between the arch darkened. Emily could no longer see the other side of the room. Just a black shadowy mass, like clouds moving against a moonlit sky.

"Let's—" Nimue started to say, but her words froze on her tongue as she stared back at the door. Emily whirled around to see the White Knight and the Morrigan standing in the doorway. There was a moment of frozen silence, then Nimue turned and jumped toward the gate.

"Hurry!" she shouted.

The knight surged forward, a snarl twisting her golden features. Emily closed her eyes and jumped into the darkness. For a moment she felt as if she had been caught in a spiderweb, frozen in place, then there was a lurch, and she was yanked downward.

A second later her face was resting against a cold flagstone. She quickly rolled to her feet, staggering as a wave of dizziness overwhelmed her. Jack and Wren were lying close by, groaning. Against the wall was another wooden archway, similar to the one they had entered in the Faerie Tree. As Emily tried to keep her balance, Nimue appeared through the opening. She staggered a few steps, then skidded to a halt and whirled around, facing the arch.

But no one else came.

Nimue allowed herself to relax slightly.

"Where are they?" asked Emily.

Nimue glanced at her. She held up the key to the gate. "I yanked it out as I came through."

"So they're gone?" asked Jack, pushing himself to his feet.

"No. The gate would have stayed open for a few seconds, so they probably still made it through. The key was set for this location, but if we're lucky they've been dropped a few miles away."

"And if we are not lucky?" asked Wren.

"Then they could be waiting in the next room."

Emily took a moment to survey their surroundings. The cold flagstone floor was a design element the builder obviously liked, as the walls and roof were made from the same thing. They were basically in an empty stone room with a single arched window allowing the weak gray light inside. Emily approached it. She could see it was raining outside, a steady downpour that looked like it would carry on for days. The rain spattered against the stone sill, bouncing up and gently prickling against her face. She stood on her tiptoes and leaned out the window, taking in their surroundings.

There were two colors outside. Green and gray. The green of a vast forest that coated the hills surrounding them, and the gray of the sky. A cold breeze ruffled her hair as she gazed out over the trees. Far in the distance, she thought she could just glimpse a huge towering castle with spires piercing the gray clouds.

She turned from the window. "Are we in Faerie?" she asked.

Nimue nodded. "The Valley of Forgotten Dreams."

"Charming name," muttered Jack, peering out the window. "It doesn't look very . . . fairylike, does it?"

"We are far from the beaten track here. This is the Unforgiven Forest." Nimue looked puzzled. "But what exactly were you expecting?"

"Magical cities. Golden elves. Ogres and things traipsing around the landscape. Magic everywhere you look."

"Oh, we have all that. You should see the Floating City of Arberlast. A place of such beauty you will weep. But now is not the time for such things. We must move quickly. Follow me."

Nimue strode across to a heavy door and pulled it open, revealing a rather dank, dark castle foyer. A wide set of stone stairs rose up from the middle of the room, separating and curving up and around to either side.

"Charming place," muttered Jack.

"It was the best we could do at the time," said Nimue. "We were rushed . . ." She hesitated, then sighed. "Look, I know what you think about me. But the stories have it all wrong. Merlin *agreed* to be interred here. It was part of a plan—"

"Agreed?" asked Emily, surprised. "Why would anyone agree to such a thing?"

"It was the only way to stop Morgan Le Fay."

"Sorry," interrupted Wren. "Morgan Le Fay? *The* Morgan Le Fay? From the stories? Half sister to King Arthur?"

"The same. Morgan was half-fey herself. And she had many followers. Followers who wanted the same as Kelindria. The eradication of humankind. But Arthur and his knights vowed to stop her."

"The Knights of the Round Table?" asked Wren.

Nimue nodded. "Or to give them their original name, the Knights of the Invisible Order."

There was a pause while they took this in.

"So . . . ," began Jack. "All those legends. The knights. Arthur. Mordred. They were all true?"

"The people existed, yes. Although the legends that survive today are more . . . *distortions* of what really happened. Morgan Le Fay was very dangerous. She thirsted for power and didn't care how she got it or how many people had to die. Merlin tried to stop her, but by this time, her power was simply too much."

"She was stronger than Merlin?" asked Emily, surprised.

"In some ways, yes. Merlin had a conscience to stop him from going too far. Morgan Le Fay did not. That gave her the edge, as there was nothing she wouldn't do to achieve her aims. Titania had no love for Morgan and wanted her stopped just as much as Merlin did. For the first time in history, the fey and humans actually agreed on something. So a plan was hatched. And I was the bait."

"I don't understand," said Wren. "How were you the bait?"

"Merlin and I were in love. Had been for some time. When Titania found this out, she wanted to use it to our advantage. I was to pretend allegiance to Morgan Le Fay, take her information about Merlin and the Invisible Order. It took me a long time to gain her trust, but I did it in the end."

Nimue trailed off, a sad look on her face.

"And?" prompted Jack.

"There was no way Morgan Le Fay could capture Merlin on her own. He was too wary, too powerful. So Morgan had an idea. I was the only person in the world who Merlin would allow inside his defenses. I was the only one who could capture him. So she . . . it's hard to describe. She took most of her power and put it inside me. It left her weak, defenseless, but it enabled me to 'trap' Merlin and lock him away here in Faerie."

"Didn't he fight you?"

"Don't you understand? He knew what I was doing. He was the one who came up with the plan. He sacrificed himself so that Morgan Le Fay could be leeched of her power. I locked him up here, and while Morgan Le Fay lay in her tower, weak as a newborn babe, the Invisible Order captured her."

"Did they kill her?" asked Emily, fascinated by the story.

"No. They didn't have the power. But they locked her away in a similar manner to what I did to Merlin. The plan worked. We stopped her."

"But if you were successful," said Wren, "why was Merlin kept trapped here?"

Nimue hung her head in shame. "Yes. That was where things went wrong. Titania decided to . . . alter the plan. The

Invisible Order was still a danger. It was still dedicated to fighting the fey. And Merlin was their leader. She thought it would be better for all concerned if Merlin was to ... remain where he was."

Emily was horrified. "And you allowed that?"

"What was I supposed to do? I argued, yes. But she is my Queen. And she controlled access to Merlin. This is the first time I have been to Faerie since it happened. In Titania's defense, her plan worked. Since that time there have been no major wars. A few skirmishes, yes, a few hidden battles, handled by her spies, but on the whole it has been a thousand years of peace."

"You've kept that poor man locked away for a thousand years?" asked Wren, anger rising in his voice.

"He is not a man. Not as you are. But yes, for a thousand years."

"And he expected ... what? A few days? A week?"

"He was to stay locked away till Morgan was captured."

"And how long did that take?"

"It took some time for the knights to get through her defenses. About a month."

Jack shook his head. "I don't think he's going to be very pleased to see you," he said.

"No. No, I think you are right."

"Hel-loooo!" echoed a voice.

Everyone looked up to see a face peering at them over the balcony on the floor above. "Er . . . are you friend or foe? Sorry. Have to ask. Being the guardian and everything."

"It's me, Cob. Nimue."

Emily could hear a sudden indrawn breath. The head disappeared and was replaced by the sound of pattering feet.

A moment later a small man appeared around the bend in the stairs, running as fast as his short legs could carry him. He almost fell down the last steps in his haste. He pulled up short before Nimue, struggling to catch his breath. Except for his size, he looked almost human. A straggly white beard sprouted from his face. He peered at Nimue through a pair of small, round spectacles.

"Is it time?" he asked in a trembling voice. "Can I finally go home?"

Nimue nodded. "It is time, Cob. You have done well."

The old fey danced a jig on the flagstones. "Time to go home. Time to go home," he cackled.

Nimue glanced around nervously. "Cob. We're in a bit of a hurry."

"Of course, of course. Follow me, follow me."

Cob led them up the stairs and along an echoing corridor, turning into a torch-lit room lined floor to ceiling with books. Each book was identical but for a different number on the leather spine. Cob gestured at them proudly.

"A thousand years of daily reports," he said. "You'll want to check them, obviously. Just to make sure I kept at my job."

Nimue looked confused. "Daily reports?"

"Oh yes. Not always a lot to write down, it has to be said. Twelve fifty-six was an interesting year. Merlin blinked five times in a day. Not often you get that kind of activity, let me tell you!" Cob laughed deprecatingly. "I almost sent a missive to the Queen. Was worried something was happening." Cob looked around the room fondly. "Nine hundred eighty-four was another good year. It looked like he was trying to open his mouth. I thought he was going to try and speak." Cob pressed his hands together in front of his chest. "He didn't, though."

Nimue stared around the room, her eyes wide. "Cob, you didn't have to keep records!"

"Had to, miss. Had to. How else would you know I did my job. Anyway, it kept the boredom away. Got to keep busy, yes? But you'll be wanting to see him. Come."

He took one of the torches down from the wall and opened a door nestled between the shelves of books. A dark spiral staircase led down into the darkness. Cob stepped through the door and disappeared around the bend. The others hurried to catch up.

The flagstones of the stairs eventually gave way to uneven rock as they descended far beneath the ground. These stairs eventually fed onto a ramp that opened into a vast underground cavern. The sounds of dripping water echoed around the cave.

There was a glow from up ahead, the only source of light other than Cob's torch. They moved deeper into the cave. As they drew closer, Emily saw that the light was coming from inside a huge chunk of crystal. It glowed with a white illumination, outlining a still form encased within.

Merlin.

They hurried forward, details emerging as they drew closer. Merlin looked exactly the same as when Emily had first met him, his white hair and beard sticking out at all angles from his head. His eyes were open, staring straight ahead. He wore robes of dark gray.

Nimue moved forward until she stood face-to-face with him. She laid her hands on the crystal, bowing her head as if in prayer.

At first nothing happened. Then the crystal started to melt, like ice turning to water. It dropped away from around Merlin's body, gathering in hollows and dips on the floor, crawling slowly outward until finally Merlin and Nimue stood in the center of a large silver pool.

The others watched in rapt fascination as Merlin blinked, then took a great, shuddering breath of air. Nimue couldn't look at him. She stared down at her feet. Merlin glanced around the cavern, then turned his glare on Nimue.

"A thousand years, Nimue." His voice was hoarse and grating. "A thousand years!" he shouted. His voice reverberated around the cavern. Cob quickly ducked behind Jack.

"I'm sorry," she whispered, and her voice was so filled with pain and anguish that Emily felt tears rise to her eyes.

Merlin stared at the top of her head, his frown gradually easing away. Finally, he sighed.

"Come here, my lady Nimue," he said softly.

Nimue finally looked up. She and Merlin locked eyes, then they reached out and held each other in a tight hug. They stood like that for some time.

Emily looked away, feeling as though she were intruding on their private moments. She gestured for Jack to do the same, but he just waggled his eyebrows at her and grinned.

Finally, Merlin disentangled himself. "Now," he said. "I'm assuming something bad has happened, yes? Time is of the essence, and all that? And I'm assuming it involves these three creatures, as well? Hello, Cob. I see you hiding there. Bet you're glad I'm awake, eh? Now you can get on with your own life again."

Cob stepped out from behind Jack and bowed shyly. "It's been an honor to watch over you, milord."

Merlin started to walk out of the pool, but as he did so his legs suddenly gave way beneath him. Nimue reached out and caught him as he fell to his knees.

"Merlin! Are you all right?"

"I . . ." Merlin put a hand to his head. "I don't think so." He glanced back at the pool of silver. "Your spell kept me alive, but . . . I think the years are trying to catch up with me." He gripped hold of Nimue's arm and pulled himself up. "You must take me to my workshop," he said urgently. "It is of the utmost importance that I reabsorb my powers immediately."

Nimue nodded and helped him over to the others. When he stood before Cob, he gestured for Nimue to wait.

"Cob," he said slowly. "Before I go, I must thank you for all that you have done."

Cob looked confused. "But I haven't done anything. Except my duty."

"Not so. You talked to me. You visited me. Every day for a thousand years. This was as much your prison as mine. I look on you as a friend, Cob. A very good friend. And I thank you."

A smile as bright as a sunrise spread across Cob's face. His eyes disappeared into the laugh lines around his eyes. "Do you really mean that?"

"I do. Now be off with you and go visit that family you

were always talking about. I'm sure they are eagerly awaiting your return." He turned to the others. "Let us leave this place, and you can explain to me what has been occurring." He frowned. "Although with all the gaps in my memory, I'm not sure I can be of any help to you."

⊰⊱ Chapter Twenty-four ⊰⊱
Newgate. The forgotten prison.

Although Newgate had been used as a prison for over six hundred years, its original purpose had been to act as a gate in the old Roman wall that ran around what was then Londinium. But as London expanded beyond this wall, some of the gates found other uses.

William stared at the prison critically. "It still looks like a gatehouse," he said.

And indeed it did. A hefty slab of brick with a large arched door in the center and a portcullis to lock people out. Small barred windows overlooked the street.

"That's still part of the original wall," said Corrigan. "But it's been changed, expanded."

"And how are we supposed to get in?" asked William.

"That's where you get to thank me for coming along," said Katerina. She turned and pointed to a large, Gothic-looking church a short distance down the street. "That's St. Sepulchre. Where the priest who rings the execution bell comes from."

"And how does that help us?" asked William, staring at the forbidding spires outlined against the dark sky.

"It helps us because there is an underground tunnel linking St. Sepulchre with Newgate. It's how the bellman gets from the church into the prison."

Corrigan turned around and gave his full attention to the church. "Is that so," he said thoughtfully. "Well that *is* good news. Well done, human. Maybe you're good for something after all."

Before Katerina could respond, Corrigan trotted away from the both of them, heading toward the church.

"If he speaks to me like that one more time," muttered Katerina, "I'm going to tie him up inside a sack and drop him into the Thames."

⊬⊐ ⊏⊦

Getting inside St. Sepulchre was a lot easier than William thought it would be. A window at the rear of the building had been left open a crack, and Katerina simply pushed it all the way up and climbed inside. William and Corrigan followed after, hopping from the window onto a small desk covered with parchment. Corrigan knocked over an inkwell, the black ink soaking into the paper and obliterating the writing.

"Be careful!" snapped Katerina

William dropped onto the floor and looked around the small office they found themselves in. "Now what?" he whispered.

"The crypts. The tunnel is below ground."

She led them from the office and through narrow wooden corridors until they entered the main body of the church. It was much larger than the one where they had found Thomas the Rhymer. Moonlight streamed in through windows all around the walls, illuminating the high, arched ceiling and picking out the expensive paintings and decorations. Katerina hurried over to a heavy door with an inscription above the lintel.

William squinted up at it, but it was in Latin.

Katerina took a torch from the wall and lit it with the flint she kept in one of her pockets. She pushed the door open and disappeared, the light fading as she went. William swallowed nervously and followed after. The stairs didn't go on for long. After only a minute or so they found themselves in the cool, dark rooms of the catacombs. William looked around, pleasantly surprised. He had expected cobwebs hanging from every surface. Spiders and beetles scuttling across the floor.

But in fact, the room was quite clean. The priests obviously took the time to make sure everything was kept neat and tidy. He supposed it made sense. If someone had to come down here to access the tunnel into Newgate, it was only logical they wouldn't want cobwebs hanging everywhere.

They made their way through the room, walking past crypts and coffins mounted on stone bases. There was only one other door in the room, and that was against the far wall. The door was a heavy slab of solid oak. There was a ring of keys hanging from a nail next to the door.

This surprised Will for a moment, before he realized that Newgate wasn't really concerned with people sneaking *in*. It was people getting out that was the problem. And seeing as the door was locked from this side, any escape attempts by the prisoners were doomed to failure.

Katerina quickly unlocked the door, revealing a low brick-lined tunnel that disappeared into the darkness. She left the door slightly ajar, and they hurried along the passage. After about a hundred meters, they arrived at a second door, identical to the first. Katerina put her ear against the wood and listened. William wasn't sure why, as the door was so thick he doubted you could hear anything through it. A moment later she straightened up and inserted the key in the lock, turning it carefully and pulling the door open a short distance. She put her eye to the crack and peered through, and only when she was satisfied did she open it all the way and lead them into Newgate Prison.

William followed her through and found himself in what had to be one of the cells. It was tiny and cramped, a concrete room with a single door in the wall opposite. The door was locked, but Katerina tried the other keys on the key ring until she found one that unlocked the door.

"Are you two ready?" she asked.

"Of course we are," snapped Corrigan. "And stop acting as if you're the leader. You're not. Now open that door."

Katerina glared at him, but pulled the door open. A dark corridor lay beyond. William could hear someone moaning. He peered out and saw a line of doors identical to theirs. He stepped into the corridor. The doors had numbers painted on them, exactly like the doors in Tom the Rhymer's vision. The one closest to the cell they were in had the number 13 painted on it.

They hurried out of the cell, moving quickly along the corridor. The sound of moaning and cursing grew louder, different sounds coming from each of the cells.

They finally arrived at number 40. The cell door was unlocked. William pushed it open to find it empty. Not even a cot.

They stepped inside and quickly closed the door behind them. William turned in a slow circle.

"There's nothing here," he said, disappointed.

Corrigan moved forward. "There has to be."

Katerina moved slowly along the walls, holding the torch close to the stones. "It has to be this cell. It's the only one not being used to hold prisoners. There must be a reason."

Katerina carried on moving the torch along the wall. Eventually, the flame flickered, as if a gust of air had blown across the flame. She smiled triumphantly at them. "You see? You just have to know what to look for."

The three of them then spent the next fifteen minutes pushing and prodding the stones, looking for some kind of catch that would release the hidden door they now knew was there. Katerina finally found it, a tiny switch hidden in a long groove formed by the meeting of wall and floor. But the catch wouldn't budge. It was only when she dug the end of one of the keys into the groove that the mechanism released, a small door scraping outward to reveal a dark opening.

Katerina shone her torch inside to reveal a square platform made from wood. The platform was supported at the four corners by heavy ropes that were in turn attached to a second supporting rope looped through a pulley system.

"Interesting," said Katerina. She stepped carefully onto the platform, then stood still to see if it would hold. It swayed under her weight but didn't show any signs of giving way. William and Corrigan slowly joined her. The wood creaked and groaned but held strong. Katerina unhooked the rope that worked the pulley and started to lower them. The platform lurched, bumping against the walls of the shaft as Katerina carefully lowered them down. William moved over to help her, and they soon got a rhythm going that dropped them down at a smooth speed.

Will could feel the excitement building inside. They were close. He was sure of it. A section of Newgate Prison, walled away and kept secret. It had to be what they were looking for. What they would find was another matter, though. Surely not the Raven King? Not here. Unless he was under some kind of sleeping spell, locked away somewhere? It was possible, he supposed, but he didn't dare hope. He didn't want to face disappointment again.

It took them almost ten minutes to reach the bottom. The platform bumped against the ground and the ropes fell slack in William's hands.

"Looks like we're here," said Katerina. She held the torch over William's shoulder and leaned forward out of the shaft. A deserted, dusty corridor lay beyond. Silence filled the air. Nothing moved.

They stepped gingerly off the platform. The air was oppressive, filled with a heaviness that weighed on William's spirit. There was a strange smell. It took him a while to place it, but he finally realized it was the smell of decay. But it was old, weak, an odor that tainted the very air they breathed.

William paused before the first door they came to. It was made from wood. He pushed it open, curious to know what had to be kept so far belowground. He took the torch from Katerina, slowly entered the tiny room, and raised the torch high above his head.

A horrific sight greeted him. There were chains fixed to the walls. Inside these chains was the skeleton of a huge creature, hanging from the manacles by its wristbones. The skeleton was easily over nine feet tall and was topped by huge, bull-like horns.

"A minotaur," said Corrigan quietly.

William turned to find the piskie staring up at the skeleton. Then he gestured at the chains.

"Iron. They kept the poor thing locked up with chains of iron."

"And they just left it to die?"

"Looks that way."

"Do you think the other cells are the same?" asked Katerina.

"I have no idea." Corrigan looked around with distaste. "At least now we know what they were hiding down here. A prison for the fey."

They left the cell and hurried along the corridor, checking through each door in turn. It was an unpleasant task, but it

had to be done, as they had no real idea what they were looking for down here. Not all the cells had skeletons in them,
something William was very grateful for. He had no love for
the fey, but to see their bones strewn about the cells like that
turned his stomach.

They kept going until there was only one door left. The
last one in the corridor. William glanced apprehensively at
the others. What would they find inside? Something to help
them? Broken hopes?

Katerina nodded, and William pushed the door. It swung
open on squeaky hinges. William moved the torch into the
doorway, pushing the darkness back into the room.

The first thing they noticed was that it wasn't another cell.
It was a large chamber furnished with tables and chairs.

But besides that, it was empty.

William entered the room. Thick dust covered every available surface, and it seemed this was all there was for them to
find. William walked slowly around the perimeter, trying to
fight off the despair that was threatening to overwhelm him.
Why had Thomas the Rhymer sent them here? Will had
been sure it had something to do with the Raven King, but it
seemed this was just an old, forgotten prison. It didn't seem
as if anyone had been here for centuries.

The torchlight revealed another door up ahead. William
brightened. Maybe there was another room. He hurried over

and pulled it open, but he was doomed to disappointment. It was just an empty closet.

He slammed the door shut and turned away. As he did so, his foot sent something skittering across the floor, raising a cloud of dust into the air. He lowered the torch and found a book lying on the floor. He picked it up and examined it. It was covered with red leather. He opened it up, skimming over the spidery, untidy scrawl until his eyes spotted a familiar phrase.

The Raven King.

"Over here," he called, taking the book to one of the tables. The book wasn't big. It was more of a journal, used to record a series of notes. Little clumps of information. Katerina and Corrigan joined him.

"'Notes on the Raven King,'" he read. "'Classification: Very Sensitive. If you are not a member of the Invisible Order, stop reading now; otherwise, your eyes will boil in your skull. And this is a promise from Merlin the Enchanter.'"

William hesitated and looked at the others. Corrigan waved his hand impatiently.

"Go on. It's a bluff."

"How do you know?"

"I just do. Now carry on."

William licked his lips, then carried on reading. "'Who is the Raven King? It is probably more appropriate to ask *what* is the Raven King. He is a protector, a watcher over Britain. The legends say that whenever Britain is in danger, the Raven King will be awoken to protect the land from her enemies.

"'It was Bran the Blessed who first came to this power. He was an early British King, a member of the Invisible Order. It happened during one of the wars with the fey. Through a series of circumstances too complicated to reveal here, he was chosen by Mother London to channel her power during times of danger. (I hasten to add, he came up with his title all by himself. *Bran* is a Welsh word. It means 'blessed crow.' So he played around with it and came up with the Raven King. Bran always was one for show and pomp.)

"'The power of the Raven King is a fearsome thing to behold. It burns bright and fast, devouring all who would stand in its way. Enemies tumble before the Raven King like trees in a gale. He is the last protector of Britain, but his is a terrible power and must only be used when all else is lost. I hasten to repeat this. If I am not there to advise you on this, make sure this is your last hope. The Raven King must not be summoned lightly.

"'And just how do you summon him? Mother London spoke an incantation, something to be repeated at the proper place at the time of Britain's need.'"

William looked at the others excitedly. "The incantation is here. Merlin wrote it down!"

"Skip over it for the moment," said Corrigan. "Finish his notes."

William nodded. "'In the end, Bran fell in battle to a fey spear, but only after he saved us all from the armies of Faerie. Even when channeling the power of Mother London, the Raven King is vulnerable to normal weaponry. Something we were not aware of at the time. After the battle, we buried Bran beneath the Tower of London. It was his final wish.

"'Even as I write this, I wonder if I am doing the right thing. But I have no other choice. Events are moving fast, and Nimue comes for me. There are a hundred things to do before Morgan Le Fey's trap is sprung, and time is running out. I do not know what will happen. I do not know if I will survive. So I have no choice but to put ink to parchment and hope that this information survives until it is needed. I will take it into the Order's prisons. They are unused now, so the information should be safe. Why even bother? I do not know. It is a gut feeling, an inkling that someday it might be needed. Am I being coerced? Is it Fate? I know not. Only time will tell whether this was a mistake or the right thing to do.'"

William paged through the book. "There's more stuff here, but nothing else about the Raven King."

The three were silent for a moment. Finally Katerina cleared her throat.

"So . . . we need to read this spell or whatever it is?"

"So it would seem. And it will wake Bran the Blessed. The Raven King."

"The Tower of London it is, then," said William.

CHAPTER TWENTY-FIVE

In which London burns and sacrifices must be made.

Merlin leaned heavily on Nimue's arm as they all climbed back up the stairs to Cob's study. As they went, Nimue tried to explain everything that was happening between Titania and Kelindria, with frequent interruptions from Emily and Jack. By the time they reached Cob's office, Merlin knew as much as everyone else about what was happening in London.

He didn't like it. Not one bit.

"The Fire King!" he sputtered weakly. "What kind of a fool summons such a creature? It will devour the whole of Britain before the week is out. And what if it gets aboard a ship? It can hibernate in a lantern. The whole of Europe could be consumed."

"The question we have to ask ourselves," said Wren, "is how *do* we stop it?"

Merlin glanced at him and frowned. "You seem to be going through something of a growth spurt."

Emily looked at Wren. It was true. He was taller, about half his normal human height. Plus, his features weren't so goblinlike. She could easily see his normal features beneath the wrinkly skin. She turned to Jack. He was changing as well. Even as she watched, his hair returned to its original brown color, his skin fading to its normal shading. He smiled at Emily.

"Nice to have you back, Snow," he said.

Emily raised her hands and saw that her disguise spell had also worn off. They were back to their natural forms again.

"I think you should tell me exactly who you are and why you are here," said Merlin.

Emily took a deep breath. Merlin had no idea what he was asking. But it had to be done. If Merlin was to understand the enormity of what was going on, he had to know exactly how they got there.

Emily told him everything, starting with her stumbling across Corrigan back in her own time, about finding out the information about the Raven King. Everything.

After she had finished, Merlin and Nimue both stared at them in amazement.

"And you accomplished all this by yourself?"

"Not by myself, no." Emily nodded at Jack. "I had help."

Jack saluted her and grinned.

"Still," said Merlin. "That is a lot to happen to someone so—"

"Please don't say, 'someone so young,'" said Emily. "I've had to be a grown-up for a long time now. Young was when my da used to read me stories in bed. That was a long time ago now."

Merlin looked at her sadly. "As you wish," he said.

"So how do we stop this Fire King?" asked Jack, eager to change the subject.

"How do we stop him? *Can* we stop him? It depends on how much he has fed. The Fire King sends his minions out into the flames. They spread with the wind, growing stronger, burning more and more. And while they do this, he feeds on their power. The more the fire spreads, the stronger he gets. If we want to have any hope of stopping it, it will have to be soon."

"You won't be stopping anyone, meddler," said a scratchy voice.

Everyone whirled around to find the Morrigan and the White Knight standing in the doorway. The knight had a heavy crossbow pointed at Merlin.

"This is what I'm thinking," said the Morrigan. "I'm

thinking you should have sensed us. I'm thinking you're weak after your little confinement. I'm also thinking that Kelindria is going to be very grateful to find you locked away in her prison."

Nimue tensed, ready to attack, but Merlin grabbed hold of her arm. "Not now," he said in a low voice.

The Morrigan turned to Emily. "And you. Quite the bonus. Kelindria's been wanting words with you all day. Now that she's Queen, she'll most likely just cook you over a fire. Me, I'd eat you. Slowly. Fingers first. Then the arms and legs. So you can watch yourself bleed out. There's nothing like a meal with the music of screams to accompany it. Makes the whole thing so much more tastier. Now move."

They moved reluctantly toward the door. The Morrigan led the way while the White Knight brought up the rear, her crossbow pointed at Merlin's back. They moved back through the castle to the room with the Faerie Gate in it. When they were all gathered, the Morrigan pointed at Nimue. "Take the key out. Slowly."

Nimue did as she was instructed.

"Bring us out at the Hyde Park Gate," said the Morrigan. "Kelindria's place isn't far from there."

Nimue rearranged the tiny branches and shoots of the key. "Put it in the gate."

Nimue looked at Merlin, but the old man just nodded

wearily. He looked exhausted, as if the walk up the stairs had taken all his meager energy.

Nimue placed the key into the wooden circle, and the wall behind it was replaced by roiling clouds.

The Morrigan gestured at Jack. "You go first. Then come back." She looked at Nimue. "Just in case you've opened the gate into one of the Forbidden Lands."

"Um …" Jack looked deeply uncertain. "Forbidden Lands?"

"Don't worry," said Nimue. "It opens into Hyde Park."

Jack still hesitated.

"I'll go," said Emily, stepping forward.

The Morrigan grabbed her by the arm, her black nails digging into Emily's skin. "You're not going anywhere, little one. I'm not letting you out of my sight."

"Fine," said Jack, He stepped into the gate.

They waited, and a moment later he came back through again. "All clear."

The Morrigan nodded. "Let's go, then." She pushed Emily forward. Nimue helped Merlin limp into the gate. Emily followed behind, stepping into the clouds.

Darkness washed over her. Emily's stomach lurched. Her heart thudded painfully in her chest. She staggered, almost falling. The Morrigan released her grip.

And then she was falling to her knees on the dry grass of Hyde Park. Emily pushed herself to her feet and looked around. It was the same tree where she had met the Dagda back in her own time. The tree where the battle had been fought and she and the others had escaped. The Morrigan stepped through the gate, followed quickly by the White Knight.

The Morrigan had the key in her hand. She tucked it away into a pouch on her belt, then held out her hand to Emily.

"And yours."

Emily had no choice but to hand her key over. She watched in anguish as the Morrigan pushed it into the same pouch. "Now follow me," she ordered. "And if one of you so much as breathes in a way I don't like, you'll get a crossbow bolt through your neck. And I don't think you want that. Besides the difficulty breathing, you'll get blood all over your nice clothes."

She cackled and headed off through the park. Jack moved forward to walk next to Emily. "What are we going to do now?" he whispered. "We can't just let them lock us up. That will be the end of everything. The Fire King will win."

Emily had been thinking exactly the same thing. But so far she hadn't managed to come up with any kind of plan. "I don't know what we're going to do," she answered. "Just keep your eyes open and hope something turns up."

It took them an hour to walk through London, and all the while Emily couldn't take her eyes off the orange glow that lit up the southern sky. She'd already known that Kelindria had released the Fire King, but to see the flames actually casting their eerie glow against the smoke and clouds made her realize just how badly they had failed. The Fire King was free. His hands were spreading out across London, burning everything they touched, claiming everything to feed his hunger.

What surprised Emily most of all was that there was no panic in the areas they passed through. Everyone was aware of the fire. People were out in the streets, watching the distant flames and discussing how much of the city they thought would burn. But none of them seemed overly alarmed. They had seen it all before and had survived (according to those she overheard) much bigger blazes than the one that had started up just after midnight.

Emily wanted to scream at them, to tell them to pack up and leave, but she knew it would be pointless. She was just a girl, after all. They would look on her with pity, pat her on the head, and tell her not to worry. That the grown-ups would deal with the nasty fire.

By the time they reached their destination, Emily could hear the distant crackling of the flames, could see the sparks bobbing and weaving up into the night sky, pushed higher and higher by the fierce, hot winds that breathed extra life into the flames, urging them farther and faster through the dry alleys and streets of the city.

It was hard to focus on her own problems with everything around them cast in dark shades of orange and red, but when Emily finally looked at the house the Morrigan had brought them to, she realized she had been here before.

It was Kelindria's dwelling, where Emily and the others had been captured and locked away.

"You can't keep us here," she said. "The fire is coming. We'll be burned alive."

The Morrigan chuckled. "Maybe better for you if that did happen, but don't worry yourself. The Fire King will leave Kelindria's places alone. He knows better 'n that. Fact is, this is probably the only safe place left in London. Once the Fire King gets going, he's going to eat his way through everything." The Morrigan grinned. "So take a good look around. It's the last you'll ever see of your precious London."

The Morrigan pushed open the gate and entered the garden. The White Knight herded the others through. Merlin and Nimue walked in front; Emily, Jack, and Wren behind them; with the White Knight bringing up the rear. The Morrigan walked confidently along the overgrown path that led to the house. Emily hesitated, staring around the weed-choked garden. The White Knight prodded her in the back.

"Move," she said.

Emily reluctantly stepped forward. It wasn't just because she didn't want to be locked up. It was because the last time she had been in this garden, they had been chased by the Sluagh and had only just managed to escape with their lives.

A movement in the shadows beneath an ancient willow tree froze her in her steps. The shadows shifted, a dim outline moving against the darkness.

And then it came, drifting toward them, a roiling, heaving mass of dark cloud and shadows.

"Walk," repeated the knight.

The Morrigan paused to see what the problem was. When she saw Emily staring at the Sluagh, she waved her hand in irritation.

"I have permission to be here. Just stay on the path, and you'll be fine."

It seemed she was telling the truth. The Sluagh stopped before crossing the path's border. Emily stared at it in horrified fascination. She could see the faces inside, bobbing to the surface every now and again like rotten apples in a stagnant lake. The faces were snarling, angry, snapping at the air.

But they didn't attack. They were held back by Kelindria's instructions.

The Morrigan turned away again. Emily felt the White Knight push her in the back, sending her stumbling forward into Jack. She steadied herself, grabbing onto his arm, then looked up . . .

. . . to lock eyes with Nimue. Tears were coursing down her face. She nodded respectfully at Emily and gently disentangled herself from Merlin. She gave him a trembling smile and mouthed the word *good-bye*.

Then she stepped from the path directly into the Sluagh's embrace.

There was a moment of frozen horror.

"No!" Merlin shouted. He tried to follow after her, but Wren had enough presence of mind to grab the old man and hold him back. The Morrigan stared at the Sluagh, her mouth hanging open in amazement.

They all heard the hissing. It grew in volume as the cloud formed into tendrils, spinning around Nimue like a whirlwind. The tendrils entered her mouth, pushed into eyes, slid into her ears. Then it settled over her face like a funeral shroud. Nimue's features were still visible through the thin layer as some of the tendrils formed into a large funnel hanging above her. It paused there for a second, a snake ready to strike, then dropped over her like a mouth devouring its prey.

A moment later Nimue was gone.

Merlin stared at the cloud, tears rolling down his cheeks. Emily didn't know what had just happened. Why had she done that? Why sacrifice herself? Was she running away?

Was she a coward? Had she taken what she thought was the easy way out?

But no, that wasn't it at all, and Emily soon felt utterly ashamed that she had even entertained such thoughts.

The cloud was agitated. The faces were rising and falling quicker and quicker, jerking, snarling, and hissing as if in pain. It was as if the faces were trying to escape, trying to pull free from the seething darkness.

Then the cloud seemed to turn in on itself, the outer mass pulled in toward the center. There was a pause, then it pushed out again, like a great breath releasing.

One face rose to the surface, a face of smoke and highlights.

It was Nimue.

Emily drew a shocked breath. The face turned to her, and she suddenly realized that she had seen Nimue like this before. It was here, when they had escaped Kelindria's cells. It was Nimue who had saved them as they ran through the garden, Nimue who had stopped the Sluagh from taking Emily.

The cloud surged forward and swallowed the White Knight. She let out a scream of horror, frantically trying to wave the cloud away. She tried to run, but instead tripped over a bush and sprawled onto the ground. The cloud draped over her, settling like a low bank of fog. She continued screaming, but her voice was muffled as the cloud sank into her mouth, filled up her lungs. Her screams turned to chokes. Her feet hammered the ground.

The cloud settled over her entire body. The noises stopped. A moment of stillness, then the cloud rose slowly into the air.

The White Knight was gone.

Nimue's face turned in the direction of the Morrigan. A ghostly smile formed on her features.

The Morrigan turned and ran.

She was aiming for the door to the house, obviously thinking the dwelling would offer her protection. But Nimue moved faster. The cloud darted forward, soaring up into the air and dropping straight down onto her head. The Morrigan screamed in fury, gouging at her face, actually succeeding in yanking strands of the cloud away. But it was not a fight she could win. The Morrigan carried on moving, stumbling blindly along the path. She dropped to her knees, then pushed herself up and moved another step before collapsing once again.

Emily realized with a jolt that the Morrigan still had the keys to the Faerie Gate. Without their key they wouldn't be able to go home. She darted forward, ignoring the shouts from the others. The Sluagh had dropped over the top half of the Morrigan. Her screams of anger and fury were terrible to hear.

Emily stopped just behind her. She could see her pouch hanging from her belt. It was untouched by the cloud, but the tendrils were slowly wrapping around her ribs, moving downward.

Emily reached out and opened the pouch. But as soon as her fingers touched the Morrigan, the cloud bunched up and a face lunged down toward her, snapping at the air. Emily jerked back. The face snarled and growled, then was yanked back into the cloud to be replaced by the face of Nimue. Emily quickly withdrew the two keys while she had the chance.

You helped me free Merlin, Nimue said. *For that I will always owe you a debt.*

Emily remembered the words Nimue had spoken back in her own time, when she had stopped the Sluagh from attacking her. The words that had so puzzled Emily at the time. *My debt is repaid, Emily Snow.*

The words made sense now.

Go, said Nimue. *I am using what power remains to me from Morgan Le Fay, but I am not sure how long I can hold them back.*

The ghostly face of the White Knight rose to the surface and sank back again. Emily remembered seeing her in the cloud as well. Her and the Morrigan. Although she hadn't really registered seeing them at the time. They were just two faces among many, faces she was too terrified to take proper note of.

A hand dropped onto Emily's shoulder. She looked up to see Merlin standing behind her, shoulders hunched in grief, his eyes locked on Nimue's ghostly face.

Emily looked away, not wanting to intrude on his pain. She hurried back along the path and rejoined Jack and Wren.

"I think we should wait outside," said Wren, ushering them down the path.

They opened the gate and stepped outside. Emily turned just as the gate was closing, and saw Merlin standing on the path facing a ghostly image of Nimue. She had forced the cloud into the shape of her body.

Merlin raised his hand. Nimue did the same.

They moved their hands close together, stopping just short of touching.

The gate closed.

❧ CHAPTER TWENTY-SIX ❧

In which events move toward their conclusion.
An extremely narrow escape.

Kelindria knew the moment the Morrigan was taken by the Sluagh. She was connected to her guardian, could see what it saw, could feel what it felt. So she heard the Morrigan's infuriated scream of rage as soon as she died.

Kelindria closed her eyes.

"What happened?" she asked the Sluagh.

The Morrigan pushed herself forward from the maelstrom of spirits suddenly clamoring for Kelindria's attention, begging to be released.

It was the girl! raged the Morrigan. *She and Nimue rescued Merlin. She has the key.*

Back in the Faerie Tree, Kelindria's hands gripped the throne until her knuckles turned white.

"What else?"

She has a plan, that one. I fear she will be your undoing.

"Did she speak of the Raven King?"

She did. She asked Merlin about him, but the old man was evasive. You must stop them, Kelindria. Send the Fire King after them. Send your soldiers. Send everyone. Stop them now before it's too late. She is pushed by destiny, that child. I could sense it in my bones. If she is not stopped now, hers will be the hand that slays you.

Kelindria opened her eyes and blinked. The Dagda still stood before her, complaining. As always. He was growing wearisome.

"I repeat, how are you going to stop him? The Fire King is not someone you summon lightly."

Kelindria rounded on him, her fury causing even the mighty Dagda to take a step backward.

"Don't you think I am aware of that? Look at me! *Look at me!* I gave everything to make this plan work, so do not *dare* stand there and lecture me! Leave me now. And if you are unhappy with what I have done, feel free to take your followers and depart London. In fact, I think it may be better for all concerned if you did just that."

Black Annis moved over from the wall, followed closely by Jenny Greenteeth. "You should remember who supported you, Kelindria," she said. "It is not wise to turn your back on those who helped you into power. Loyalty is a coin that should be collected and held close."

"Is that so, Annis? And who are you to talk of loyalty? Do you think I did not know you and Greenteeth were spying for the Dagda? Did you think I was so stupid not to have you followed when you reported back to him?"

Annis glanced uncertainly at the Dagda. That look alone, that brief look of fear, was enough to send a warm glow through Kelindria's stomach. And speaking of warm glows . . .

Kelindria stood up and approached one of the torches attached to the wall. She looked into the flames.

"Attend, Fire King. I have a task."

Kelindria stepped back just as the flames shot up the wall, revealing the roaring outline of the Fire King's head. He turned his red eyes to Kelindria.

What do you want? I am feeding.

"I have some morsels for you." Kelindria turned and pointed at Black Annis and Jenny Greenteeth. "Take those two. They are water spirits. You cannot kill their essence, but their bodies are yours. Burn the moisture from the bodies."

Black Annis paled and turned to the Dagda. But he hastily backed away.

"My lord," said Annis. "Protect us—"

Her words ended in a shriek of pain as a fire blossomed into life inside her body. It flickered through her sodden rags, bursting out of her chest in an explosion of steam. The same was happening to Greenteeth. She dropped to the ground, writhing in pain as her body was burned from the inside. Annis tried to slap the fire out of existence, but all she did was set her arms alight.

She turned to Kelindria, fury giving her strength. She took a step forward, her clawed, burning hands outstretched. He mouth was open in a snarl of pure hatred. Flames flickered from her mouth, drying up the black water that trickled down her chin. Fire burst out of her eyes.

She screamed, then collapsed onto the floor. The flames quickly consumed the bodies.

Kelindria waited for the fire to die down, leaving behind a black smear on the tiles. She smiled at the Dagda. "Your services are no longer required. Leave now, or suffer the same fate."

"You go too far, Kelindria. This was meant to be *our* plan. Not yours."

"Things have changed."

The Dagda hesitated, then swept out of the room, his followers running to keep up. She had made an enemy there, she knew. But so be it. He wasn't strong enough to challenge her. She had made sure of that.

"I wish to be alone," she said.

Her new court bowed and backed hastily out of the throne

room. Kelindria waited for the doors to close before turning her attention back to the Fire King.

The Morrigan had been right. She had to stop the girl before it was too late.

⊢≫ ≪⊣

"Where are we going?" asked Emily as she, Jack, Wren, and Merlin moved as fast as they could through the London streets. Jack and Wren were supporting Merlin, trying to keep him upright as the enchanter attempted to lead them through the city.

Merlin ignored her, turning onto a side street. He paused and swore beneath his breath, staring at the flames licking across the roofs of the buildings at the far end. There was no way they would get through that. He turned back onto the main road and carried on moving northward. He was trying to get around the fire, but for what reason, Emily had no idea.

"Merlin?" she said.

"I need to get to my workshop," snapped Merlin. "It's as simple as that. I can't even *begin* to do anything to stop this Fire King if I don't get to my workshop."

"So you *can* stop him?" asked Emily hopefully, running to catch up.

Merlin hesitated. "I don't know," he admitted.

"Can't you just"—Jack wiggled his free hand in the air—"cast a spell or something?"

Merlin stopped walking so suddenly that Emily bumped into him. Wren almost pulled the old man off his feet before he realized they had stopped walking. Merlin turned a furious gaze on Jack. "Number one: I can't cast *any* spells right now, because I have no power. I hid it away before Nimue captured me. Just in case Morgan Le Fay came sniffing around and tried to steal it. *That's* why I need to get to my workshop. Right now I'm as much good to the fight against the Fire King as you are. I can't even walk unassisted!"

"Excuse me!" snapped Jack, offended. "I've done my bit. You wouldn't be standing here if it wasn't for us."

"And number two," said Merlin, ignoring Jack's outburst, "even if I *did* have my power, you don't just"—he wiggled his fingers in the air, mimicking Jack—"'cast a spell or something.' It doesn't work like that. Spells have to be prepared, tailored to requirements. It can take days to prepare a really good enchantment."

So William had been right all along, thought Emily. Merlin really couldn't help them. "What about the Raven King?" she asked.

Merlin rounded on her. "Where did you hear about the Raven King?" he asked hopefully.

Emily cast a doubtful look at the others. They had already

told him about the Raven King. Back in Cob's office. Was his memory really that bad?

"Uh . . . Someone from the Invisible Order was looking for him."

Merlin cackled and clapped his hands together. "Splendid. Change of plans, then. Take me to this person."

"We can't. He's dead."

Merlin's face fell. He glared at Emily. "It's very cruel to get peoples' hopes up only to dash them," he said. "It's bad for the heart."

"Uh . . . excuse me," said Jack. "But should we be worried about that?"

The other three turned to see what Jack was talking about. They had been heading east using Thames Street and had already turned onto Trinity Lane, intending to use the narrow road to head north and then circle around the fire to wherever Merlin wanted to go on the east side of the city. At the speed the flames were going, they should have had plenty time.

They didn't. Somehow the fire had converged behind them, traveling quickly along Thames Street to enter Trinity Lane at the southern end. They could clearly see a swarm of salamanders crawling over one another in haste, skittering across buildings and roofs, leaving trails of flame in their wakes.

"Are they . . . are they *looking* at us?" asked Emily.

"It would appear so," said Merlin. "It seems the enemy is aware of our escape."

They turned and moved as fast as they could go, but with Merlin unable to walk on his own, that wasn't very fast at all. The fire was gaining. Emily could feel the heat against her back, pushing her, daring her to slow down even slightly. Merlin was trying to move faster. His face was pale and slicked with sweat. His white hair was plastered against his skull, and every time he threw a worried glance over his shoulder, Emily could see the fire reflected larger and larger in his eyes.

The noise behind them was horrendous. The crackling of flames, the crashing of collapsing buildings, the screams of those trying to escape this unexpected change in the direction of the fire. Those who lived around the area had probably thought themselves safe. Probably thought they had until tomorrow before they had to leave. But now the fire had come to them sooner than expected, and no one was ready for it.

And then they lost Jack.

Merlin had ordered them onto a narrow street, saying they could use it to bypass some of the busier roads that would now be filled with panicking Londoners. Emily had turned around to check on the fire, and when she turned back, Wren was the only one holding Merlin up.

She skidded to a halt, staring wildly around. "Jack?" she shouted. "Jack!"

There was no sign of him. The fire was only twenty paces away. The salamanders leapt and scrambled across the cobblestones, their eyes glowing orange, tongues of flame darting in and out as they ran straight toward them.

Wren was looking around frantically.

"Where is he?" Emily shouted.

"He was here only a moment ago," Merlin replied, struggling to be heard over the roar of the flames.

Emily looked around in despair. She could see in Merlin's eyes that he thought Jack already dead.

"We don't have time," Merlin shouted. "Not if we are to stop this from spreading."

"You already said you don't know if you can stop it!" she screamed. "I won't leave Jack behind!"

A small alleyway opened off to their right. The salamanders climbed the wall of the building on one side, leaping across the gap to land on the thatched roof opposite. In seconds, the building was ablaze.

Wren hurried over to Emily. He leaned close to her ear and shouted, shielding them both from the flames with his arm. "You'll die here if you don't move," he screamed. "I know it's painful, but we must leave, Emily!"

And then Emily saw a shadow behind the flames that

now draped across the small alley like a curtain. She stared at it a moment before realizing it was growing darker and darker. Her eyes widened.

"Move!" she shouted, pushing a rather startled Wren aside. He staggered away, Emily quickly following. And just in time, two massive horses leapt over the flames and landed directly where they had been standing. The first horse's hooves struck sparks as the rider yanked the reins, guiding the horse quickly away from the heat and the smoke. The second horse was attached to the first by a length of rope. It moved forward and the rider leaned forward to pat its neck.

It was Jack.

"Jack!" shouted Emily, struggling (and failing) to keep the joy from her voice. She tried to sound firm. "Did you steal those horses?"

He grinned down at them. "No. I *saved* them. There's a difference. Now. Who wants a ride?"

<hr>

William, Corrigan, and Katerina had retraced their steps through the fey prison and along the tunnel that led back to St. Sepulchre. After that it had only been a matter of cutting an almost direct line east through the city as they traveled the one and a half miles to the Tower of London.

The fire hadn't reached this far north, but they could still see it in the distance, still smell the choking smoke, still hear the screams and curses of the Londoners. They passed plenty of them as well, pushing wheelbarrows filled with belongings, carrying children on their backs. They all had one thing in common: a confused, dazed expression on their faces, as if they couldn't believe this was actually happening to them.

William breathed a sigh of relief when the imposing stone walls of the Tower of London came into view. It wasn't just the tower, of course. The tower itself was simply one of many structures inside the walls of the fortifications. They slowed as they approached. The gates to the tower enclosure were wide open. He could see some men pushing wide barrows covered with blankets. A tall man was shouting at them to hurry and catch up with the others.

Of course, thought William. Weren't the crown jewels held here? And he was sure there were other valuables, as well. This must be the last of the trips to protect anything of value from the approaching fire.

The wide barrows trundled through the gates and turned north into the city. The gates were left open behind them, so they had no trouble slipping inside. A second wall confronted them, with a smaller gate set into the thick stone. It was also open. They hurried through and finally found themselves within the walls of the Tower of London.

A wide sward of grass lay before them, receding into the

darkness. The grass was dotted with houses and buildings. It looked as though hundreds of people lived here. But within the entire enclosure there was only one building that could be the actual tower.

William stared up at it, outlined against the dark sky. It actually wasn't really a tower. It looked more like a castle—a huge, square structure with four turrets reaching into the sky above the battlements.

They hurried across the grass. The building stretched almost a hundred feet above them, an imposing fort with gaping black windows that stared down at them. The door to the tower was raised high off the ground, reached by a set of wooden stairs. They hurried up the stairs and tested the door. It was unlocked, and it led into a corridor brightly lit by torches. William opened the first door he came to and saw bags of flour piled up against the walls. Another door revealed casks of wine, and yet another folded linen stacked neatly onto shelves.

"Excuse me for asking," said Corrigan, "but what exactly are we supposed to do here? That journal was rather vague."

William hesitated. He wasn't sure himself. He had been rather hoping an answer would present itself when they arrived. Where were they supposed to speak the words of the spell?

There was a set of stairs at the end of the corridor. Maybe

there was something on the other levels of the tower? He ran up to the second floor. The doors here led into richly furnished apartments and bedrooms. But there didn't seem to be anything that would help him. What had he been expecting? A shrine? A crypt with an inscription that read HERE LIES THE RAVEN KING?

That would have been nice, but when was life ever as simple as that?

He kept looking. And it was only when he opened a door at the far end of the passage to find a chapel that he thought maybe life *was* as simple as that after all.

William stepped inside. Arched windows let in the flickering orange light of the fire. Thick pillars circled the walls, linked together to create high stone arches that surrounded an empty space in the center of the room.

William looked around hopefully. Maybe this was the place? A chapel made sense. Maybe there was a hidden crypt somewhere that held the Raven King, and he would wake up when the incantation was recited.

William took the journal from his pocket and opened it to the relevant page. He cleared his throat and read:

"Acht'in segara. Betan mie alora ti. Vitaj'kel, amata yi."

William finished reading and stared dubiously at the book. It didn't seem much of a magical spell, did it? What did it even mean? What language was it?

He waited. Nothing happened. The orange light of the fire seemed to have grown brighter, the fiery light pulsing against the walls. Maybe he had he read it wrong?

"You'd better see this," said Katerina, appearing at the door.

William turned, but Katerina had already disappeared. He hurried after her, following her up a winding staircase that led to the battlements and out into the night air. William had a brief hope that maybe the Raven King had awoken somewhere in response to his words and was already battling the Fire King, but one look at Corrigan's face told him this wasn't so.

He joined the piskie and Katerina and stared out over London. From here he could get a clear view of the fire, could see the extent of the damage to the area of the city to the north of London Bridge.

"Look there," said Corrigan, pointing to the east, then to the north, areas the fire hadn't touched yet.

For a few seconds William couldn't see anything untoward. But then he saw figures moving in the darkness, streaming through the streets in their direction. It was fey. All kinds of them.

And they were all armed.

"Are they coming for us?" he whispered. "How could they know what we are doing?"

Corrigan shrugged. "The question is, do we stay and try

and raise this Raven King, however we're supposed to do that, or do we get out while we can?"

"We can't run," said William. "Not after all we've been through."

"Have you tried it yet?"

William looked away.

"Didn't work, did it?"

William didn't reply. He gazed out over London and noted something flitting through the sky. He squinted against the smoke that was hanging over the city. It was those white ravens, swooping above the approaching fey, hundreds of them gliding through the darkness.

"Look over there," said Katerina urgently.

She was pointing toward the fire. As they watched, the flames seemed to shift, as if blown on a wind. Except there wasn't any wind blowing in that direction. The roaring con-flagration funneled through the city streets toward the Tower.

"It's coming for us," said Katerina.

It was then that William saw the two horses. They were galloping ahead of the flames, turning corners, skidding into alleys. As he watched, the fire switched direction, leaping across a thatched roof in an attempt to catch them.

"It's not," said William, puzzled. "The fire is after those horses."

They watched the distant horses as they tried to outrun the

flames. But the fire seemed to anticipate their movements. It split and curved around buildings, leaping from roof to roof, leaving blazing trails in its wake. The horses disappeared from view every now and then, the buildings obscuring their vision as the animals tried to frantically shake off their pursuer.

When the horses next appeared, they were much closer. So William was able to see the figures on the first creature's back. He stared in shock.

"That's Emily," he said softly.

It was. It was Emily and Christopher Wren on the first horse, Jack and another person on the second. The horses were flagging, moving slower and slower as the frantic rush through the city took its toll. But still they kept going, turning into side streets, doubling back on themselves, trying everything possible to shake the stalking flames.

But nothing worked. The flames kept getting closer.

They were getting closer to the tower, and it was obvious to all who watched that this was their destination.

Jack turned his horse into the final wide road that led straight to the gates, the road the three of them had used only half an hour earlier. Jack sighted the gates and tried to coax an extra burst of speed from the horse. It must have sensed that that end was in sight, as it renewed its efforts, stumbling into a clumsy canter. Emily followed suit. The flames raced along the rooftops on either side of them, leaping, snaking across thatch and wood, slowly pulling ahead of the horses despite their best efforts. The flames arrived at the end of the street and poured from the rooftops like a waterfall of lava, pooling then flaring up into a wall, trying to block off the exit to the street.

The flames pulled together, closer, closer. They were five meters apart. Three. Then two.

Jack dug his heels in, and William could hear him screaming at the horse. The horse bunched its muscles and leapt, sailing over the flames and landing on the other side. There was the briefest of pauses, then the second horse burst through, an instant before the two sides touched together, blocking off the street.

William felt the tension rush from his body. He thought he heard Corrigan mutter *"yes!"* but wasn't sure. The horses galloped through the gates and onto the tower grounds, heading straight in their direction. William watched the fire for a second longer. It had stopped moving now. He wondered why it wasn't trying to follow Emily and the others.

But then he saw the army of fey marching along the road outside the walls, heading straight toward the gates.

That was why. The Fire King didn't want to burn his allies.

Chapter Twenty-seven

In which Emily and William are reunited
and all take refuge in Merlin's workshop.

When Emily saw William appear at the top of the stairs leading into the White Tower, she stumbled to a halt and stared in shock. She wondered if she was seeing things, if their escape from the flames hadn't addled her brain. But then Corrigan appeared, grinning ear to ear.

"Kept him safe for you, Snow," he shouted. He thumped William on the leg. "Look at that. Good as new."

Emily and William locked eyes. There was relief there. For both of them. But things needed to be said. Things needed to be sorted. And now wasn't the time.

"Oh, and just so you know," said Corrigan, "there's an army of about a hundred angry fey marching toward us. We should probably barricade ourselves inside."

Merlin winced and turned stiffly to Emily. "Do you know this creature? Or should we just kill him now?"

"I know him. This is Corrigan. The piskie who has been helping us."

"Ah. He doesn't look like much."

Corrigan glared at Merlin. "Who's the old man, Snow? You picking up strays now?"

"This is Merlin," she said, her eyes flicking across to William as she said it.

Corrigan stared at him critically. "Are you sure? He looks a bit . . . decrepit."

"I've been locked in a block of crystal for over a thousand years!" snapped Merlin. "Why don't you try that, and let's see how spry *you* look."

"I hate to interrupt," said Jack, "but if there really is an army on the way, shouldn't we get to your workshop?"

"Yes. Of course. Follow me."

Merlin climbed the steps, brushing past Corrigan and nodding amiably at William. He led them toward the stairs and was just about to climb them, when Emily realized someone was missing.

"Where's Katerina? Wasn't she with you?" Emily fervently hoped so, because otherwise it meant she had simply deserted them back at Cavanagh's house.

William and Corrigan paused, looking at each other in puzzlement.

"She was right here," said William. "She came down the stairs."

They hurried back to the door and peered outside.

"There," said Jack, pointing toward the gate. They could just see Katerina sprinting across the grass.

"What's she doing?" asked William.

"Probably what we should be doing," answered Corrigan. "Running away."

"She's not running away!" snapped William. "She can't be."

Katerina disappeared through the gate, vanishing from sight.

"Looks like it to me," said Corrigan.

"We don't have much time," called Merlin. He hadn't moved from the stairs. He nodded at Wren, who helped him up the steps.

The others reluctantly followed. Merlin led them along a corridor and into the chapel. He approached a blank piece of wall and rested his hands against the stone. A grinding sound echoed through the chamber, and a faint line appeared in the wall, widening until it revealed a door.

Merlin pushed it open, and Wren helped him through. The others followed, descending a long flight of stairs that ended at a round green door with a doorknob set exactly in its center. Wren turned the doorknob and stepped aside so Merlin could enter first. The enchanter hobbled inside, breathing a great sigh of relief.

As he entered his workshop, there was a loud whoosh of rushing air, and a blue pillar of fire leapt into life in the center of the large room. Merlin moved to the side and waved everyone in.

"Welcome to my lair," he said, then frowned. "Sorry, that sounded rather ominous. Welcome to my workshop."

Emily stepped across the threshold and looked slowly around. It *was* a workshop. But it was also a library. And a study. And a sleeping chamber. It was all these things and more. Books were strewn everywhere. On desks, on the floor, on wooden bookshelves. A huge table ran the length of the room, covered with odds and ends. Emily peered along its length. The section closest to her was strewn with tiny gears and cogs. A half-finished bird made of metal was lying on its side, its body complete except for wings. Emily reached out to touch it, and it turned its head and whistled softly, a note of inquiry. Emily swallowed and drew her hand back. She moved to a nearby reading desk. A huge book was lying here, a book that Emily had seen before. It had the emblem of the Invisible Order on the front, the two entwined dragons devouring each other's tail. This was the *Historia Occultus*—the Hidden Histories. The book that Sebastian had shown her and William only a couple of days ago in Somerset House, the book that held all of the history of mankind between its pages.

She looked up to find her brother. He was approaching Merlin.

"Are you going to summon the Raven King?"

Merlin was leaning against the long table. He laughed bitterly. "Me? Boy, I can't even summon the strength to walk, never mind summon the Raven King." He looked thoughtful for a moment. "And as it turns out, even if I *did* have the strength, it wouldn't make a difference."

"Why?" asked William.

"Because I have no memory of how to wake him. I can remember some of it, but the spell itself . . ." He tapped his head. "Gone. Or rather"—he turned and pointed to a section of the workshop that had been curtained off—"over there." He sank down into a chair. "So to save everyone a thousand years ago, I've doomed us in the here and now."

"Then why did you want to come here?" asked Emily. "What was the point if we can't do anything?"

"I told you. I need to restore my magic. If I don't do that, I'll be dead in a matter of hours. Once I have my magic restored to me, we'll see what can be done."

"And how long will that take?" asked Wren.

"It took a full day and a half to complete the process the first time. It will take the same amount of time to reverse it.

"A day and a half!" exclaimed Emily. "But it will be too

late by then. London will be gone. So will half of England. Thousands of people will be dead!"

Merlin looked wretched. "I don't know what to tell you," he said. "You did the right thing. You rescued me. But sometimes we're just not successful in what we set out to do. Sometimes we have to settle for what we can get. Right now, I don't know how to summon the Raven King. We will just have to wait."

"Excuse me," said William, "but will this help?"

William handed over a slim leather book to Merlin. Merlin took it from William and flipped through the pages, his eyes widening as he did so. "I remember this! I wrote it down before I started siphoning off my magic. It was all the knowledge I was afraid to lose."

"What is it?" asked Wren.

"Information. Spells and notes. Among many other things, this book holds my instructions on how to summon the Raven King."

Emily stared at William in wonder. He had done it? He had actually succeeded in finding a means to summon the Raven King?

"Where did you find it?" asked Merlin.

"A fey prison. Beneath Newgate," said Corrigan.

"Ah, yes. I contemplated leaving it in the library of the Invisible Order, but I didn't think it was secure enough. So

I left it at the prison. I was the last person alive who even remembered it existed. I thought it the safest place."

"Why not leave it here?" asked Emily.

"If Arthur and his knights hadn't succeeded in capturing Morgan Le Fay, there was a chance she would have found my workshop here. Of course, the tower wasn't built yet. That came much later. If she found the information contained in this book, then all would have been lost."

"So you can summon him?" asked William excitedly. "You can wake Bran the Blessed?"

Merlin frowned in confusion. "Bran the Blessed? Bran is dead, my boy. Even I can't bring someone back from the dead."

"But it says in there. It says he is the Raven King."

Merlin opened the book and quickly scanned the contents. "Ah, I see. No, Bran *was* the Raven King, yes. But I didn't mean he would be awoken from death when the need arose. What I meant was that as long as Bran's *bloodline* exists, then the Raven King will live. The power of the Raven King flows down through Bran's descendants." He stared at his book with some distaste. "I really wish he hadn't used such a name, though. The Raven King. The true name of Britain's protector is the Pendragon. As long as the blood of the Pendragon clan lives on, Britain will have her protector."

William's face fell. "Wait. So the Raven King—the Pendragon or whatever—might not even be in London?"

"Oh, he'll be here. Whoever he is, he will be drawn to London. It is as if he is pushed by fate. The Pendragon will always be involved in tumultuous affairs. Will feel drawn to events that will one day become history. The blood of the Pendragon pulls them to trouble like iron filings to a magnet. It has always been so. Just look at King Arthur."

William gestured at the book. "So wake him up. Say the words!"

"I can't! The words must be said at the site of Bran's grave."

"But Katerina said he was buried beneath the Tower of London. That's why we came here!"

"Ah, I see," said Merlin softly. "Some of the legends say that, yes, but Bran was not buried beneath the Tower of London. He was actually buried beneath Tower Hill. Come here."

Merlin limped over to what appeared to be a well built into the floor of his workshop. But as they approached, Emily saw it wasn't a well at all. It was one of the crystal dragon eyes she had used to look inside Somerset House.

Merlin touched the glass. A pale pink glow surrounded his hand, spreading out like ripples in a pond, washing up against the edge of the glass and bouncing back again, growing brighter and brighter as it did so.

An image appeared, showing a bird's-eye view of the

White Tower, the tower above Merlin's workshop. Surrounding the tower (and within the walled enclosure) was the fey army they had seen approaching. They appeared to be waiting for something. Outside the Tower enclosure they could see a massive wall of fire stretching along the street.

Merlin moved his hand over the image, and it slowly shifted to the northeast. He pointed at a small hill just outside the walls of the enclosure. "Tower Hill. It is a magical place, the oldest spot in London. The first stone of the city was laid here. *That* is where the blood of the Pendragon must be awoken."

"Except we now happen to be surrounded by a small army," pointed out Wren.

"Yes. So it would seem."

"So what do we do?" asked William. "We can't just sit here waiting to die."

"You are entirely correct." Merlin winced and walked over to a table. He picked up a small stone and held it up. The entwined dragon symbol of the Invisible Order was engraved into the stone. "We have the means of getting into Tower Hill." He held up the journal. "We have the means of waking the blood of the Pendragon." He put the two objects back on the table and moved across his workshop to the curtained-off area. He pulled the curtain aside, revealing a ghostly figure lying on a long stone plinth. The figure was Merlin, looking like he was peacefully asleep. The real Merlin climbed up onto the plinth, his hands moving through the half-seen figure. "But first, I need to restore my magic, because if I set off to wake the Raven King now, I do not think I will make it back alive." He lay down. The ghostly image seemed to shift and sink over his real body, so that the only way you could tell there were two was a slight blurring around the edges of Merlin. He opened his eyes again. "Trust me. I don't like doing this. But sometimes waiting is the best way forward. My advice is to get some sleep. My workshop is warded. They could burn the tower down around us, and they still wouldn't be able to get inside."

Emily stared at him hopelessly as he closed his eyes once again. She felt angry at Merlin. She knew it wasn't fair. If he didn't do this, he would die, and then what would happen? They would need him in the days ahead. But he had been the focus of all her hopes. Right from the very beginning, she had thought that he would be able to fix everything. And now she was expected to just sit here and wait? While people died and London burned?

No. That wasn't the type of person she was.

The others were still peering into the dragon's eye, watching the fey army. Emily quickly picked up the stone and the journal and slipped them inside her coat. Then she joined the others. The fey had completely surrounded the White Tower.

There was no way she could get through their lines without being caught. But Emily wasn't about to let that stop her. She touched Will on the shoulder. When he turned and looked at her, she put her finger to her lips and nodded toward the door. He stepped away from the eye and followed her.

Emily carefully pulled the door open and slipped out onto the small landing at the bottom of the stairs. When William joined her, she closed the door and fished out the journal and the stone.

"The way I see it," she said. "We were both right. We need the Raven King, and you found the way to summon him, but without Merlin we wouldn't know about Tower Hill and we wouldn't have this." She raised the stone into the air. "In which case your journal would be useless anyway. Agreed?"

Will thought about it, then nodded.

"So I think what we should do is sneak out of here and summon this Raven King ourselves. Then we can put a stop to all this nonsense once and for all. Are you in?"

William nodded. "I'm in."

⇥ CHAPTER TWENTY-EIGHT ⇤
In which Emily and William attempt to wake the Raven King.

Emily and William crouched down just inside the door to the White Tower, making sure to keep out of sight of the fey milling around on the grass below them. Emily could see a lot of the Tuatha guards mixed in with the smaller fey. They looked incredibly frightful, standing in small groups with their spears resting against their shoulders, casting dark glances at the tower.

"What now?" asked William.

Emily wasn't sure. She'd been hoping for some kind of a gap, something they could slip through. They couldn't even look for a back window or anything, as the tower was completely surrounded.

A ripple of movement ran through the fey. Some of them

turned and looked over their shoulders. The Tuatha straightened to attention, their eyes fixed on something.

"What's going on?" asked William.

Emily got down on her stomach and crawled forward. A line of fire burned higher than the walls, a fiery barrier that blocked off the main gates. Walking across the grass toward the tower were the silhouettes of two figures. One was huge, the other slightly smaller. The firelight glinted against the larger figure, striking highlights from its metal armor.

It was Kelindria and the Crimson Knight. And if it was the Crimson Knight, that meant . . . Emily stared hard into the darkness. There. A few feet behind the knight. She could just make out the red glow of two pairs of eyes. The two remaining Hounds of the Hunt.

"Do you think she'll burn the tower down?" asked Will.

"I don't think so. She'll be after the key to the Faerie Gate. She can't risk its being destroyed."

"That's something, I suppose," said Will. "Still doesn't help us, though."

He was right. They needed a distraction. Something big. Something that would shift all attention away from them. Then they could try to escape through one of the other gates, seeing as the wall of fire seemed to block only the western wall.

Emily and William were watching Kelindria as she walked toward them. So it took them a few moments to realize something was happening off to their left. It was subtle at first, a few clashes of sound, but after a few seconds there was a scream, then a shout taken up by the other fey. All attention shifted to the south side of the enclosure. One or two of the fey standing below them started to run, then more and more, until a wave of fighters swept toward the sounds. Even Kelindria and the knight shifted direction and started running off to the left.

The field of grass outside was deserted. Emily and Will looked at each other in amazement, then quickly clattered down the stairs to see what was going on. Their view was blocked by a tower that jutted from the southwest corner of the enclosure.

Emily knew they should turn around and head to the north end of the fort in an attempt to find another way out, but she couldn't help herself. She had to see what was happening. She hurried out onto the grass, facing toward the south wall. The fire was now off to her right, the flames casting a demonic glow over the scene before her.

It was a battle. An army had appeared from nowhere, surprising the fey who were surrounding the White Tower. It was hard to make out what was going on in the dim light, but a moment later, a small skirmish involving a Tuatha and two children staggered into view.

"It's Katerina!" said William. "She didn't run off. She went to get help. I told you!"

Will was right. It was Katerina's gang. But many, many more than had surrounded them at the Thames when they had first arrived. Emily skimmed her eyes over the escalating battle, feeling a tentative hope spring to life in her chest. It looked as though the fey were evenly matched in numbers.

And then Emily saw Katerina. She was slicing an iron sword through the air, a look of fierce determination set on her features. A goblin fell before her blade, dissolving into a smoky black puddle. She quickly stepped over it and attacked one of the Tuatha. The tall creature was caught by surprise. He tried to parry with his spear, but Katerina's blade cut it in half. She darted forward through the opening and stabbed the creature through the chest, yanking her sword out and turning to look for her next victim.

As she did so, she caught sight of Will and Emily. She raised her sword in a hasty tribute, then turned to block an axe that was swinging for her. She pushed her attacker back, a squat creature that appeared to have no neck. The creature stumbled, and Katerina put her boot against it and pushed, shoving it onto its back. She finished it off with one swift thrust.

"Come on," said Emily. "She's given us our distraction."

Emily and William turned and ran across the grass, heading for the north end of the enclosure. There was a series of structures built up against the wall, sheds of some kind.

They hurried along a path that wound between them and arrived at one of the towers that was built into the wall. They ran through the exit, only to be confronted with a lowered portcullis blocking their escape.

There was a small door set into the wall to their left. Emily pushed it open and found herself in a small guard-room. There was a huge iron cog set into a hole in the floor. A thick metal chain was looped around the cog, disappearing into a slit in the roof.

"Help me here," she said, grasping hold of the iron wheel.

She and Will leaned on it with all their weight, pushing it toward the ground. It moved slowly, grudgingly. They struggled with it for a full minute until they had raised the portcullis enough for them to slip under.

They found themselves in the outer ward of the fort, stuck between the two walls. There was no gate in the wall ahead of them, though. Emily looked to her left, but she could still see the flames lighting the sky. They couldn't go that way. There *had* to be another gate, because Katerina and her gang had entered from the south side.

"This way," she said, turning to her right and running along the wall.

The sounds of fighting grew louder as they approached the south end of the enclosure. Sure enough, she could see a gate up ahead. More of Katerina's gang were arriving, streaming in from the streets, raising their weapons to join the battle.

Emily and Will hurried beneath another portcullis and out through a heavy gate set into the outer wall. They had made it. They were free of the tower. Emily paused to take a breath. Now they had to head back around the wall to the northwest to get to Tower Hill.

"Let's go," she gasped, setting off at a run.

Emily and William finally rounded the north side of the Tower of London and sprinted across the road to Tower Hill. It wasn't much of a hill, though. It was more of a gentle slope that spread away to either side of them. A small sward of grass.

They hurried toward the crown of the hill. Emily cast frequent glances behind her as they did so. She could see the line of fire that had chased them to the tower. It still wasn't moving. As they ran up the hill, Emily fished out the stone that Merlin had shown them. The one that was supposed to get them into Tower Hill. What was she supposed to do with it? Find a keyhole somewhere?

They arrived at the hill summit. It wasn't even high enough to let them see over the tower walls to the battle happening inside. Emily turned in a slow circle, looking for anything that might help. She could see nothing.

"What do we do now?" asked William.

"I don't know," said Emily. She inspected the stone.

"Put it on the ground," said William.

Emily shrugged and placed it on the grass.

A deep rumbling echoed beneath her feet. The rumbling grew stronger, a vibration that threatened to throw them to the ground.

A small hole opened up at Emily's feet. She staggered backward, grabbing William as she did so. The hole grew in size, earth and grass crumbling away. The bottom edge of the hole pushed down and flattened the grass so that after a few seconds it was no longer a hole in the ground, but a dark entrance into a tunnel.

The rumbling stopped. Emily and William walked hesitantly forward. Emily kicked something, and she looked down to find the stone lying at her feet. She scooped it up and dropped it into her pocket.

William looked at her. "You ready?" he asked.

Emily nodded. She wasn't, not really, but she didn't think Will was, either. They simply had no choice.

Emily held her hand out. William hesitated, then took hold of it, and they both stepped into the darkness.

The light from outside gave them a small amount of illumination. But only for a short while. As they walked deeper into the tunnel, the decline grew steeper and steeper, and the darkness folded in around them, leaving them totally blind.

After they had been walking for about five minutes, a flare

of light froze them both in their tracks. To their left and right small flames had leapt up inside half-moon bowls that were built into the walls. There was some kind of aqueduct linking the two bowls with another two farther down the tunnel, then to the next and to the next. Emily and William watched as the flames traveled along these aqueducts, lighting each bowl in turn until there were fires dwindling into the distance.

They could now get a good look at their surroundings. The tunnel was massive, easily wide enough to fit twenty people walking side by side. The ceiling arched high above them. The walls were made from old stones fitted neatly together. Despite the obvious age of the tunnel, the stones didn't even crumble beneath her touch.

"Impressive," said Emily. Her voice echoed into the distance.

Judging by the bowls of fire, the tunnel moved in an absolute straight line down into the earth. It looked as though they had a long way to go, so they started to run, aware that every passing second meant added danger to Katerina and her friends. She and her gang were tough, and they matched the fey in number, but who knew how long they could hold out. Emily didn't even know if summoning the Raven King would help them. What if he was too far away? What if he was out of the city? Traveling somewhere else?

These were all doubts that Emily tried to force from her mind. Thinking such thoughts did nothing to help the situation.

She became aware that the scene up ahead was changing. The two lines of fire, which up until now had seemed to meet up in the far distance, had gradually begun to separate. Emily realized this was because they were coming to the end of the tunnel.

"Nearly there," grunted William.

They put on an extra burst of speed and because of this almost fell into the huge hole in the ground at the end of the tunnel. Emily skidded to a halt when she saw the vast darkness that swallowed the light from the fire bowls. She reached out to grab Will, and they both slid to a stop, teetering over the edge of the vast pit.

William swayed backward and managed to yank Emily with him. They both fell to the ground, panting from fear and exertion. Emily got to her knees and crawled forward. She couldn't see anything. Just a black . . . *nothingness* that seemed to swallow light. She found a small stone and dropped it over the edge.

She didn't hear it land.

She stood up and brushed off her hands. "Over to you, William," she said, handing him the journal.

William slowly pushed himself up and took the book

from Emily's hands. He opened it to the relevant page and nervously cleared his throat.

"Acht'in segara. Betan mie alora ti. Vitaj'kel, amata yi."

He closed the book.

"That's it?" asked Emily. "What does it mean?"

"I've no idea," said William.

At first there was nothing, but then Emily thought she heard a dry, whispering sound, like sand coursing through a funnel. She peered into the pit. The noise was coming from far below, but also off into the distance, as if the pit was wide as well as deep.

The sound grew louder—a scraping, rasping sound. Then she heard a fierce huff, as if something was drawing breath. She glanced at William, alarmed. His features were set in a determined look. He wouldn't back away now. Not after going through so much to get them here.

The dry rasping grew closer, and Emily heard something else, too. The scraping of stone, then the fall of pebbles. As they stood there listening, the noises fell into a pattern. First the scrape, then the fall of pebbles, then the dry rasping sound.

It took Emily a while to realize the sounds were that of a creature climbing up the wall of the pit, gripping the stone with claws before pulling itself up, scraping its stomach on the stone as it climbed. This time she did take a step back. Whatever was coming sounded incredibly big.

Emily caught a glimpse of something, a brief hint of dark blue and green, sliding into the light for the briefest second before moving into the darkness again. It reminded her of something, but she couldn't think what. She saw it again, a flash of blue and green sliding through the dark, rasping against the stone.

That was when she realized what it reminded her of. A snake, coiling and twining as it moved. And the dry rasping sound had to be the scales rubbing against the wall of the pit.

She grabbed hold of Will's arm and pulled him backward. He was about to complain, but at that moment a massive reptilian head heaved up above the lip of the dark pit and gazed down at them.

Emily's mouth fell open.

It was a dragon. She was staring at a dragon. There was no possible way she could deny it. No chance of saying it was something else.

It was a dragon.

Its head was easily half as tall as the White Tower. It filled the space, almost touching the distant roof. It pointed its blunt, pockmarked snout downward until it was no more than five paces away. Heat wafted out of nostrils the size of doors. Ruby-colored eyes stared at them.

The dragon sniffed, almost pulling them both off their feet. Then it exhaled, knocking them both onto their backsides.

Who speaks the ancient tongue? Who summons the Pendragon from her sleep? Have I not earned my rest?

The voice echoed inside Emily's head. She scrambled to her feet. "Uh . . . I, that is, *we* do. Summon you."

On whose authority?

Emily thought for a moment. "Merlin's? Britain is in danger. The Fire King has been summoned, and he is burning the city to the ground. He will destroy the whole of Britain unless he is stopped."

The dragon paused as if in thought. *You wish to summon the power of the Pendragon?*

"Yes! Please. Before it's too late."

Does the Pendragon bloodline still live on?

"We . . . we don't know. We weren't sure how this worked."

So be it. It is done.

The dragon's head lowered slowly back into the pit. They heard the sound of it climbing back down the walls. Emily drew a shaky breath and looked at William. He was pale, his eyes wide as he stepped forward and stared down into the darkness.

Then he turned to her with a huge grin on his face. "Did we just summon a dragon?"

Emily couldn't help but grin back. "I think we did. Come on. Let's get back to the others."

⫸ CHAPTER TWENTY-NINE ⫷
The Final Battle

The battle was not going in Katerina's favor. It had started off well, but that was because they'd had the advantage of surprise. But now the Tuatha guards had split up, taking charge of small groups of fey, leading them into the fight. They were keeping the fey organized, making sure they didn't scatter.

Katerina wasn't sure how many had died on her side. Lots. She knew that. But what was she supposed to do? Sit back while Will and the others fought Kelindria on their own? This was as much her fight as it was William's and Emily's. *More*, as this wasn't even their time. If they were willing to die for the cause, then so was she.

Katerina had always felt she was destined for something like this. All her life she had looked out for the little person.

Had spoken for those who didn't have a voice. It was why all the street children had flocked to her. They trusted her. Believed she wouldn't let them down. And she wouldn't. If they could somehow stop the fey from destroying London, then the sacrifice would be worth it. Think how many lives would be saved.

"To me!" she shouted. Her beleaguered followers, scattered around the field of battle, turned and ran in her direction. Her heart thudded painfully when she saw how few they were. Only about thirty or so out of how many? Over a hundred. Puck was there, urging everyone back to her. She had to admit, it had been a surprise to see him fighting by her side. After the stories she had heard from Corrigan, she wasn't sure what to think of him. But it seemed he was still loyal to the cause.

She caught sight of Jack and Wren. Even Corrigan. They must have heard the battle and come out to help. The three of them hurried toward her.

"Have you seen Emily and Will?" asked Jack. His face was covered in a spatter of blood. She wasn't sure if it was his or someone else's. Even Wren had picked up a weapon. It wasn't hard to find one. They were all over, dropped by her fallen comrades.

"They went that way," she said, pointing to the north.

Jack and Wren exchanged grim looks.

"What?"

"We think they've gone to wake the Raven King."

Katerina's eyebrows shot up in surprise. "Really? Then all that stuff is true?"

"According to Merlin, yes."

"Merlin? Ah, the old man," said Katerina. "So Emily was successful in her quest as well."

Her followers had all gathered around her. "Form a line," she shouted. They obeyed her instantly, forming into a neat line that was nowhere near as long as she wanted it to be. The fey gathered before her, their numbers disheartening to see. It had all started off so well!

The fey line parted to allow an old crone and the Crimson Knight to move forward.

"Who is that?" she whispered to Jack.

"Kelindria. The new Faerie Queen."

"Titania's gone?" asked Katerina, surprised.

"*Deposed*, I think, is the correct term," said Wren.

"Lay down your weapons," called Kelindria. "And no harm will befall you."

Katerina chuckled. She couldn't help it. "You hear that, people? No harm will befall us. What do you say? Should we lay down our arms?"

A roar of anger swept through their line. Katerina smiled at Kelindria. "There's your answer," she called.

"Surely you know you are all dead if you do not? The Fire

King will sweep through here and reduce your bones to ashes."

The Faerie Queen seemed to notice something for the first time. Her eyes swept along the line. "Where are the girl and her brother?" She stepped forward, the Crimson Knight keeping pace to protect her. In the background, Katerina could see the shadowy forms of two of his hounds. They would be hard to kill. She was sure she still had her witchbane dagger stashed somewhere about her person. Her hands slid to her belt. Better to have it at hand.

"They're not here!" screamed the Queen. She whirled around to the knight. "Find them!"

The Crimson Knight swept away from Kelindria's side, heading toward the White Tower. The two hounds padded after him. At least that put them out of the fight, thought Katerina. Made things easier on them.

The dogs loped ahead of the knight, muzzles close to the ground. As they drew close to the tower, they stopped and erupted into a frenzy of barking, running off in the direction Emily and William had taken.

Kelindria smiled as she turned back to face them. "There we go. They will not escape. Not this time." She fished something from her pocket and dropped it to the ground. Katerina craned her neck forward to see. It looked like some kind of stone. But as she watched, it cracked open and a fiery lizard crawled out of it. Not a stone. An egg.

"Attend me," said Kelindria.

Katerina's attention was drawn to the flames that had been burning steadily along the west wall of the tower enclosure. The fire flared even higher, and then a figure stepped out of the flames, a figure well over twenty feet tall. It climbed easily over the walls and stalked toward them, leaving flaming footprints in its wake.

The Fire King approached.

Kelindria turned and hurried toward the terrible creature. As it drew near, it shrank down until it was the size of a tall man. He and Kelindria spoke briefly, then the Fire King turned and followed the Crimson Knight.

Kelindria returned to her line and smiled, a terrible, cruel smile in an ancient, withered face.

"As soon as your little friends turn up, the key will be mine. And then . . . Well, and then the Fire King will embrace them both." She studied their faces. "Oh, don't look so upset. You won't even know about it. Because you'll all be kissing the mud. Tuatha! Attack!"

On her command, the lines of fey started running toward them. Katerina and her gang were outnumbered almost four to one, but still she raised her sword into the air.

Her comrades did the same. "For London!" she screamed.

"For London!" came the reply.

And then they ran forward to meet the fey in the final battle.

Emily and William were huffing with exertion by the time they arrived at the exit to the tunnel. Their first sight of the city was the orange-tinged smoke that blanketed the London sky. It was a depressing sight, but at least it meant they would soon be able to see what their summoning had wrought.

They stepped out of the tunnel. Everything seemed the same. The line of fire still wavered and burned to the south. They could still hear the sounds of fighting coming from inside the enclosure.

Emily and Will exchanged puzzled looks. They'd done it, hadn't they? They had summoned the Raven King. So why was the battle still going on? Why hadn't it stopped?

A dull *crump* caught Emily's attention, echoing through the night. Her eyes shifted to the thick wall of the tower enclosure at the bottom of Tower Hill. She stared, but couldn't see anything that could have made the noise.

She heard it again. But this time she saw some stones falling to the ground. There was a brief pause, and then the wall burst outward in a huge explosion of bricks and flame. Smoke billowed from the hole, writhing up into the sky. Loose earth and shards of stone pattered to the ground all around them, even reaching Emily and William at the top of the hill.

A figure appeared through the smoke, emerging from the flame. It ducked through the hole, then stopped and surveyed its surroundings. Emily's breath caught in her throat.

It was the Crimson Knight.

He looked up the hill and spotted them. He started running, his armor not slowing him down in the slightest.

His hounds burst out of the hole behind him, silent and deadly. They followed the knight as he hit the bottom of the hill, their long, powerful legs pushing them ahead of their master.

And if that wasn't enough, a figure of flame stooped through the hole in the wall, illuminating the thick smoke like lightning flickering inside a cloud. Brick and stone melted beneath his touch. He straightened up and walked purposefully toward them.

+≒ ≒+

Katerina was trying her best to fight her way through the fey so she could follow the Crimson Knight. Jack and the others were doing the same, everyone focusing on one thing—protecting Emily and William.

But there were just too many fey. Reinforcements had arrived, streaming through the gate to join the fight. Katerina's followers were being cut to shreds. She sobbed in frustration, watching as the Fire King sent fireballs into the distant wall of the fort. One, two, and then a third that punched through the stones like a fist through paper.

She had to get to them. Had to stop the Fire King from succeeding. The fate of everything hung in the balance.

And then Katerina started to feel strange.

Something was washing through her, filling her with a crackling energy. She shuddered, taking a deep breath. She dropped her sword, raised her hands to her eyes. Blue lightning flickered across her skin, raised the hair on her arms. The energy pushed into her, pushed up against her skin, her bones, filling every crevice of her being until she felt as though she would explode. And still it kept coming. More and more. She was aware of people and fey stumbling back, staring at her in horror. Lightning crackled between her hands, penetrating the ground, dancing across the grass, leaving scorched trails in its wake.

What was happening to her? Was it some sort of weapon of Kelindria's?

But then a voice spoke inside her head.

Greetings, my Raven Queen. The voice was rich, powerful, yet filled with amusement.

Raven Queen? What . . . ? Katerina's thoughts sped through all possible conclusions, arriving at the only one that made sense.

"Me?"

Indeed.

"But I thought it was supposed to be a King?"

Why? Do you not think a woman can hold such power? I'll wager a woman would never have forsaken my true name to come up with something so . . . theatrical.

A strange calm descended on Katerina. "What is your true name?"

I am the Pendragon, the Protector of London. One of the Protectors of the Isles.

"And who am I?"

You are my vessel. My chosen bloodline. Through you I wield my power. If you accept.

Katerina was dimly aware of Kelindria ordering a group of Tuatha to attack. They approached reluctantly. She could sense their fear. And rightly so. As they drew close, the lightning burst out of her, stabbing into their bodies, disintegrating them in an instant.

Katerina's eyes shifted to Tower Hill.

Do you accept my power? asked the Pendragon.

"What?" Katerina was confused. She thought she already had. She had to get over to the hill. Had to stop the Fire King from getting Emily and William.

You have not yet accepted. Watch, said the voice.

Images flashed through Katerina's head. Images of her ancestors, of those who had chosen to summon the power of the Pendragon. Arthur. Bran. Lud. And many others.

She saw their lives.

She saw their deaths.

Katerina didn't hesitate. She nodded.

"I accept."

⊁⊰ ⊱⊁

Emily and William had nowhere to go. The tunnel had closed up behind them while they were watching the wall explode. And now the hounds were racing toward them, already halfway up the slope. Behind them came the knight, and behind him, the Fire King.

All was lost.

Emily knew that. They were going to die. There was no chance they could outrun those dogs. They would leap upon their backs and tear them apart.

And Emily, for one, would rather face her death head-on.

She reached out and took hold of Will's hand. After all they had been through, for it to end like this. She sighed, glancing at her brother. His eyes were wide, scared. She was sure hers were as well, because she was absolutely terrified.

But at least they were together.

She smiled weakly and squeezed his hand, then turned to face her fate.

There was something odd happening within the walls of the Tower of London. She could see a strange blue light

392

shining up against the clouds, overpowering the orange and red light of the fires.

As she watched, a figure floated slowly up into the air. It was surrounded by a nimbus of blue light. Lightning crackled out from the figure, a spidery network of flickering luminescence that stabbed at the ground, flickered into the sky.

The figure started to move toward them, arms outstretched. *What now?* thought Emily, watching it approach.

It was only when the figure cleared the walls that Emily realized it was Katerina.

"No," she whispered.

But it was Katerina. She floated toward them, her eyes blazing with blue light. She turned her attention to the hounds that were almost upon Emily and Will and pointed. Lightning flickered from her fingers, and the hounds burst apart into nothing. The Crimson Knight whirled around. He pulled out his mace and swung it in circles.

Another gesture, another crackle of lightning, and he was gone. All that remained was a puddle of melted metal, ticking and cooling in the night air.

Katerina turned to face the Fire King just as a wall of fire rushed toward her and wrapped around her body.

Emily could just see her figure through the flames. She was still floating in the air, arms raised out to her sides. The Fire King stalked toward her. The flames pouring from his hands became a stream of molten lava, pouring into and strengthening the flames that surrounded her. Emily saw the fires along the tower wall lower slightly, and she realized that the Fire King was pulling his energy out of his salamanders and pumping it all into Katerina.

And still she floated, doing nothing to defend herself.

The Fire King kept coming, his eyes blazing with hatred, his mouth an open pit into the furnace of hell itself. Heat waves distorted the air around them.

Finally, the Fire King had no more. The flames along the wall winked out. He lowered his arms and stood before Katerina. By his stance, Emily could see he thought Katerina defeated.

The white-hot flames that surrounded Katerina simply winked out, leaving burning afterimages dancing before Emily's eyes. Katerina stood tall, untouched by the flames.

When the Fire King saw this, he tilted his head back, releasing a scream of fury. Flames shot from his mouth and soared up into the clouds.

Katerina floated forward and reached out with her finger. She touched the Fire King lightly on the chest.

He exploded, bursting into tiny fragments of flame. He lit up the sky, tiny red stars shooting upward in all directions, then slowly fading and blinking out into nothingness like embers from a fire. Smoke drifted on the hot breeze, and for a moment, Emily thought she could see the shape of the Fire King's face outlined against the sky. Then the wind blew the smoke apart, dispersing it across the city.

The Fire King was dead.

Katerina's head dropped. She turned to Emily and William and smiled. Then the blue light faded, and she dropped to the ground.

Emily rushed forward, dropping to her knees next to the prone figure. She took hold of Katerina's hand, wincing at the heat of her skin. She was burning hot. She felt as though she should be on fire herself.

"Katerina," she said urgently.

Katerina's eyes flickered open. "Is the Fire King gone?"

Emily nodded. "He's gone. You did it."

Will knelt down on the other side. He looked confused. "I don't understand," he said. "You were the Raven King?"

"Raven Queen," Katerina corrected weakly. "And yes. It was me. Or rather, my bloodline."

"What happens now?" asked Emily. "What do we do? Should we take you somewhere?"

"No. I'm dying, Emily."

"What? No! You can't die," said William. "That's not fair. Not after what you did."

"It's not meant to be fair. It's just the way it is. A human body can't contain the power of the Pendragon. We're not built for it. We can only channel the power and do what must be done before it burns us to nothing."

"But it's not fair!"

"It was my choice, Will. The Pendragon spoke to me. She asked if I was willing. I knew the consequences." She coughed. "I think it's a pretty good trade, don't you? One life for the whole of Britain."

She smiled at them both, then closed her eyes.

And so the Raven Queen, the Pendragon, the Protector of the Isles, died.

Emily and William stood up. As they stared down at Katerina's body, it shimmered with a white light. There was a bright flash, and then her body was no longer there.

In its place was a black raven. The raven tilted its head and cawed, then took to the air and flew toward the Tower of London. As it approached the tower, other black ravens leapt from the battlements, cawing their greeting. The birds circled in the night sky, then banked in the air and landed upon the tower.

⊱ CHAPTER THIRTY ⊰
Epilogue

Four days later, Emily, William, Jack, Corrigan, and Christopher Wren stood before the Faerie Tree in Hyde Park.

Puck had joined them, as well. After Katerina had become the Raven Queen, Kelindria had fled the field of battle. When the fey saw their leader running, they had wisely chosen to do the same.

The fire was over now. Once the Fire King had been vanquished, the flames could be battled as a normal blaze. Even so, it had been a close thing. For three days the Great Fire of London burned. Most of old London City—the part surrounded by the ancient Roman wall—had burned to the ground. But the people of London had finally managed to stop it there.

Yet their victory felt hollow. *Poor Katerina*, thought Emily. She had given her life to protect them, to stop the fire from destroying Britain. She had done so willingly, even though she'd had no idea she was of the Pendragon bloodline. And yet it made a kind of sense. Merlin had said the Raven King— Emily corrected herself—the Raven *Queen*, would be drawn to the conflicts within the city. And that was certainly true of Katerina. She had spent most of her life fighting the fey. She had been drawn into the battle from the very beginning. Her blood had known who she was, where she had to be.

"What now?" she asked Merlin.

"Now we rebuild the Invisible Order," he said. He nodded at Wren. "Wren has agreed to join us. And we have a steady stream of volunteers from Katerina's followers. A new generation to join our ranks."

Emily took the two keys from her pocket. She handed one to Wren. "This is for you. You're supposed to hide it for me to find in my time. The first part of the key—"

"Hold." Merlin raised a hand. "Do not tell him. He will do as he will, and you will learn of it when it is your time."

Emily nodded and handed the second key to Merlin. He took it from her and moved the little branches around, tweaking it until he was happy. Then he gave it back to Emily.

"There you go. That will take you where you're meant to be."

"Thank you."

"Why did she turn into a raven?" asked William.

"You must have heard the legend?" said Merlin. "It is said that as long as there are ravens at the Tower of London, then Britain will be protected. I think that grew out of the Raven King myth."

"Is it true?"

"I'm not sure. But the ravens that live at the tower *are* all of the Pendragon bloodline. That is what becomes of them after they wield the power. They do not die. They live on as watchers."

William nodded. Emily turned and put the key into the depression in the tree. It slid neatly into place. The gateway stretched and widened within the tree trunk. The last time she had entered this gate, she had seen lines of Tuatha getting ready to invade London. This time all she could see was a silvery mist.

"At least we know the name the Pendragon bloodline goes under," she said to Merlin. "If we need it again, all we have to do is find someone called Francesca."

They turned toward the gate.

"Oh," said Puck. "No, you've got that wrong."

Emily paused. "What?"

"Katerina Francesca wasn't her real name. It was just something she called herself. She liked the sound of it.

Said it made her feel exotic, more than she really was."

"So what was her real name?"

"Ravenhill," said Puck. "Her name was Katherine Ravenhill."

⊱━━⊰